TARO AND THE TERROR OF EATS STREET

Story & Art by Sango Morimoto

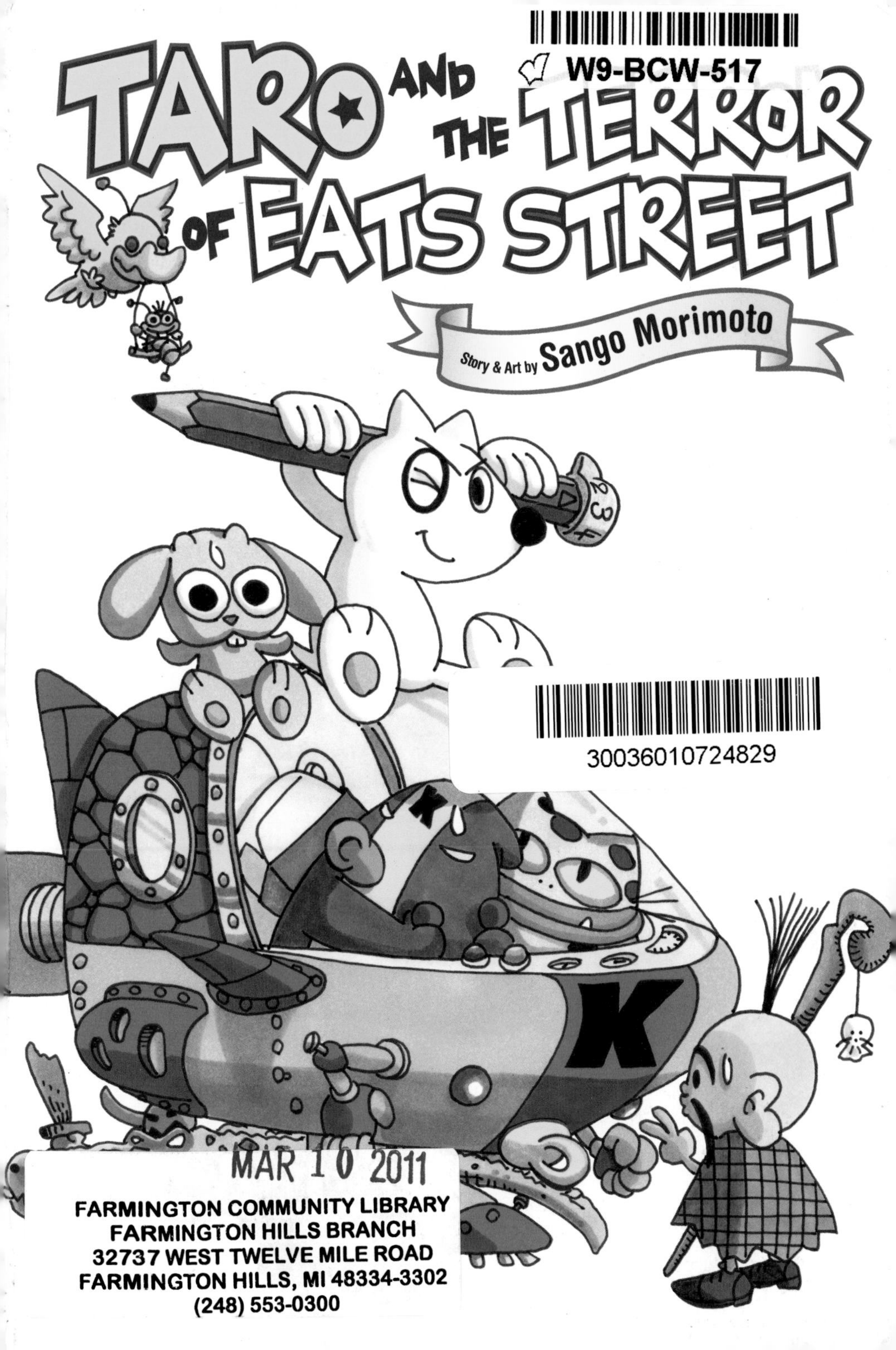

It was a lazy Sunday morning and Taro was sleeping in. But not for long.

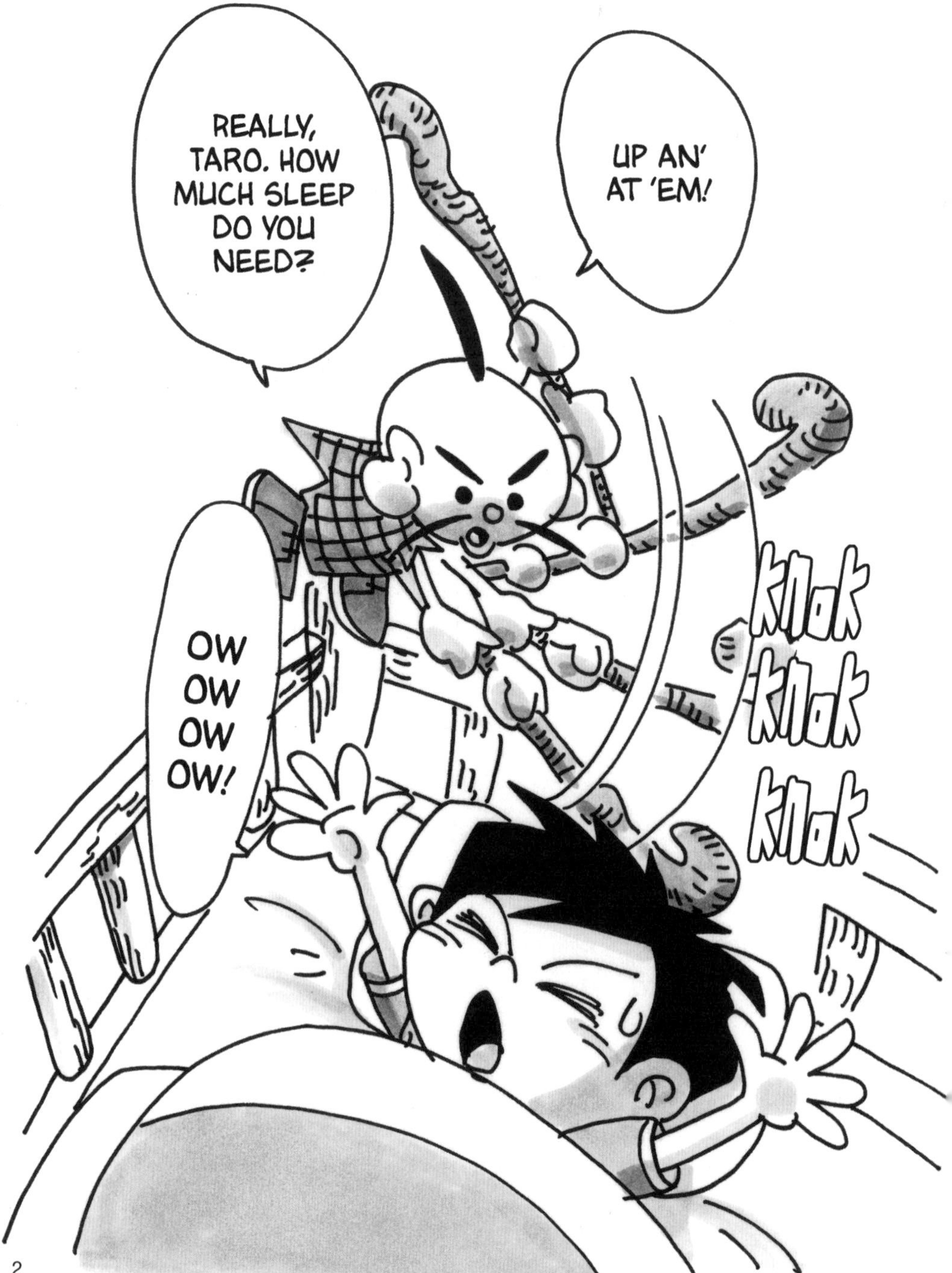
UP AN' AT 'EM!
REALLY, TARO. HOW MUCH SLEEP DO YOU NEED?
KNOK KNOK KNOK
OW OW OW OW!

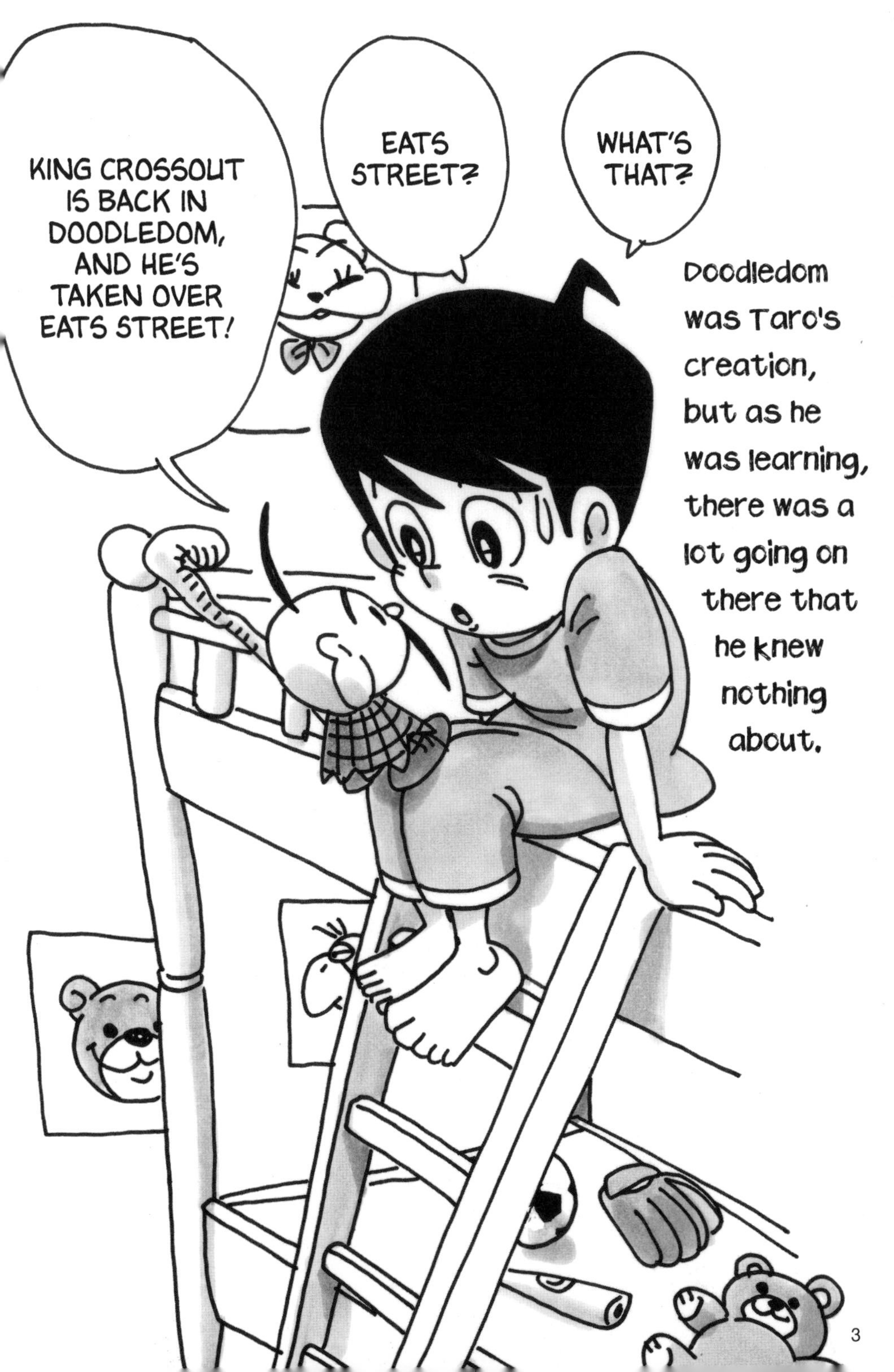
KING CROSSOUT IS BACK IN DOODLEDOM, AND HE'S TAKEN OVER EATS STREET!
EATS STREET?
WHAT'S THAT?
Doodledom was Taro's creation, but as he was learning, there was a lot going on there that he knew nothing about.

Clearly the Magician was a fan.

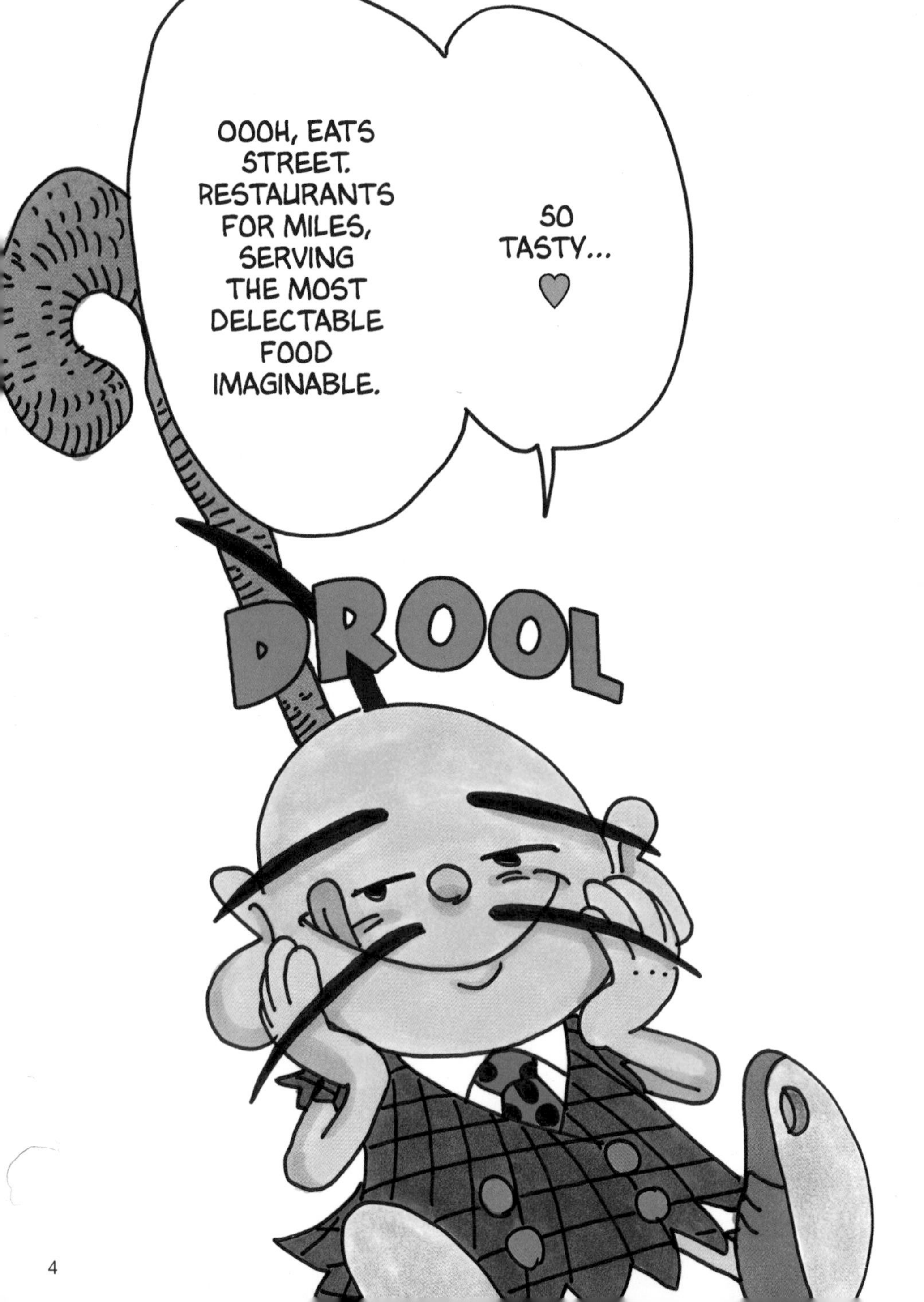
OOOH, EATS STREET. RESTAURANTS FOR MILES, SERVING THE MOST DELECTABLE FOOD IMAGINABLE.
SO TASTY...
DROOL

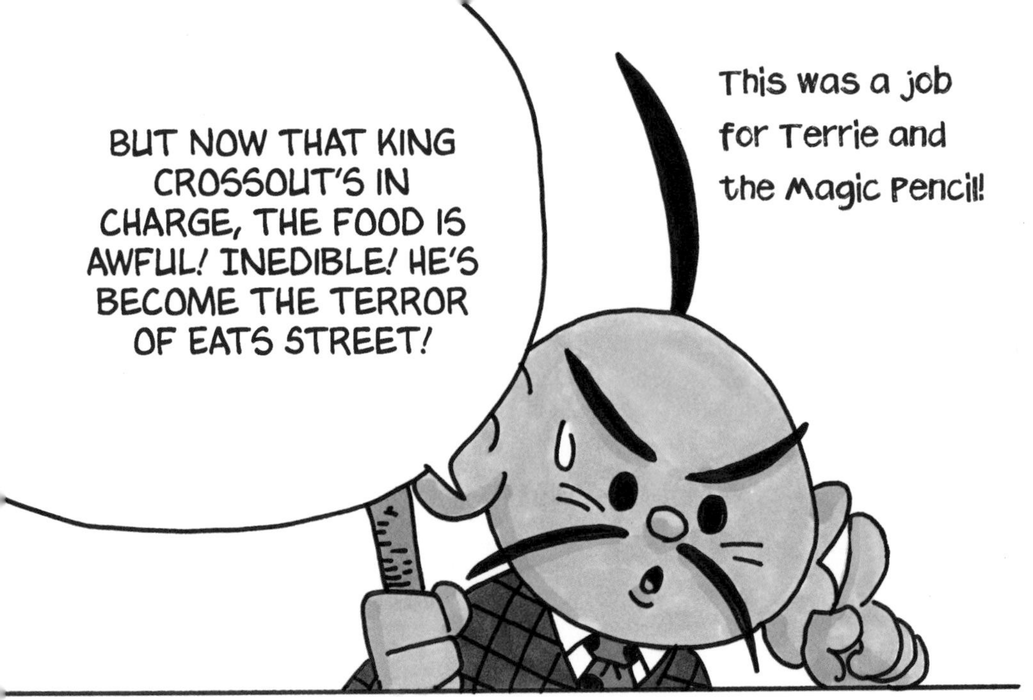
BUT NOW THAT KING CROSSOUT'S IN CHARGE, THE FOOD IS AWFUL! INEDIBLE! HE'S BECOME THE TERROR OF EATS STREET!
This was a job for Terrie and the Magic Pencil!

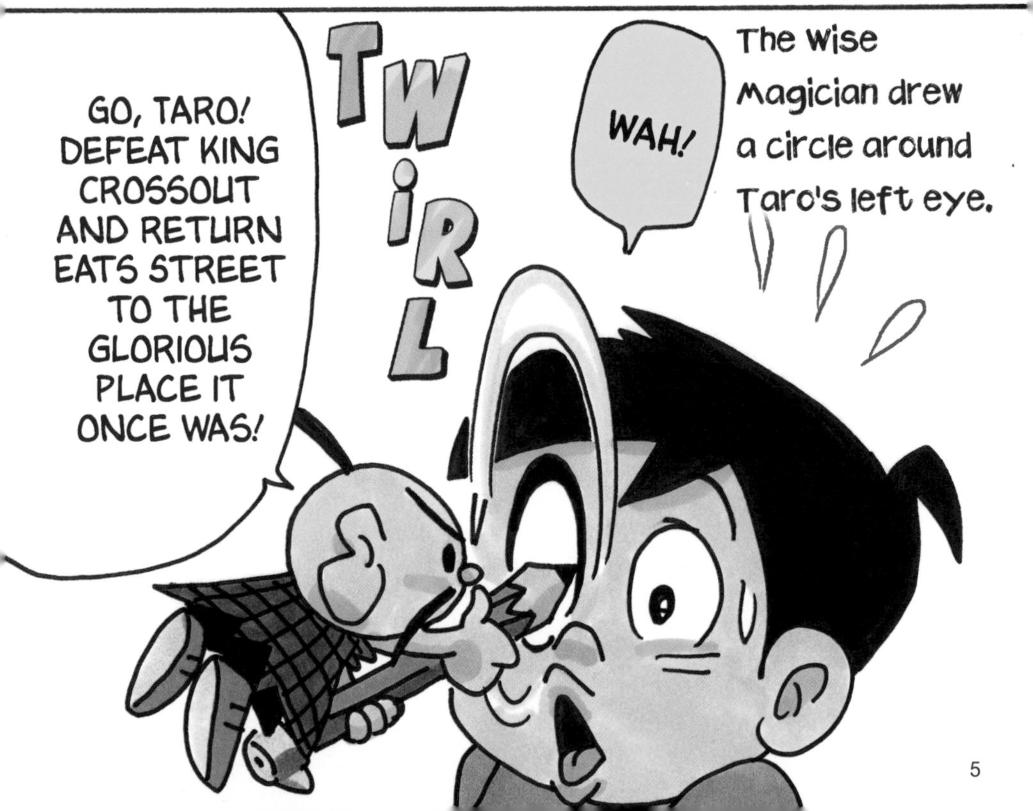
GO, TARO! DEFEAT KING CROSSOUT AND RETURN EATS STREET TO THE GLORIOUS PLACE IT ONCE WAS!
TWIRL
WAH!
The Wise Magician drew a circle around Taro's left eye.

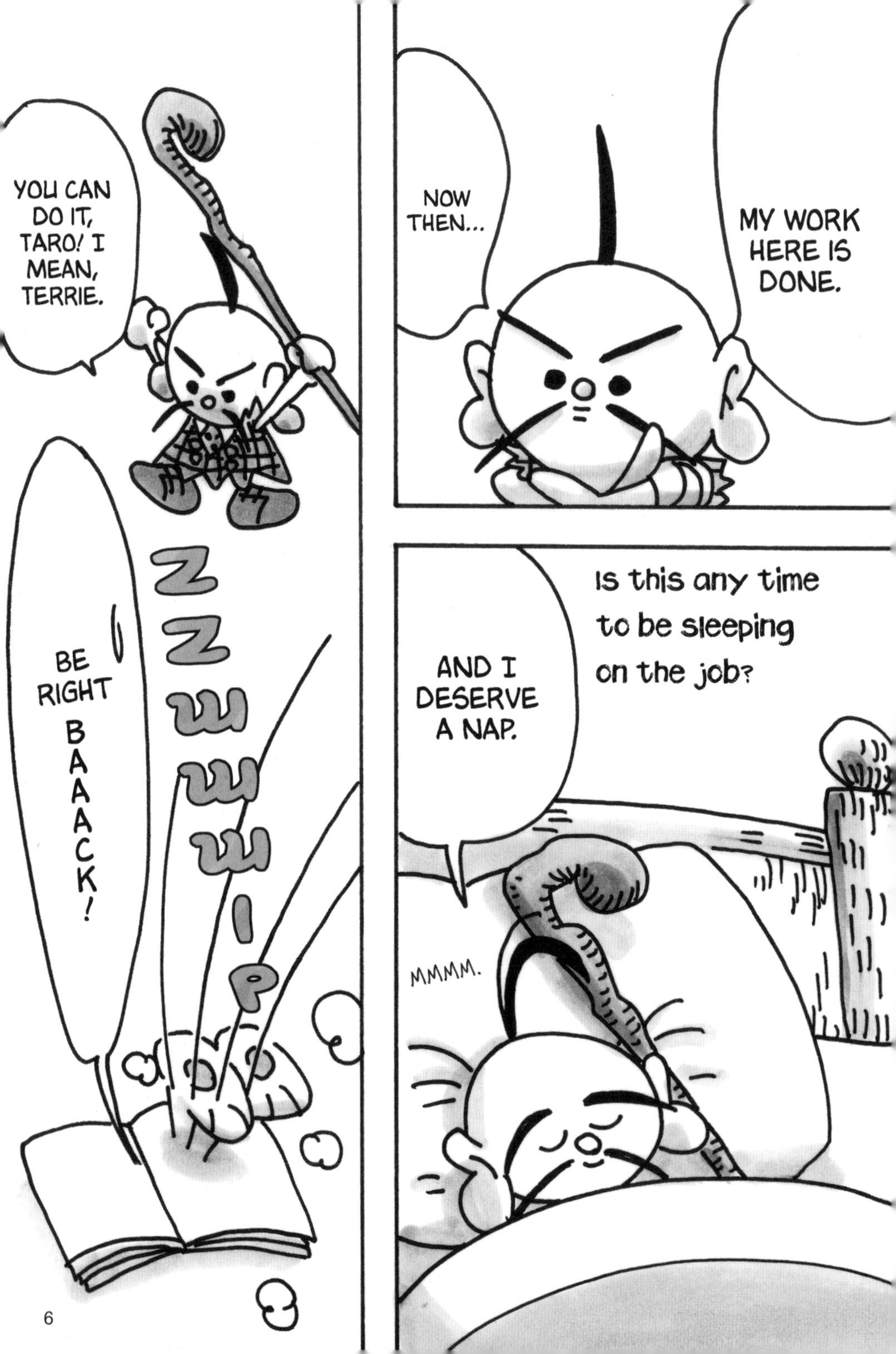
YOU CAN DO IT, TARO! I MEAN, TERRIE.
BE RIGHT BAAAACK!
ZZWWWIP
NOW THEN...
MY WORK HERE IS DONE.
AND I DESERVE A NAP.
Is this any time to be sleeping on the job?
MMMM.

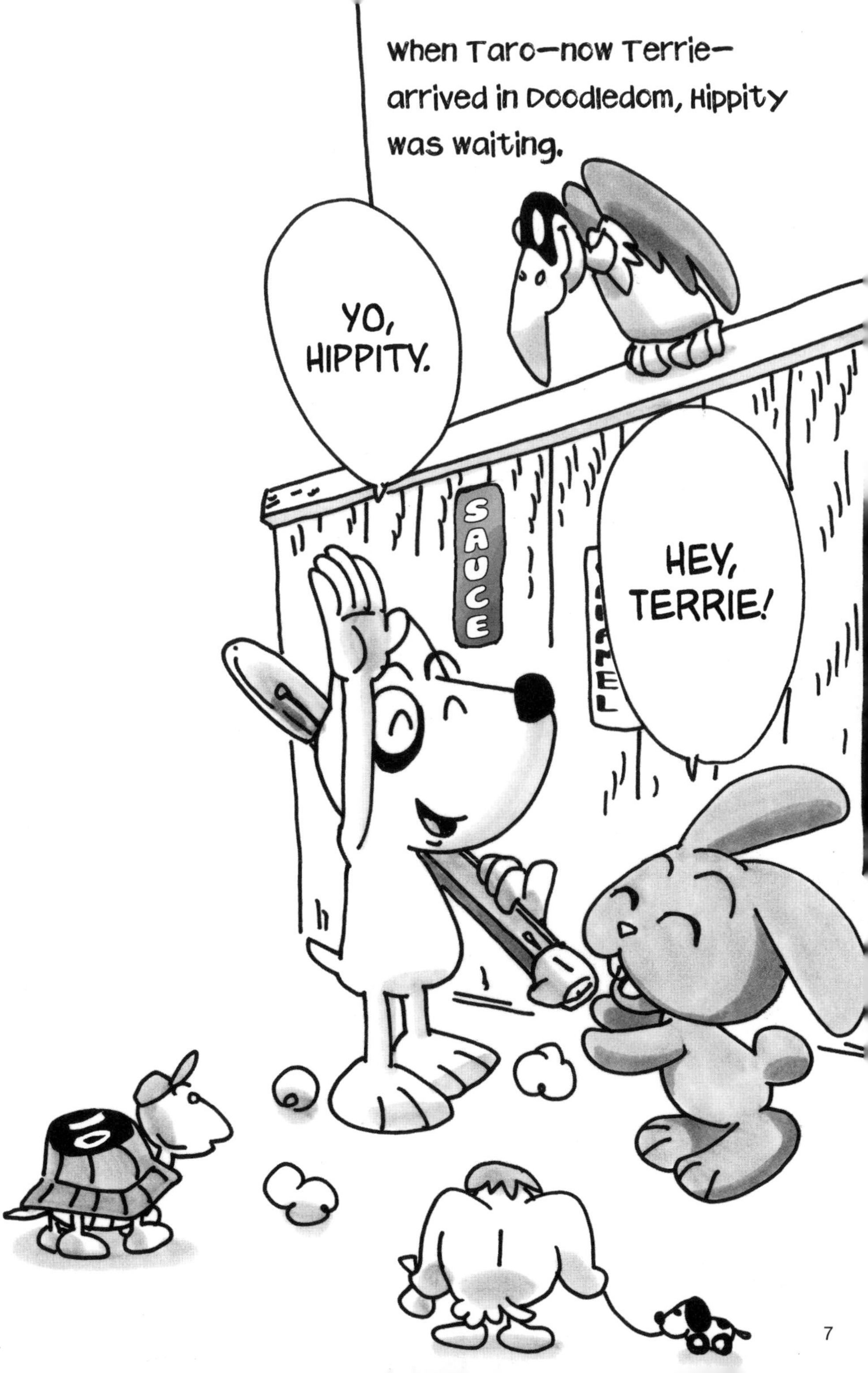
When Taro—now Terrie—arrived in Doodledom, Hippity was waiting.
YO, HIPPITY.
HEY, TERRIE!
SAUCE

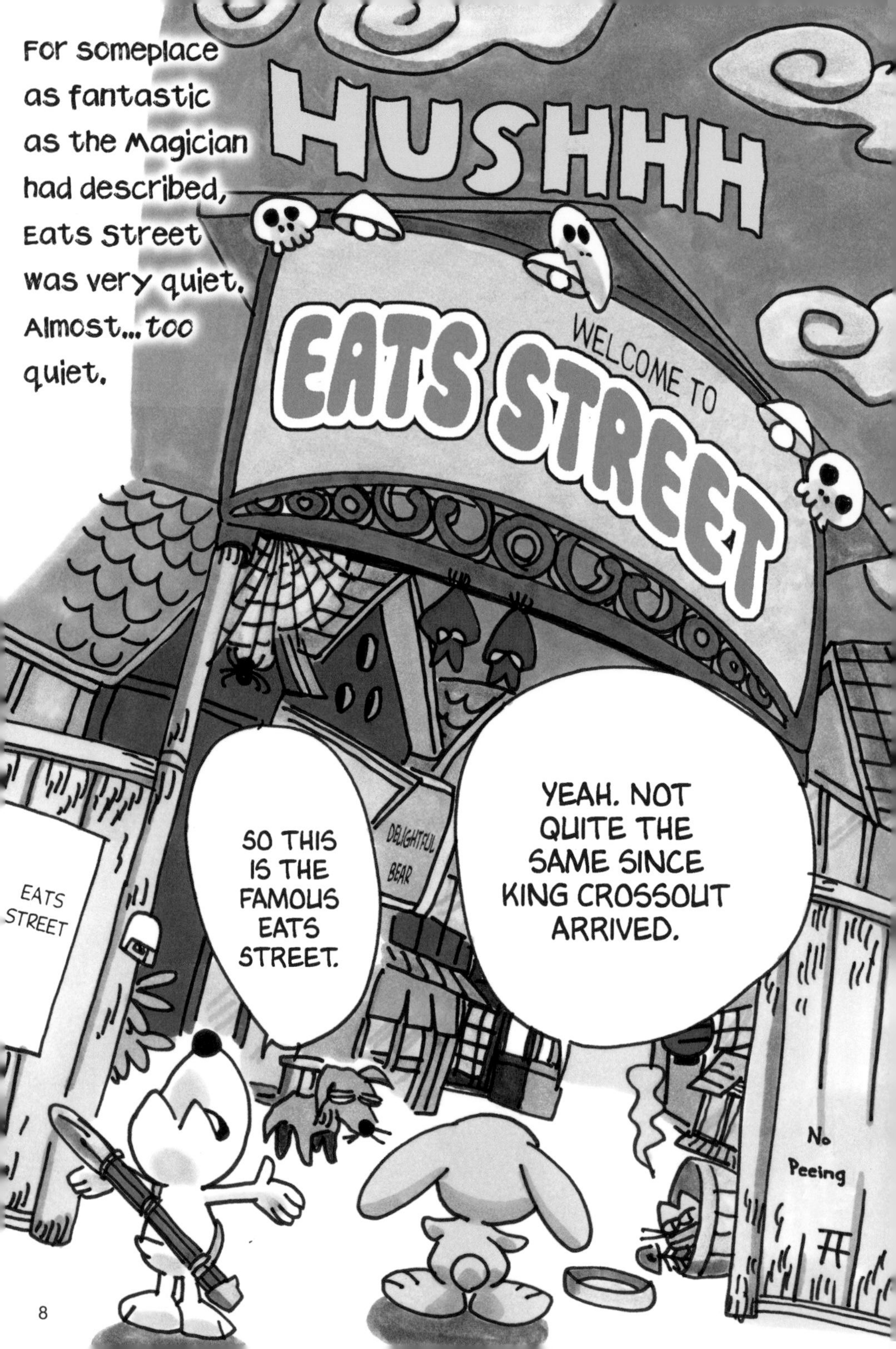
For someplace as fantastic as the Magician had described, Eats Street was very quiet. Almost...too quiet.
HUSHHH
WELCOME TO EATS STREET
SO THIS IS THE FAMOUS EATS STREET.
YEAH. NOT QUITE THE SAME SINCE KING CROSSOUT ARRIVED.
DELIGHTFUL BEAR
EATS STREET
No Peeing

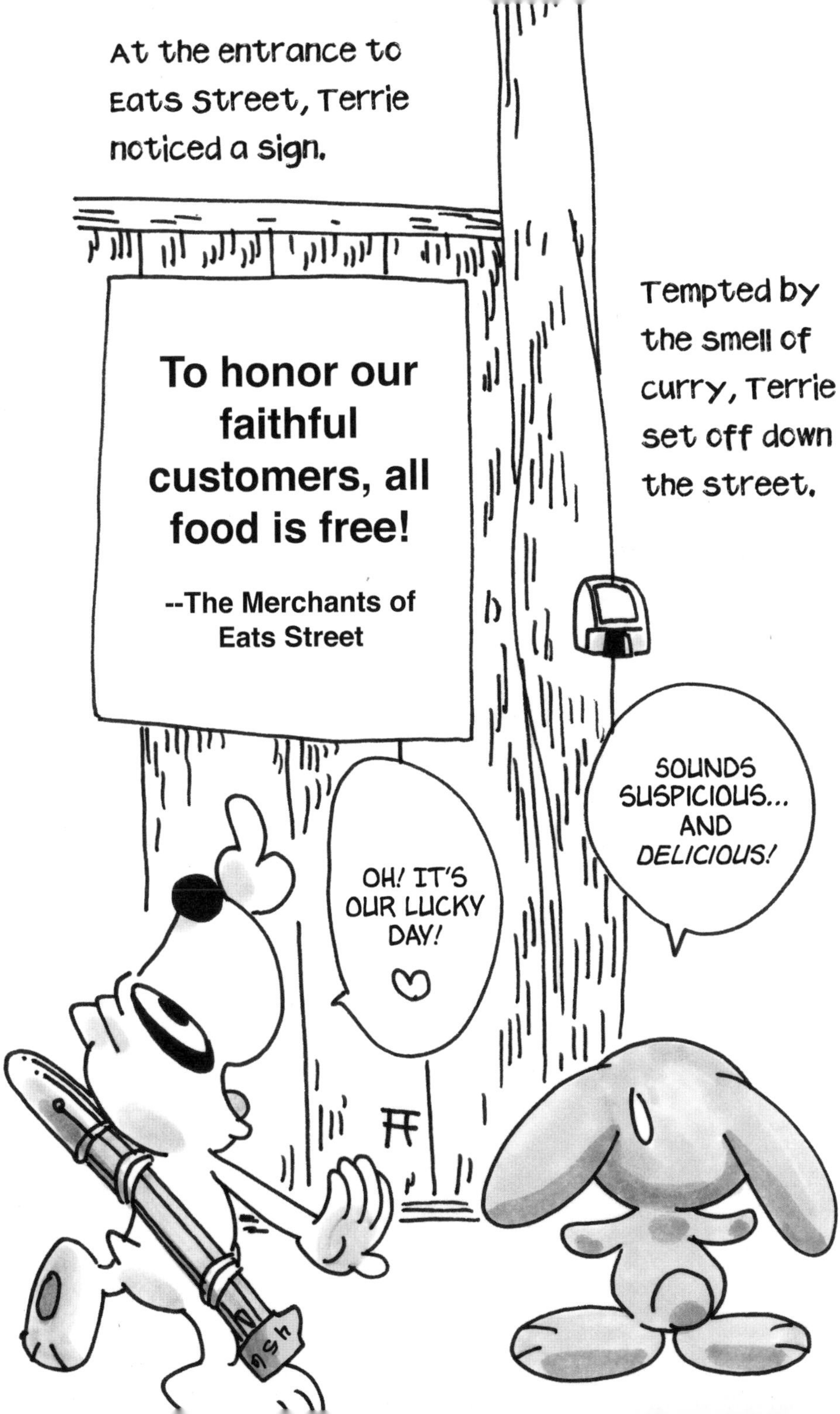
At the entrance to Eats Street, Terrie noticed a sign.
To honor our faithful customers, all food is free!
--The Merchants of Eats Street
OH! IT'S OUR LUCKY DAY!
SOUNDS SUSPICIOUS... AND DELICIOUS!
Tempted by the smell of curry, Terrie set off down the street.

The first curry shop they came to was

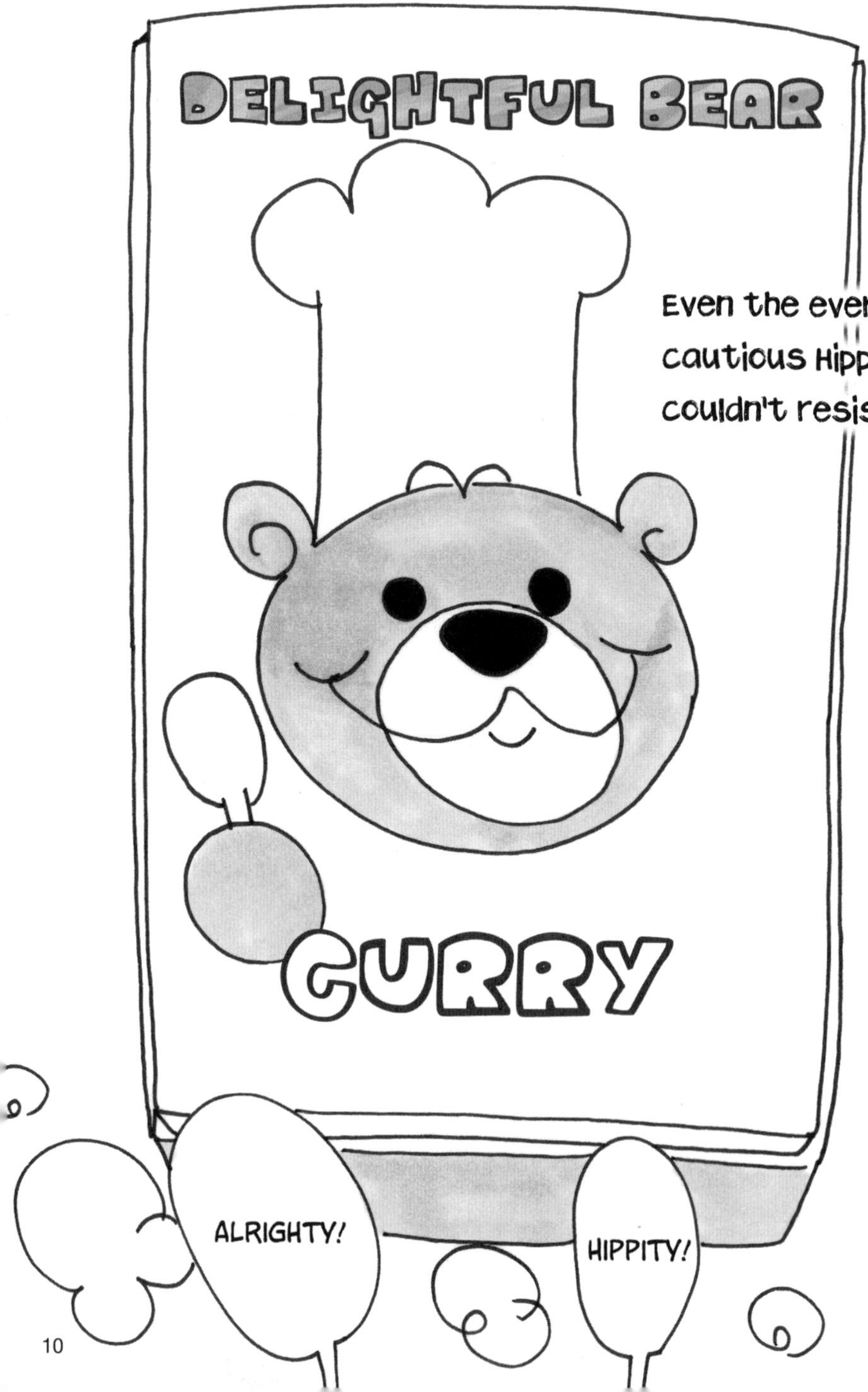
DELIGHTFUL BEAR
CURRY
ALRIGHTY!
HIPPITY!

Even the ever-cautious Hippity couldn't resist.

Little did they know, they were being watched by none other than Tattle-Tail, the royal tattletale.

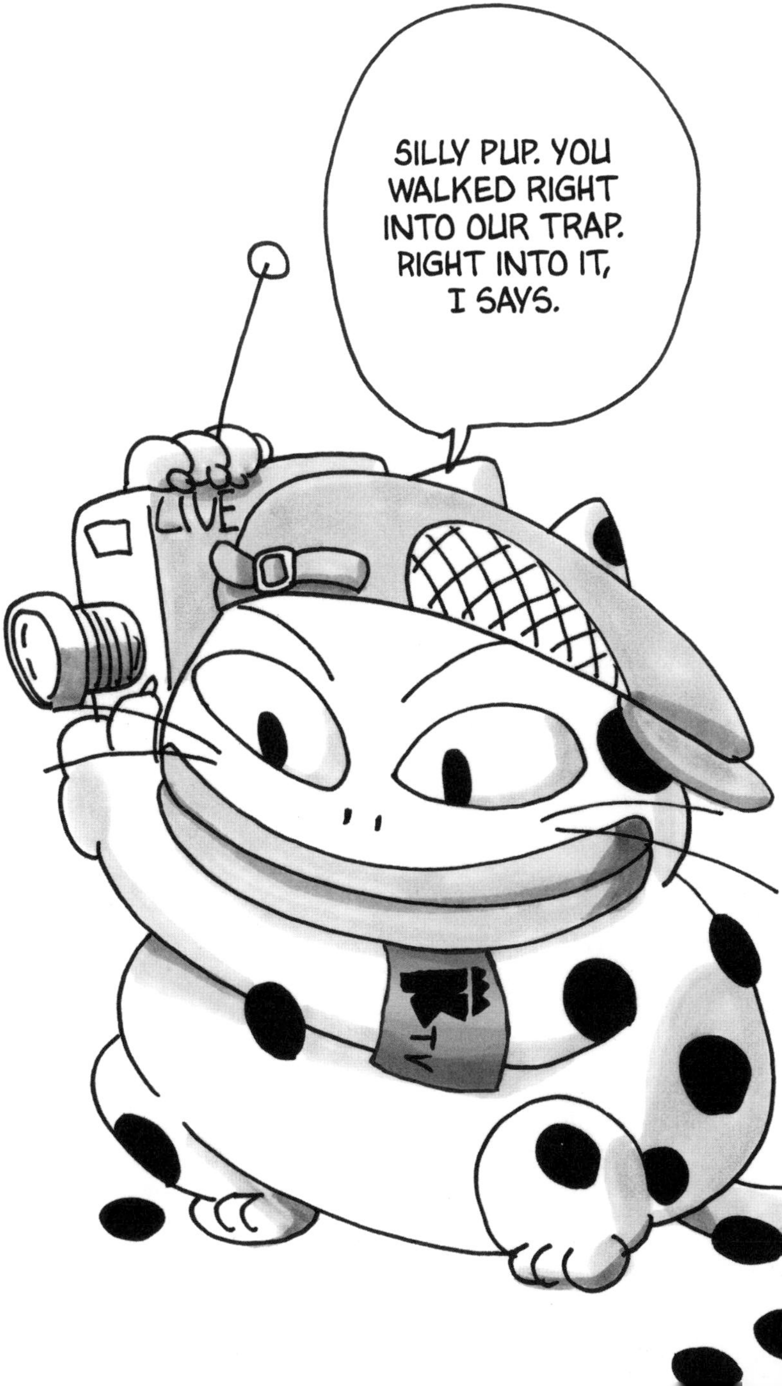
SILLY PUP. YOU WALKED RIGHT INTO OUR TRAP. RIGHT INTO IT, I SAYS.
LIVE
TV

And hidden away in an Eats Street fish shop, King Crossout was watching too.

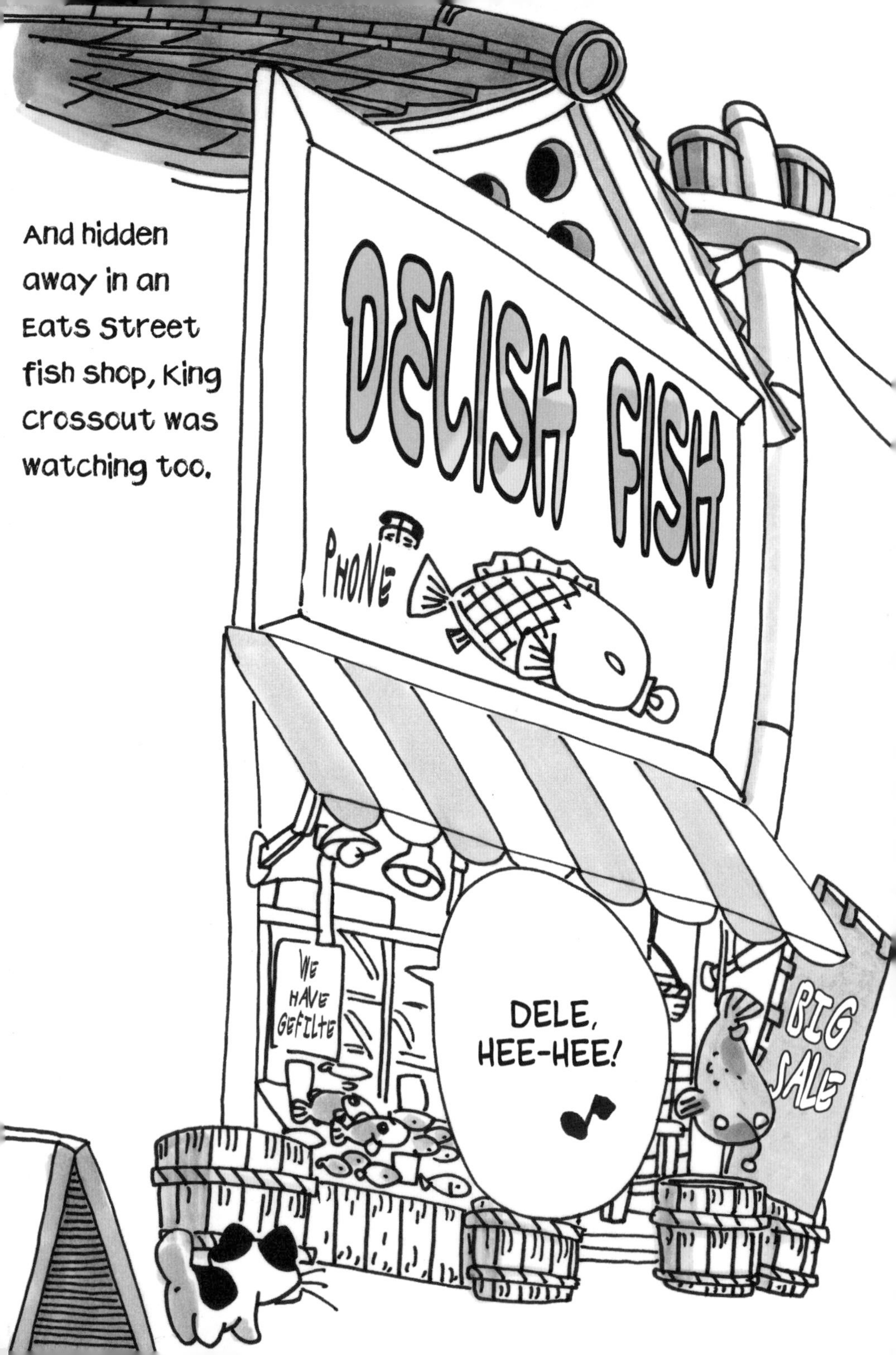
DELISH FISH
PHONE
WE HAVE GEFILTE
DELE, HEE-HEE!
BIG SALE

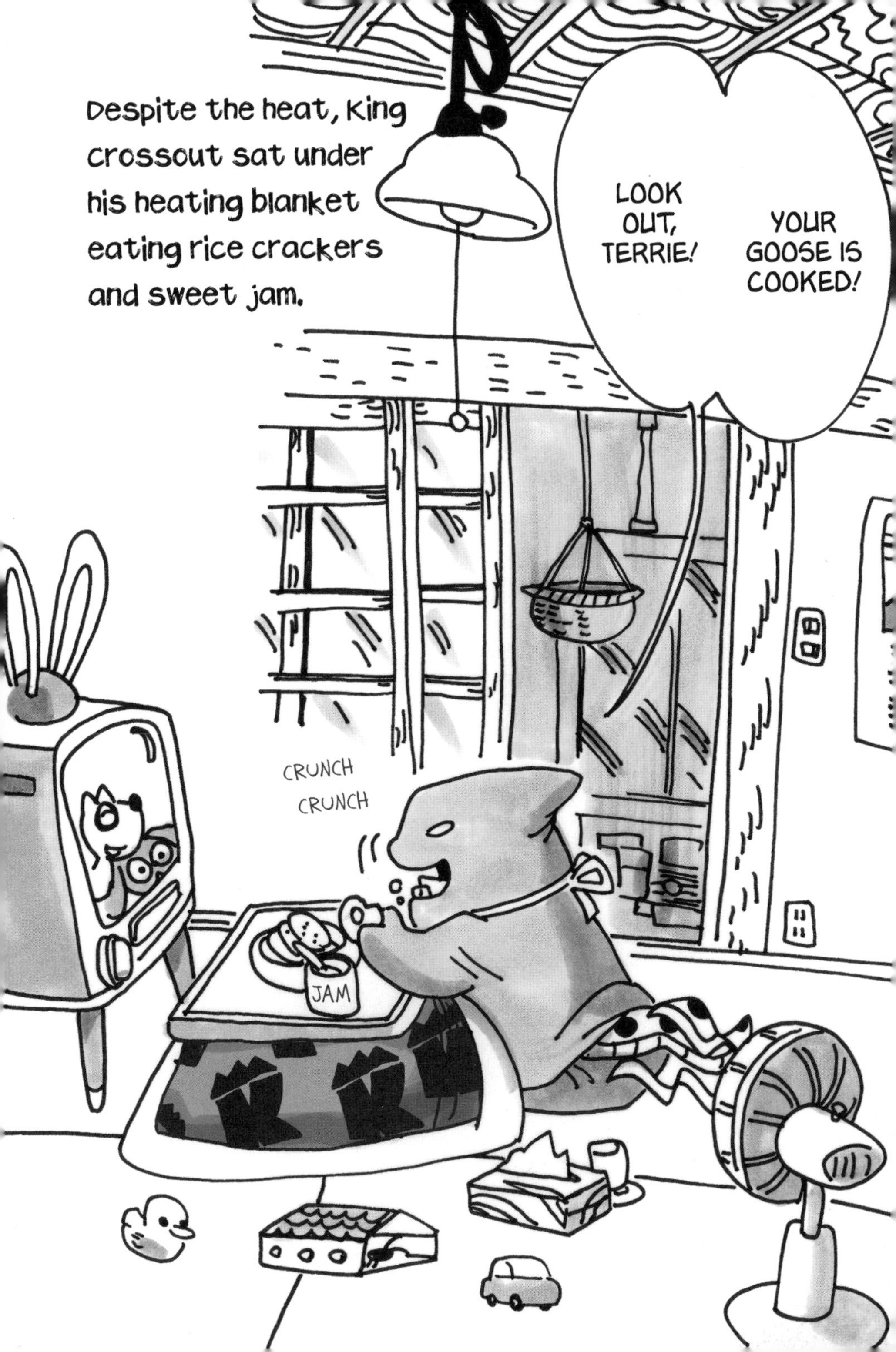
Despite the heat, King Crossout sat under his heating blanket eating rice crackers and sweet jam.
LOOK OUT, TERRIE!
YOUR GOOSE IS COOKED!
CRUNCH CRUNCH
JAM

King crossout was quite pleased with his plan.

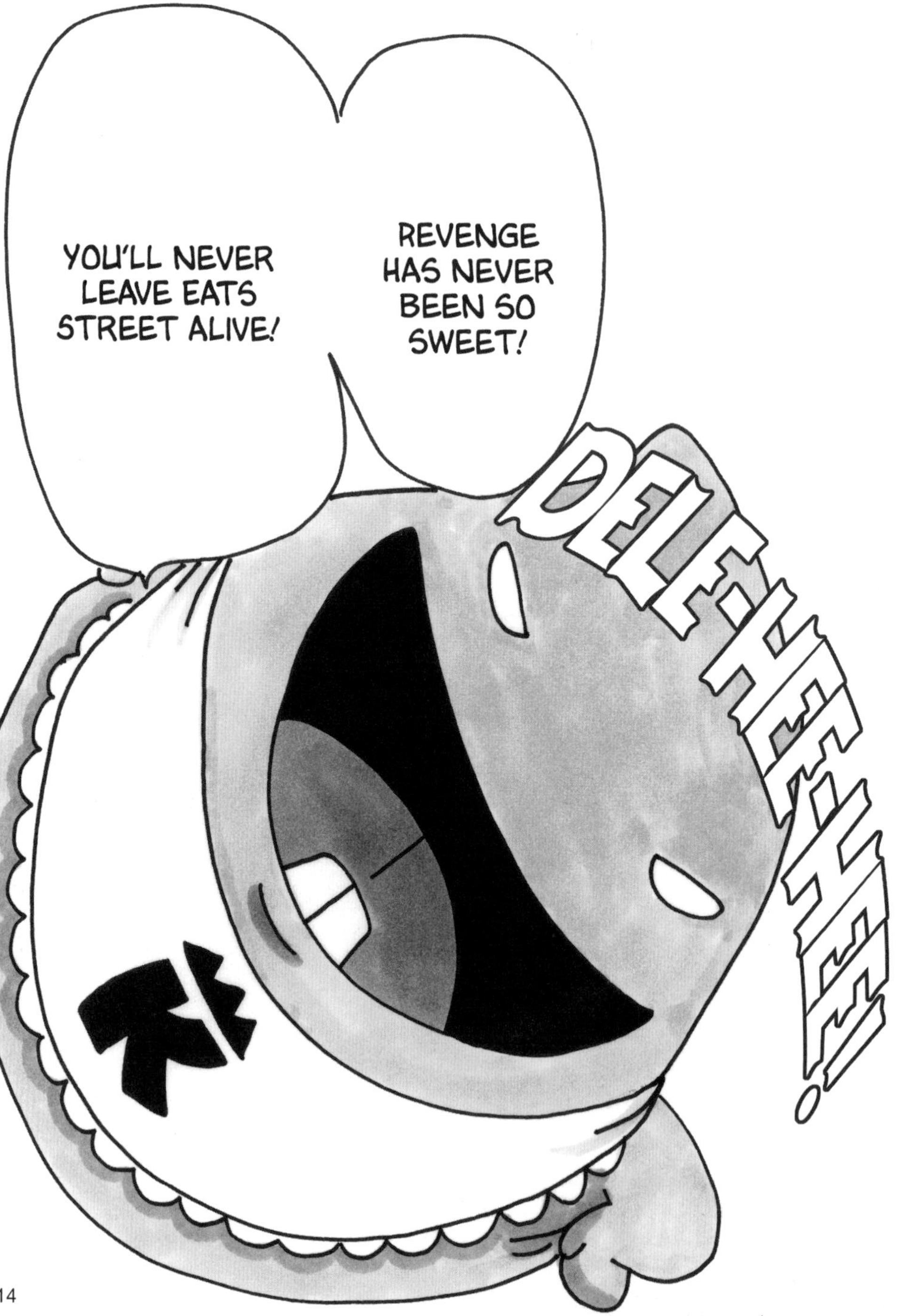
REVENGE HAS NEVER BEEN SO SWEET!
YOU'LL NEVER LEAVE EATS STREET ALIVE!
DELE-HEE-HEE-HEE!

When Terrie and Hippity entered the Delightful Bear, Mr. Delightful himself greeted them.

Perched atop Mr. Delightful's head was something that looked like a bug. A bug with King Crossout's crest on it. But Terrie and Hippity were too hungry to notice.

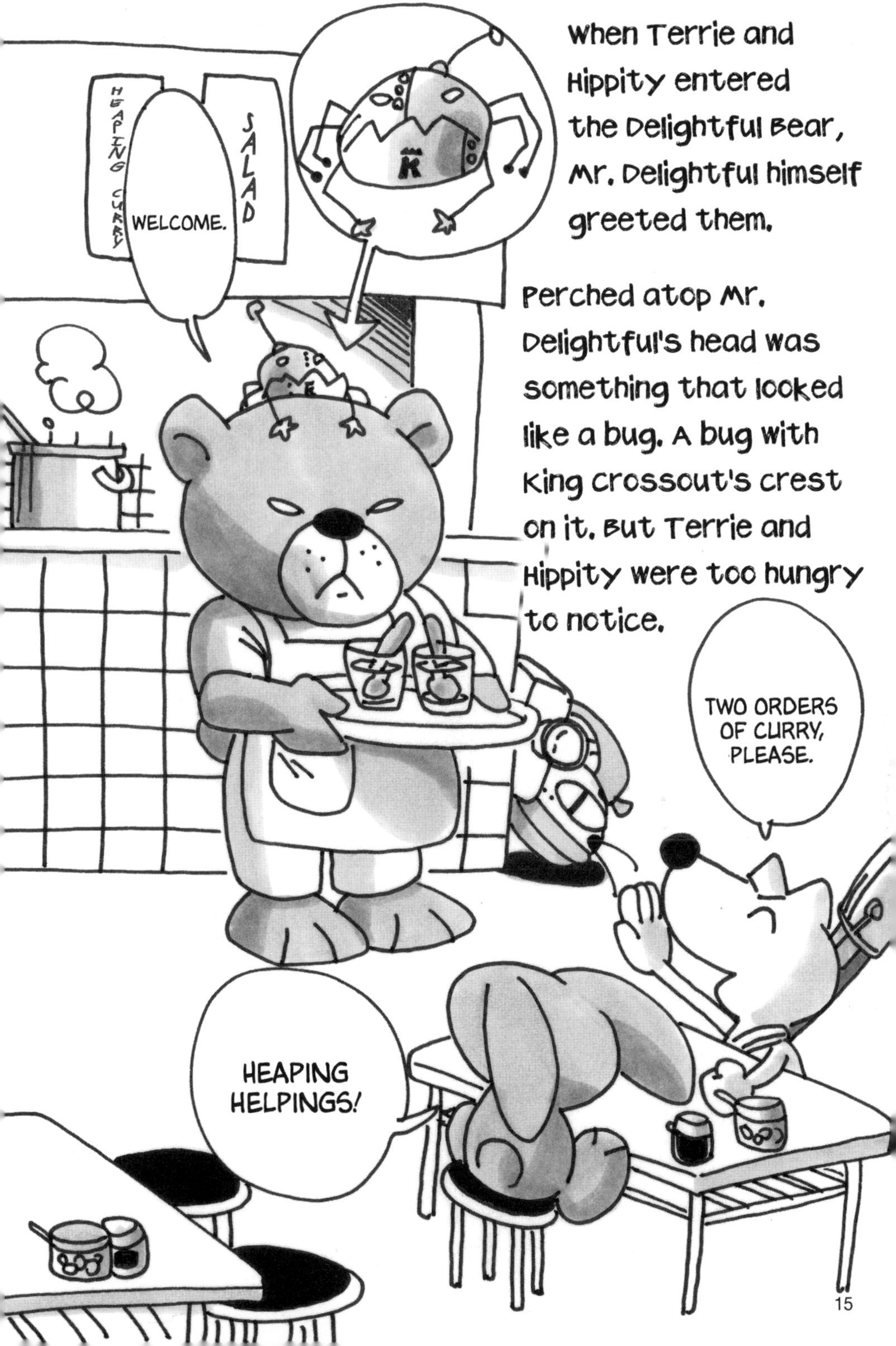

HEAPING CURRY
SALAD
WELCOME.
TWO ORDERS OF CURRY, PLEASE.
HEAPING HELPINGS!

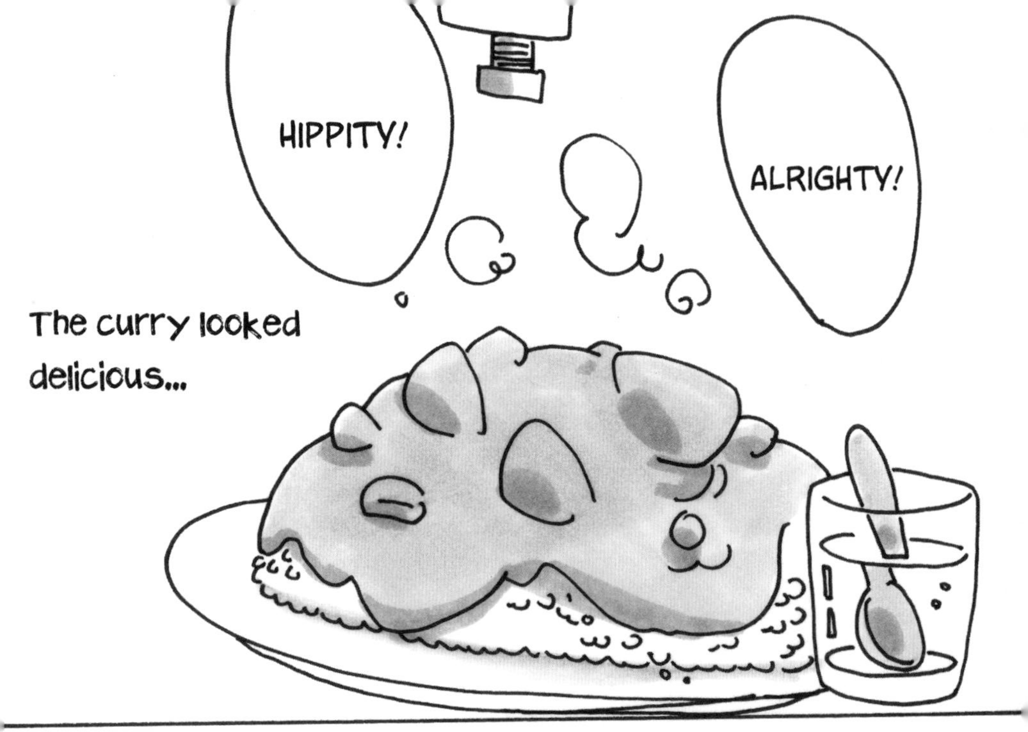
ALRIGHTY!
HIPPITY!
The curry looked delicious...
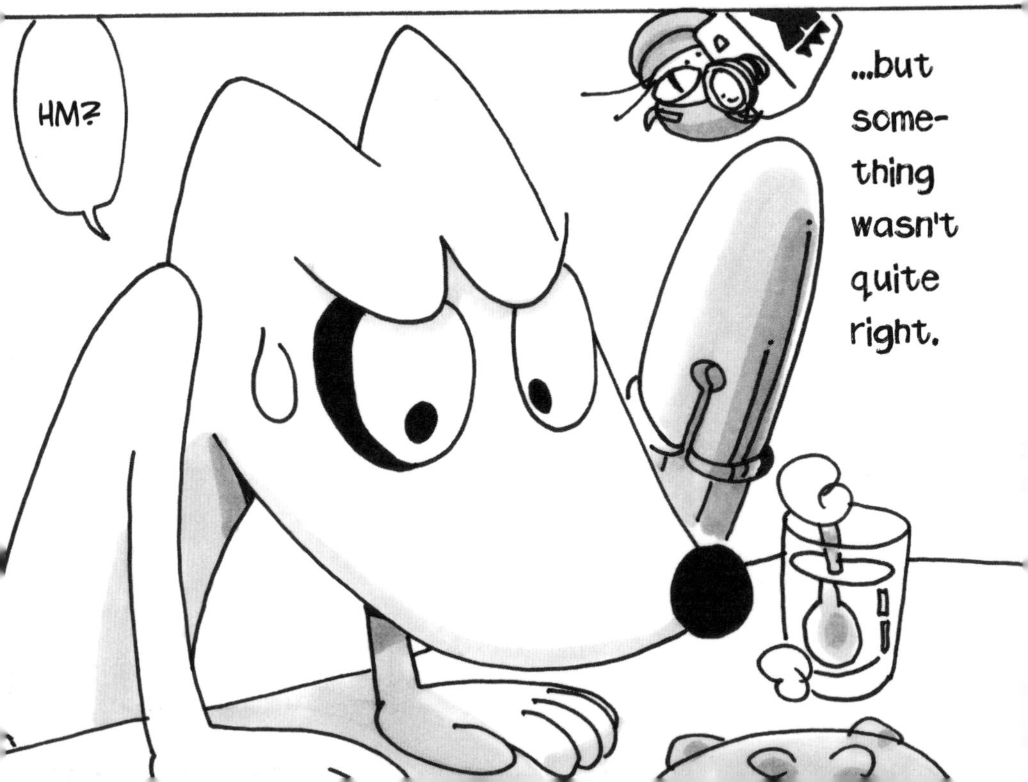
...but something wasn't quite right.
HM?

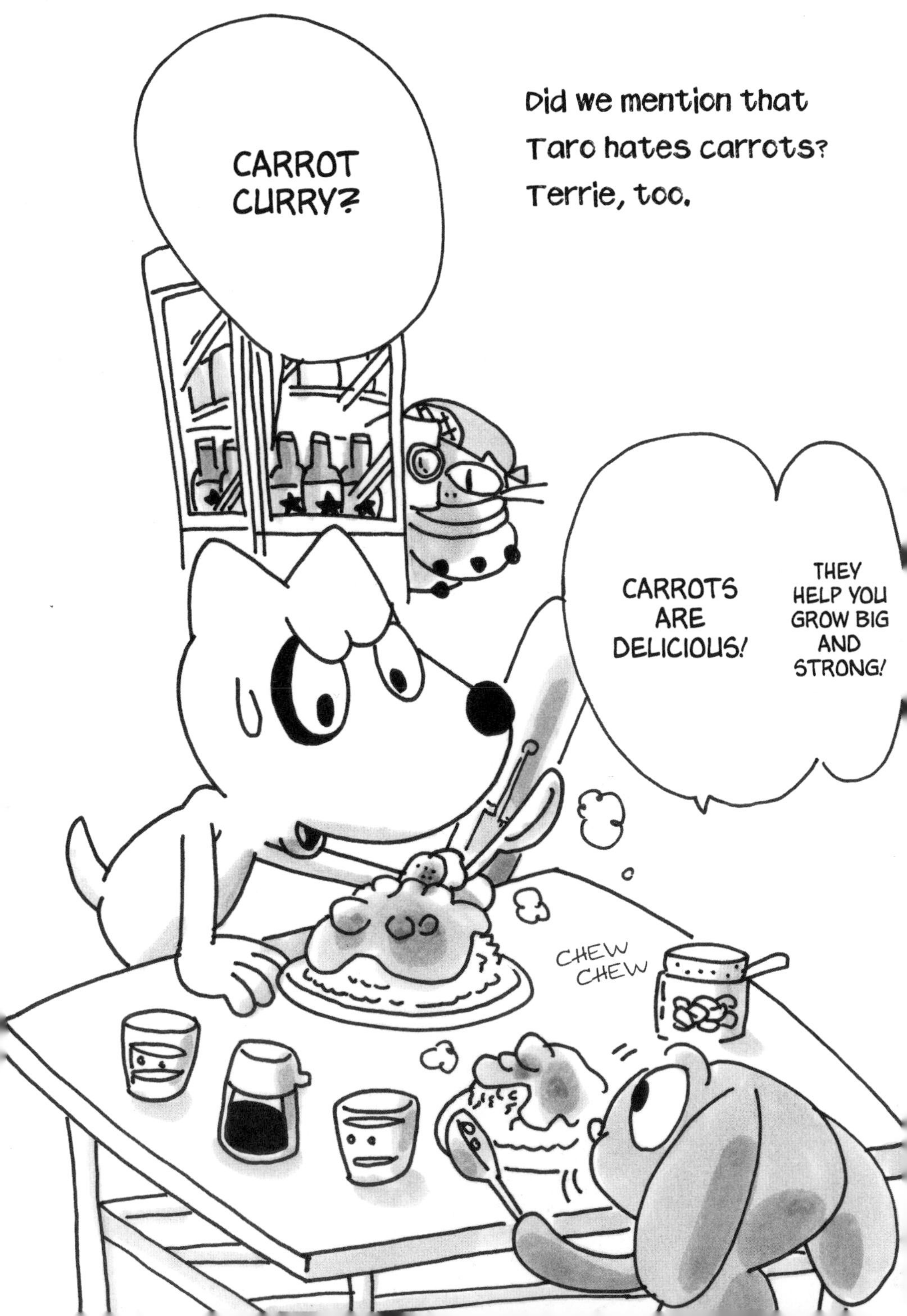
Did we mention that Taro hates carrots? Terrie, too.
CARROT CURRY?
CARROTS ARE DELICIOUS!
THEY HELP YOU GROW BIG AND STRONG!
CHEW CHEW

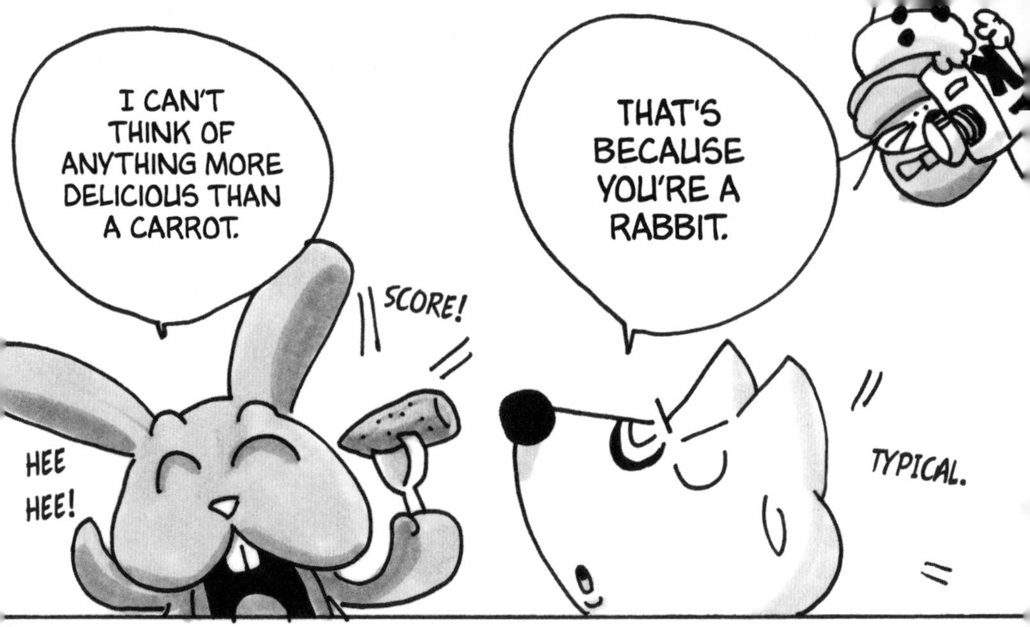
I CAN'T THINK OF ANYTHING MORE DELICIOUS THAN A CARROT.
SCORE!
HEE HEE!
THAT'S BECAUSE YOU'RE A RABBIT.
TYPICAL.
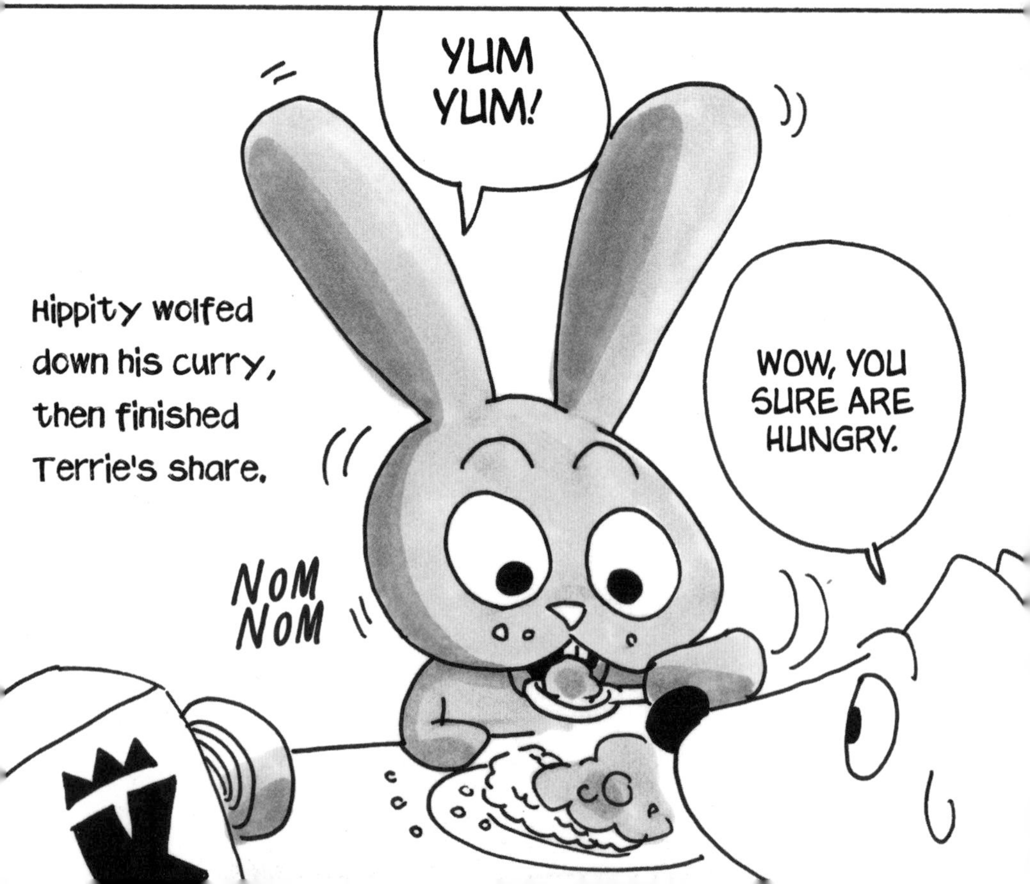
Hippity wolfed down his curry, then finished Terrie's share.
YUM YUM!
NOM NOM
WOW, YOU SURE ARE HUNGRY.

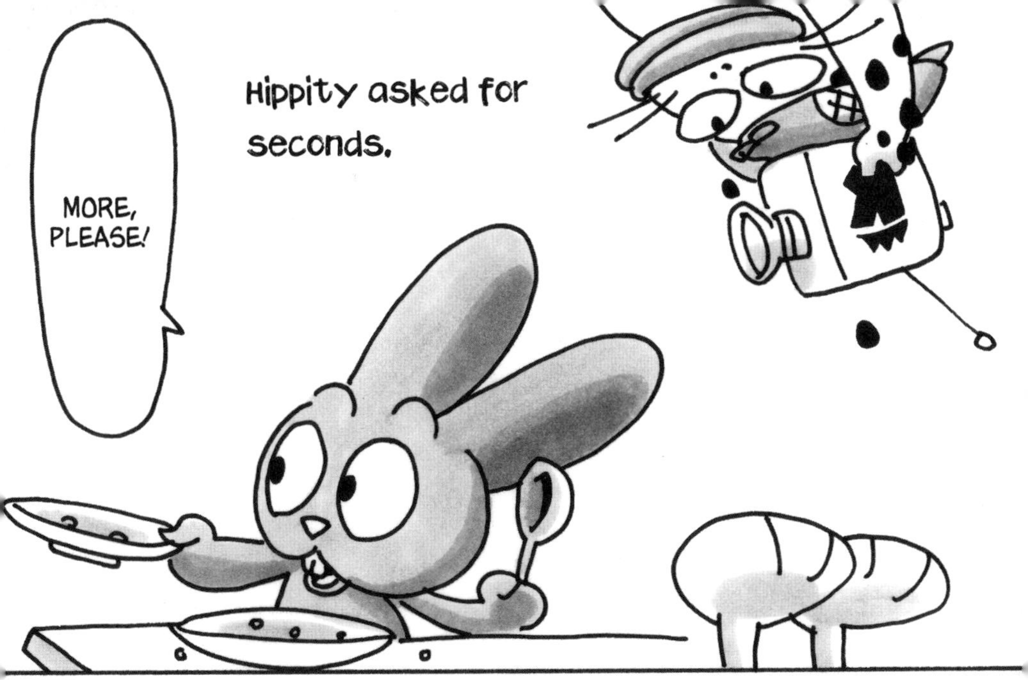
Hippity asked for seconds.
MORE, PLEASE!

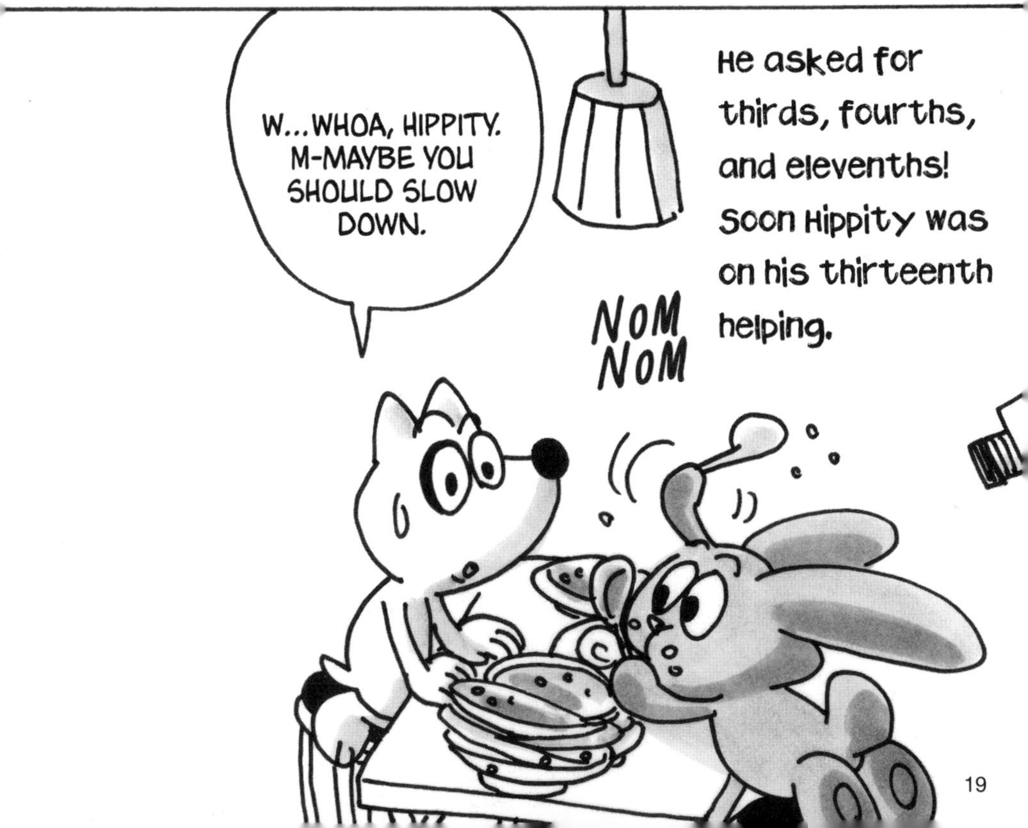
He asked for thirds, fourths, and elevenths! Soon Hippity was on his thirteenth helping.
NOM NOM
W...WHOA, HIPPITY. M-MAYBE YOU SHOULD SLOW DOWN.

But Hippity was far from slowing down. He had more helpings than Terrie could count. And then Terrie noticed a sign.

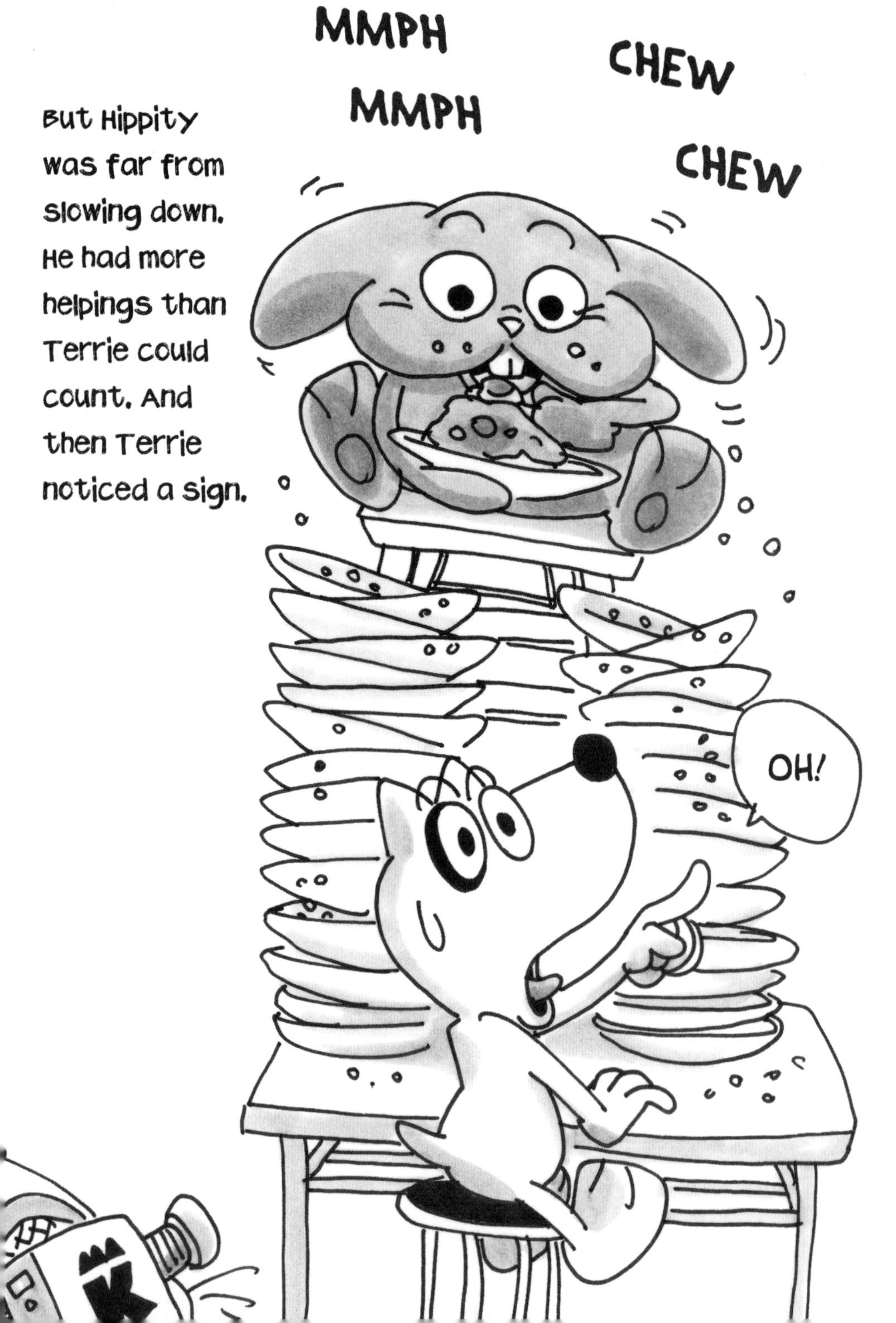
MMPH
MMPH
CHEW
CHEW
OH!

If Terrie didn't do something quickly, Hippity would never stop eating!

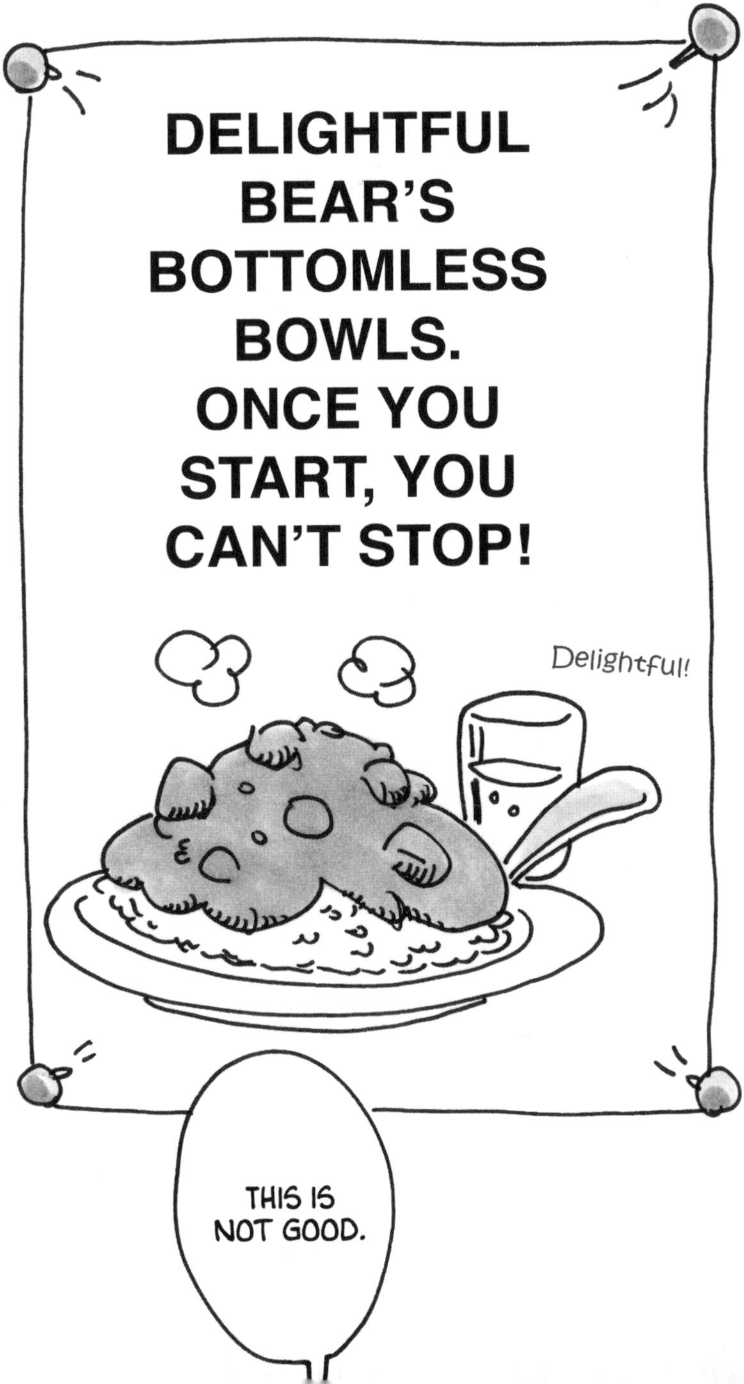
DELIGHTFUL BEAR'S BOTTOMLESS BOWLS. ONCE YOU START, YOU CAN'T STOP!
Delightful!
THIS IS NOT GOOD.

Terrie grabbed Hippity's paw and pulled him out of The Delightful Bear.

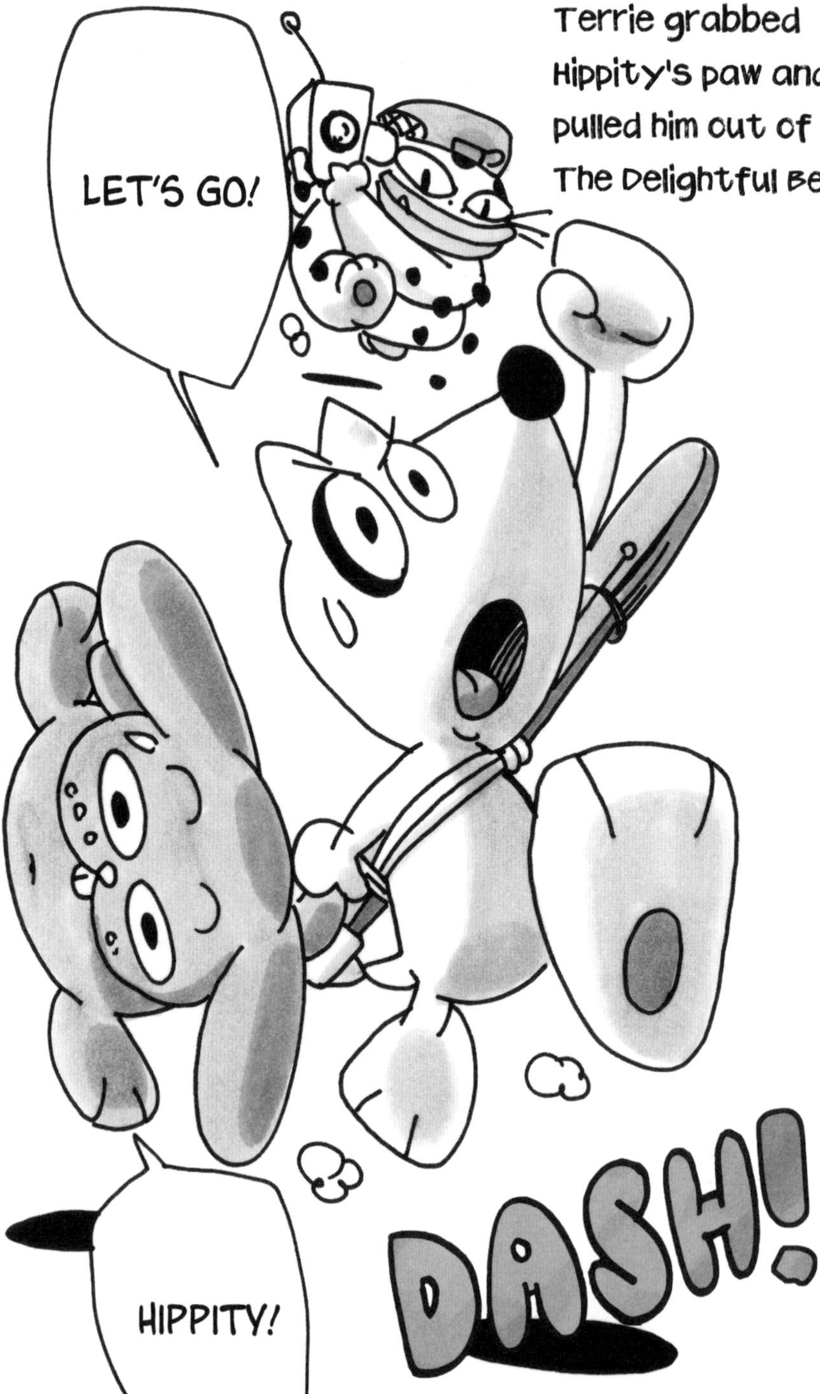
LET'S GO!
HIPPITY!
DASH!

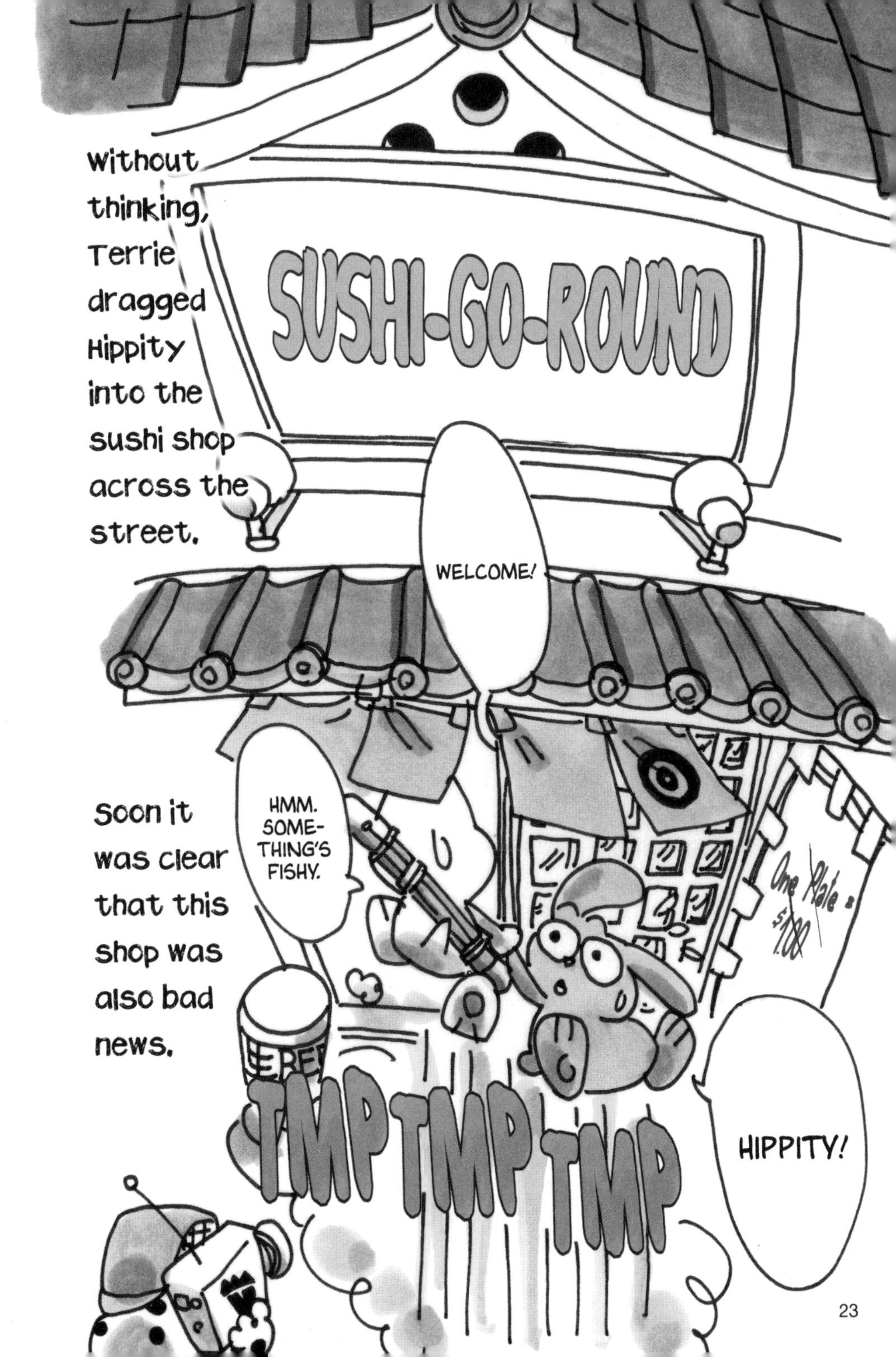
Without thinking, Terrie dragged Hippity into the sushi shop across the street.
SUSHI-GO-ROUND
WELCOME!
Soon it was clear that this shop was also bad news.
HMM. SOME-THING'S FISHY.
HIPPITY!
TMP TMP TMP

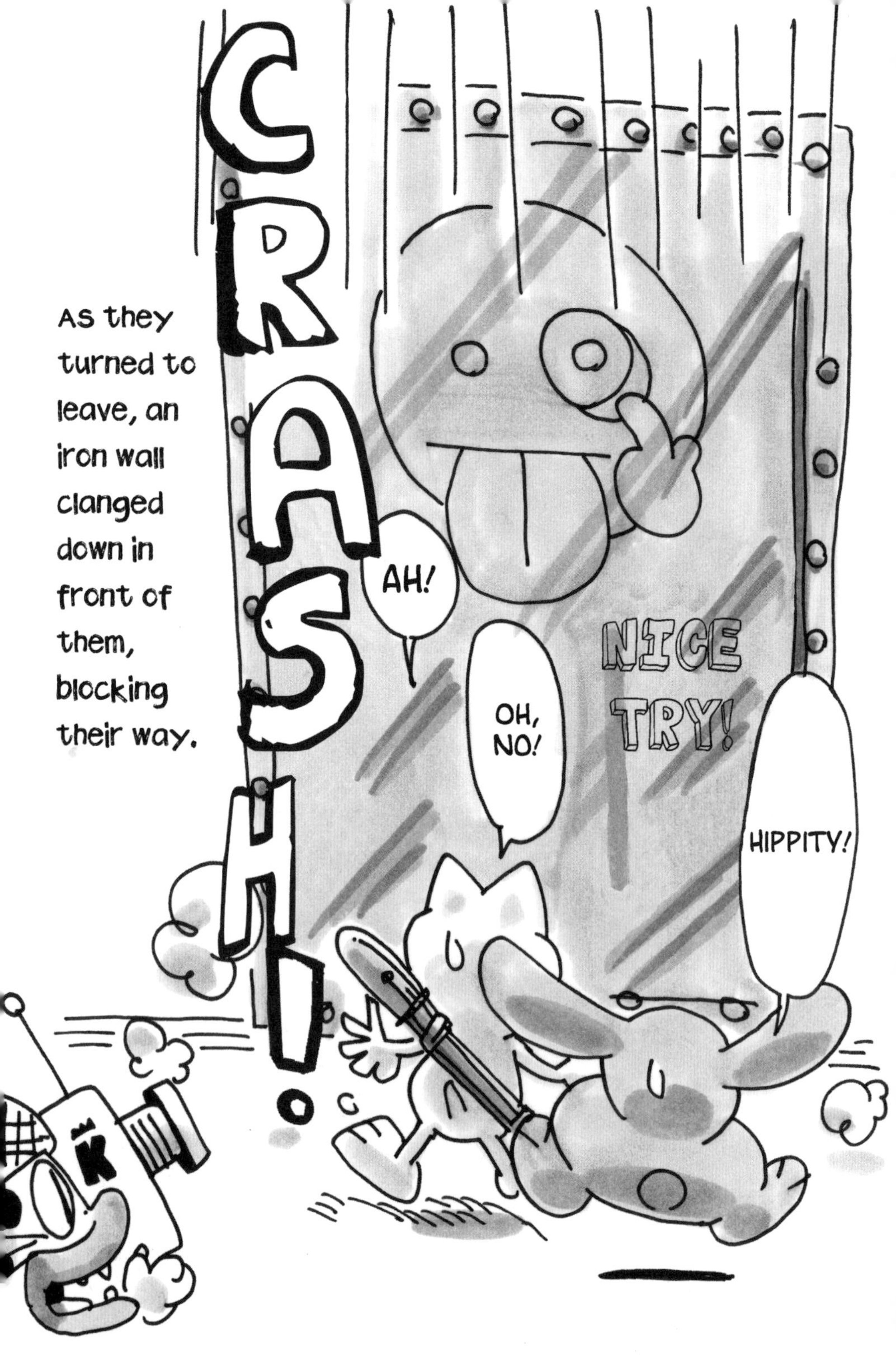
As they turned to leave, an iron wall clanged down in front of them, blocking their way.
CRASH!
AH!
OH, NO!
NICE TRY!
HIPPITY!

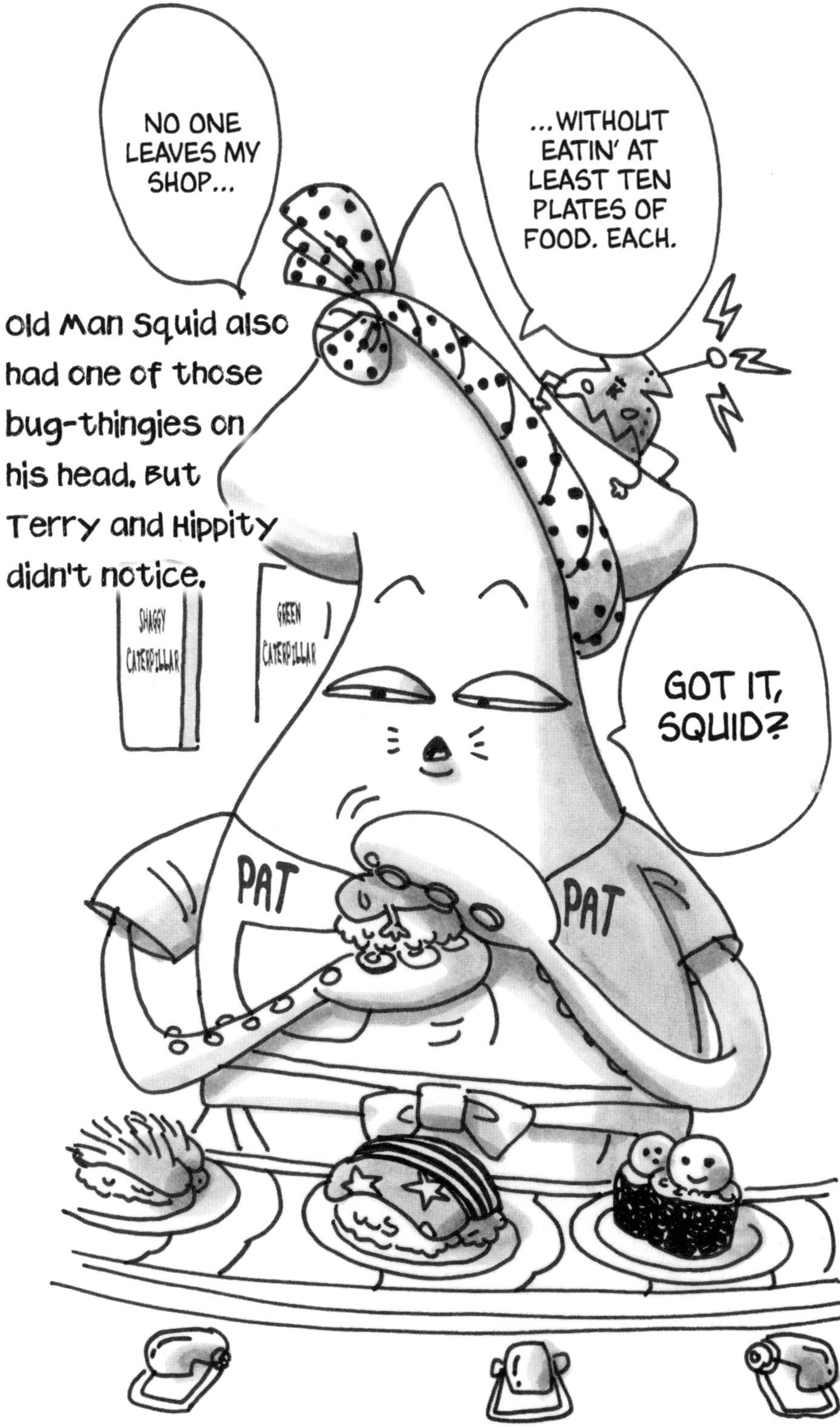
NO ONE LEAVES MY SHOP...
...WITHOUT EATIN' AT LEAST TEN PLATES OF FOOD. EACH.
Old Man Squid also had one of those bug-thingies on his head. But Terry and Hippity didn't notice.
SHAGGY CATERPILLAR
GREEN CATERPILLAR
GOT IT, SQUID?
PAT
PAT

What they did notice was the food Old Man Squid was preparing. It was unlike anything they'd ever seen.

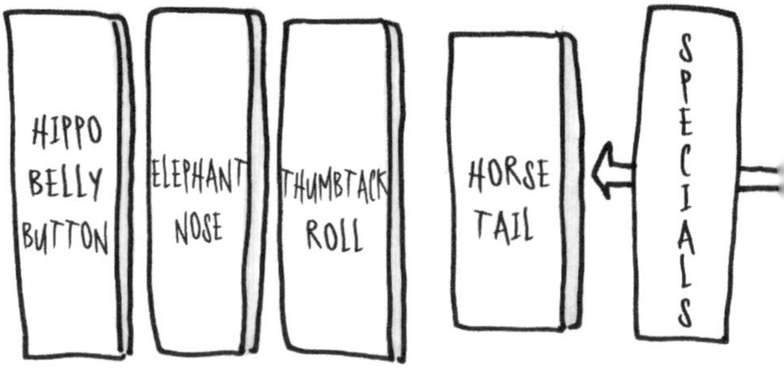
SPECIALS
HORSE TAIL
THUMBTACK ROLL
ELEPHANT NOSE
HIPPO BELLY BUTTON

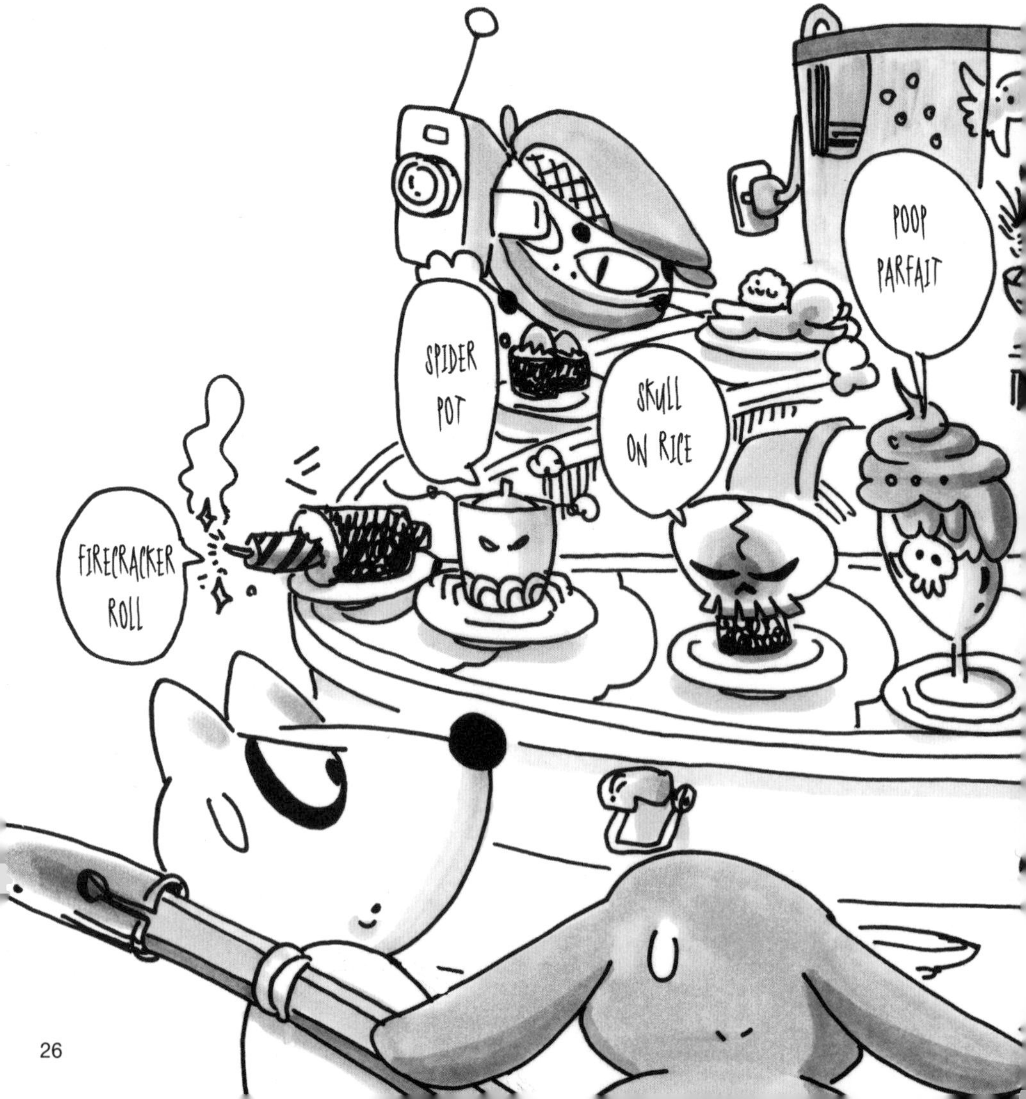
POOP PARFAIT
SKULL ON RICE
SPIDER POT
FIRECRACKER ROLL

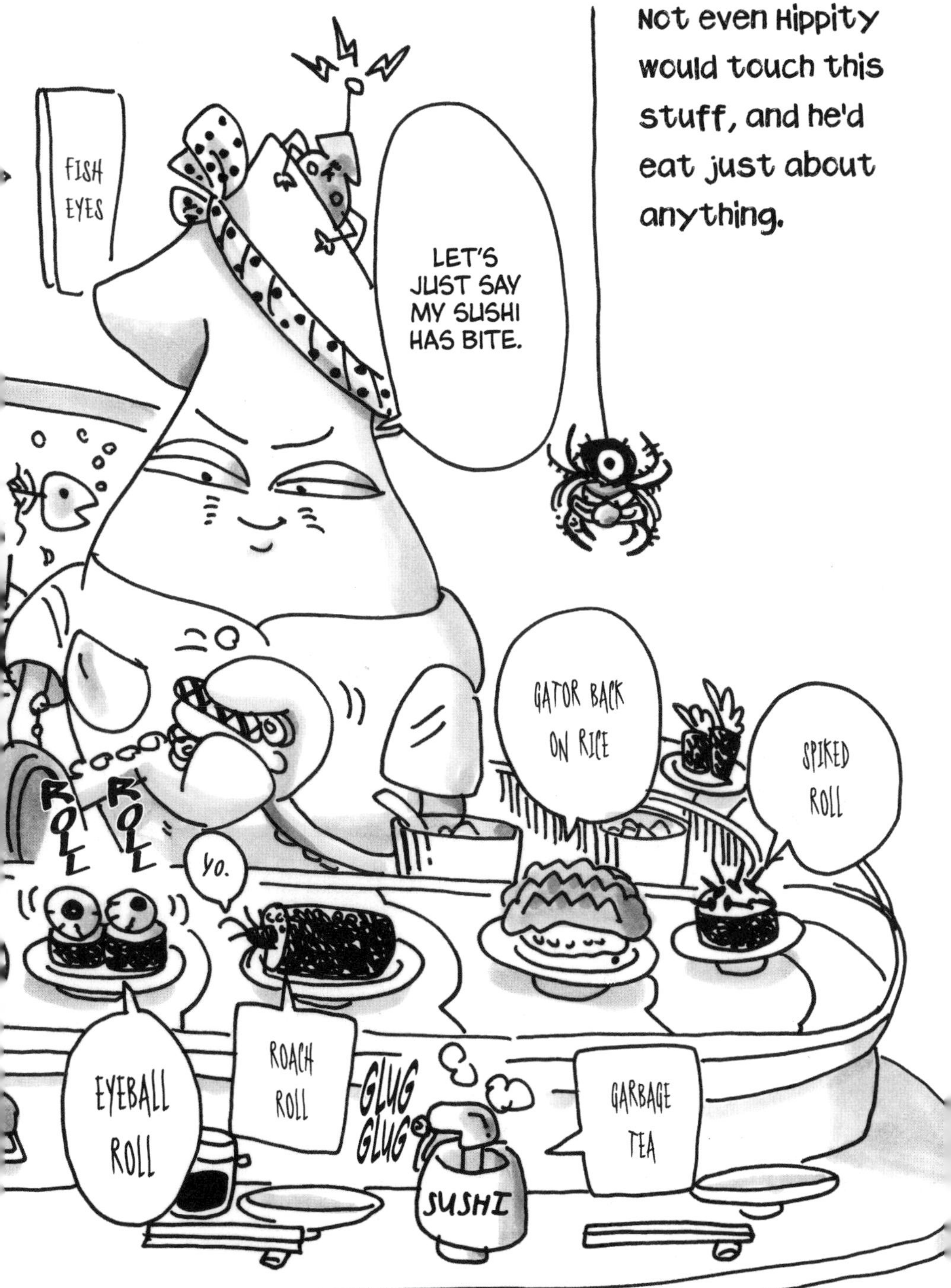
Not even Hippity would touch this stuff, and he'd eat just about anything.
LET'S JUST SAY MY SUSHI HAS BITE.
FISH EYES
SPIKED ROLL
GATOR BACK ON RICE
ROLL ROLL
yo.
GARBAGE TEA
SUSHI
GLUG GLUG
ROACH ROLL
EYEBALL ROLL

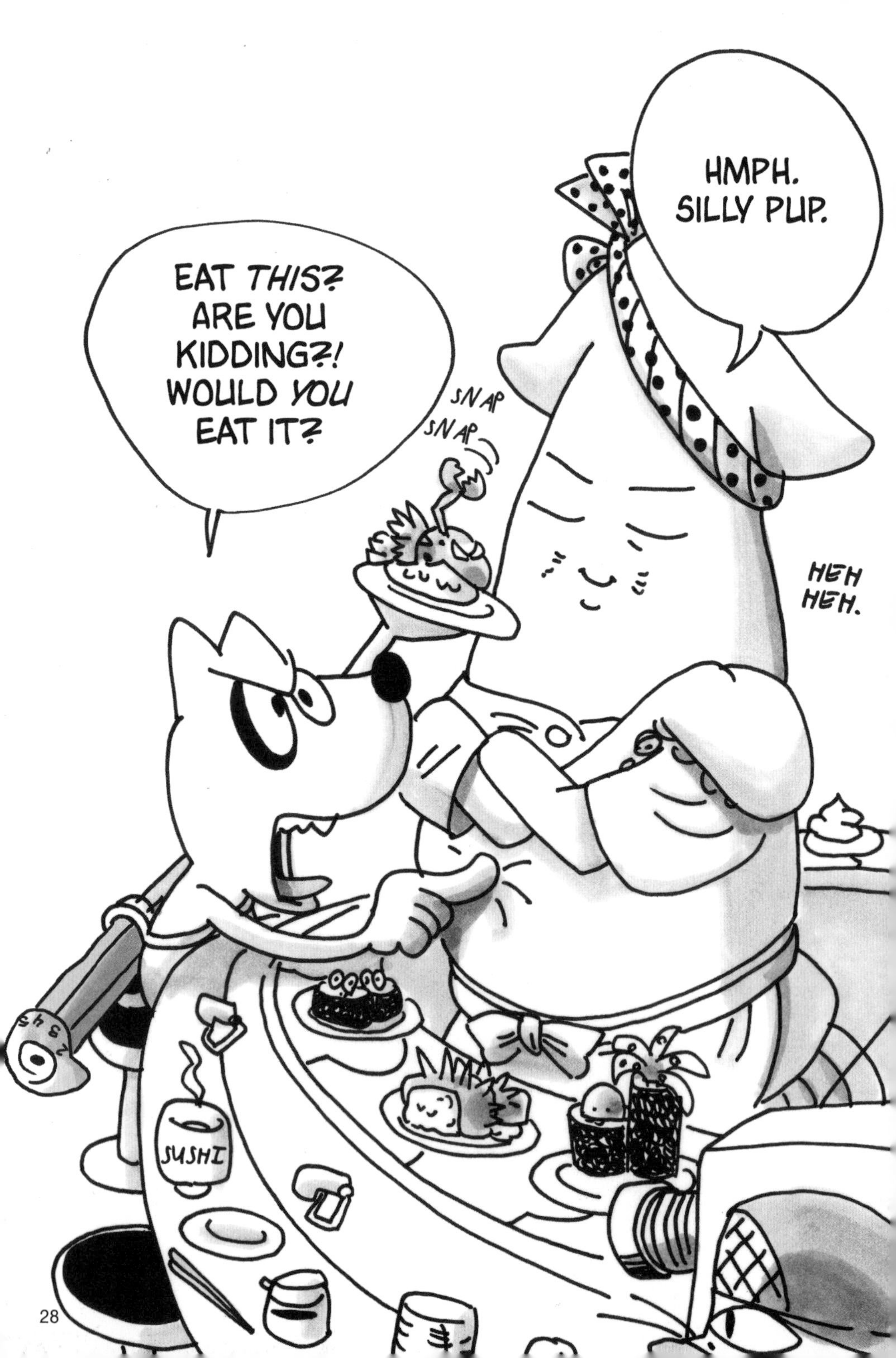
HMPH. SILLY PUP.
HEH HEH.
EAT *THIS*? ARE YOU KIDDING?! WOULD *YOU* EAT IT?
SNAP SNAP
SUSHI

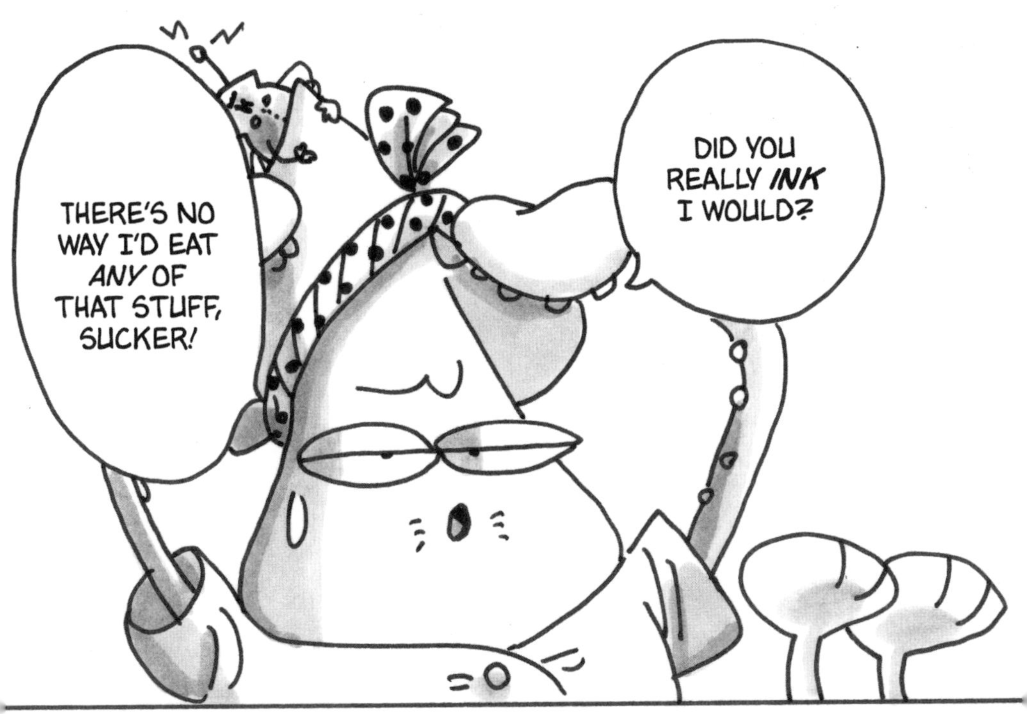
DID YOU REALLY *INK* I WOULD?
THERE'S NO WAY I'D EAT *ANY* OF THAT STUFF, SUCKER!

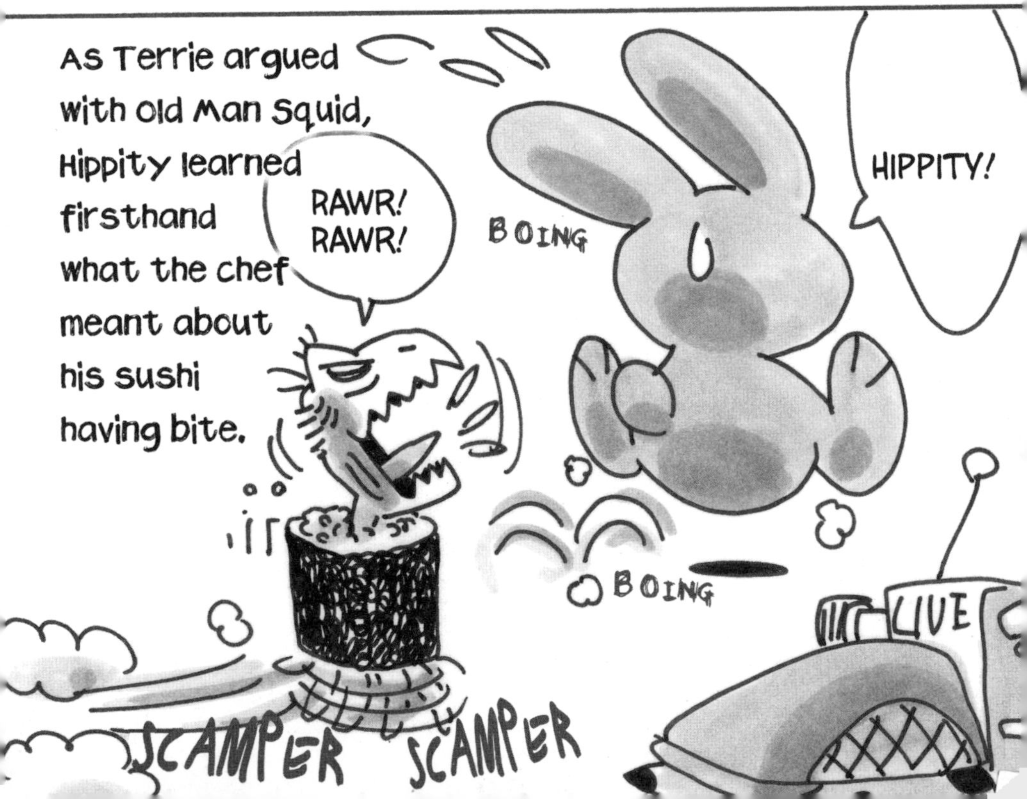
HIPPITY!
BOING
BOING
As Terrie argued with Old Man Squid, Hippity learned firsthand what the chef meant about his sushi having bite.
RAWR! RAWR!
LIVE
SCAMPER SCAMPER

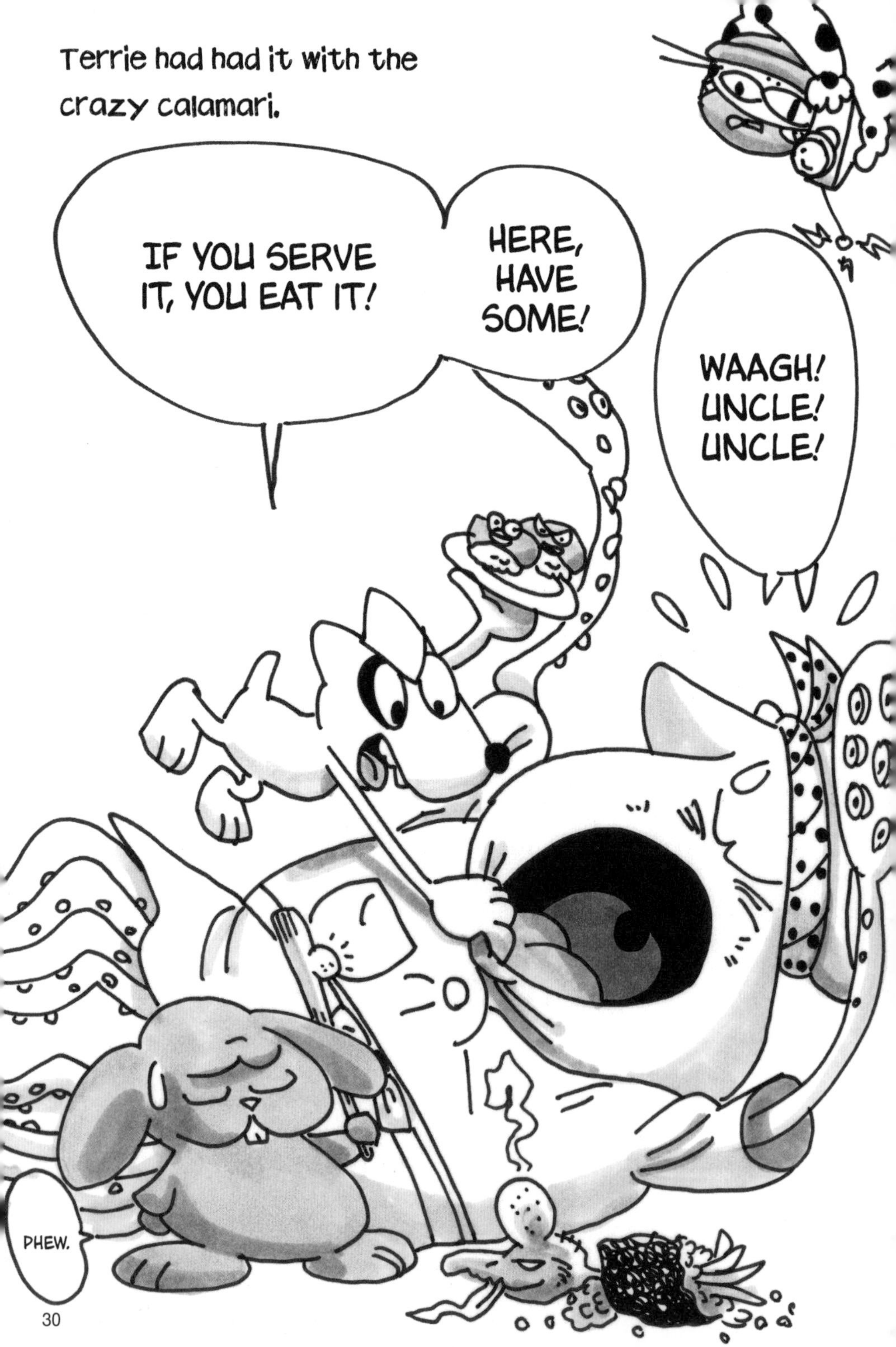
Terrie had had it with the crazy calamari.
IF YOU SERVE IT, YOU EAT IT!
HERE, HAVE SOME!
WAAGH! UNCLE! UNCLE!
PHEW.

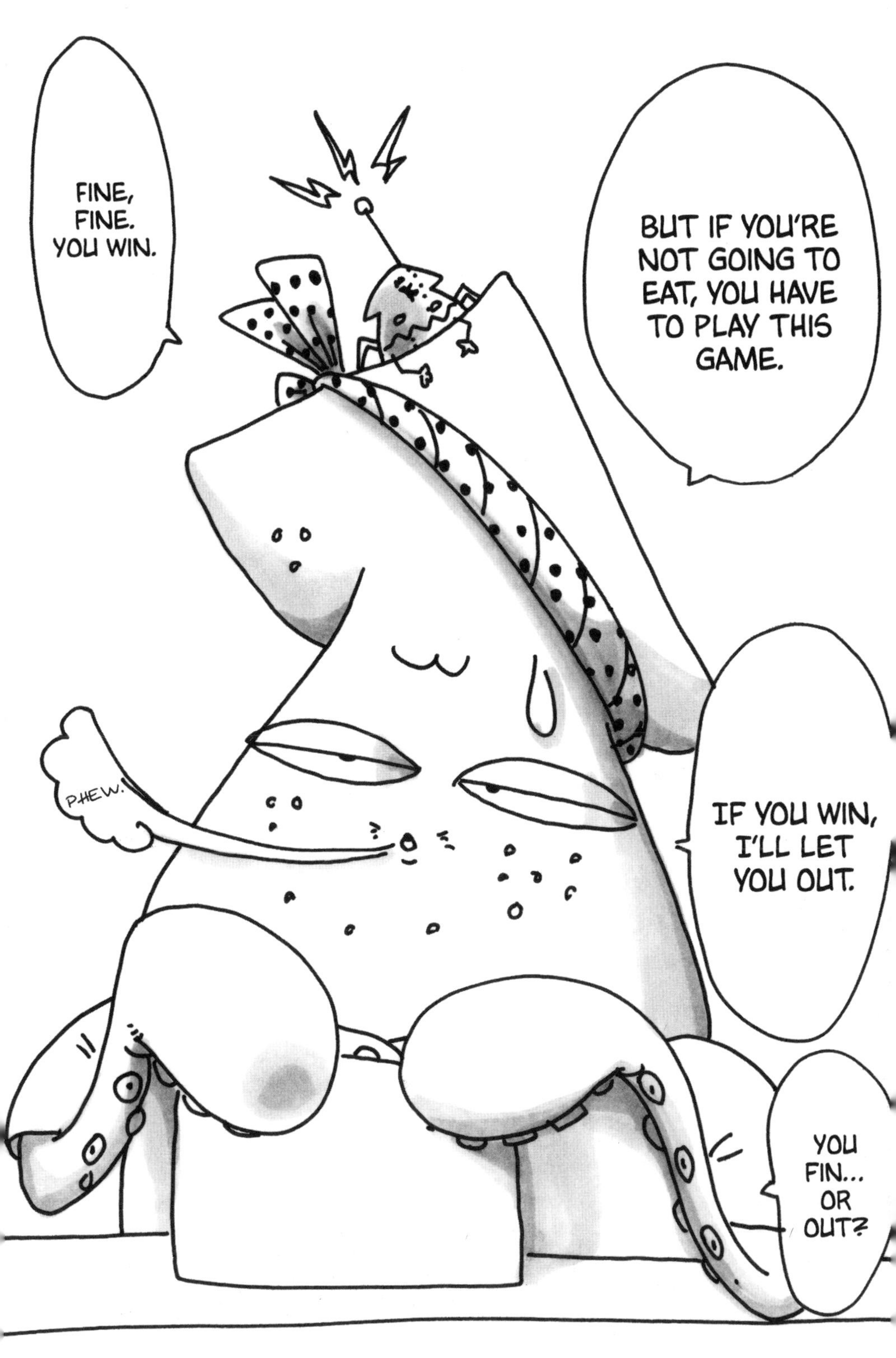
FINE, FINE. YOU WIN.
BUT IF YOU'RE NOT GOING TO EAT, YOU HAVE TO PLAY THIS GAME.
IF YOU WIN, I'LL LET YOU OUT.
PHEW.
YOU FIN... OR OUT?

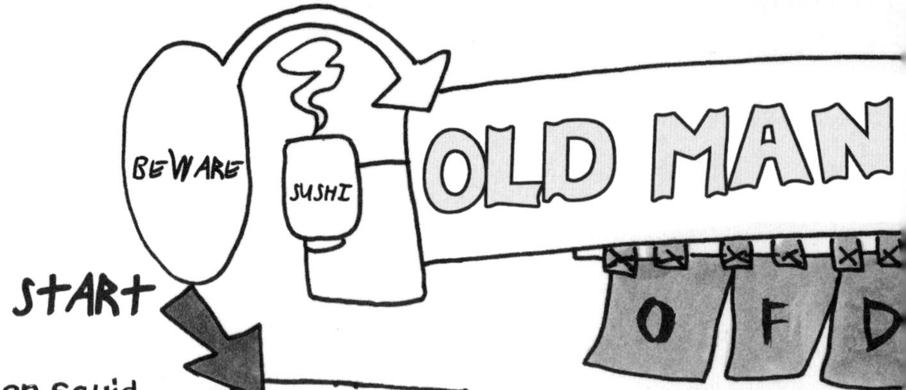
BEWARE
SUSHI
OLD MAN
O F D
START

Old Man Squid presented Terrie with a challenge. To solve the puzzle, they had to get from the carrot to the girl. To get from one word to the next, the last letter of the first word had to be the same as the first letter of the next word.

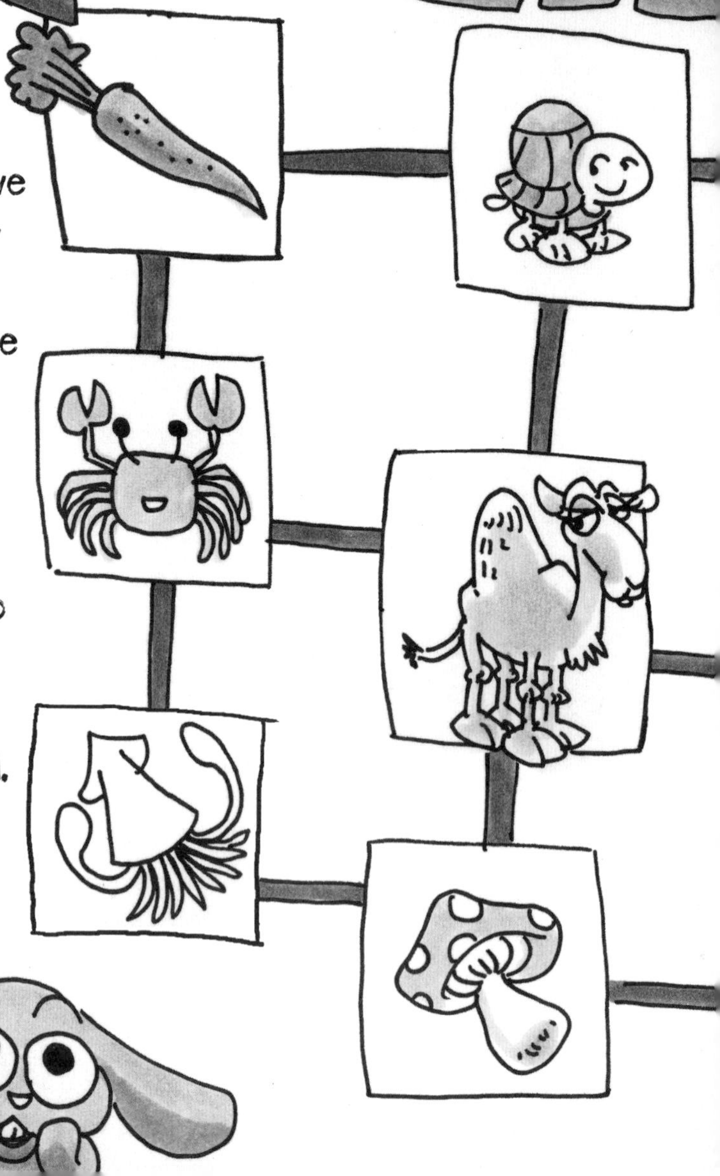

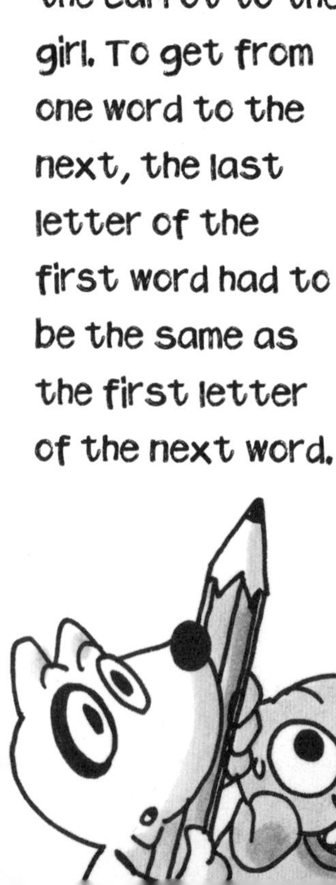

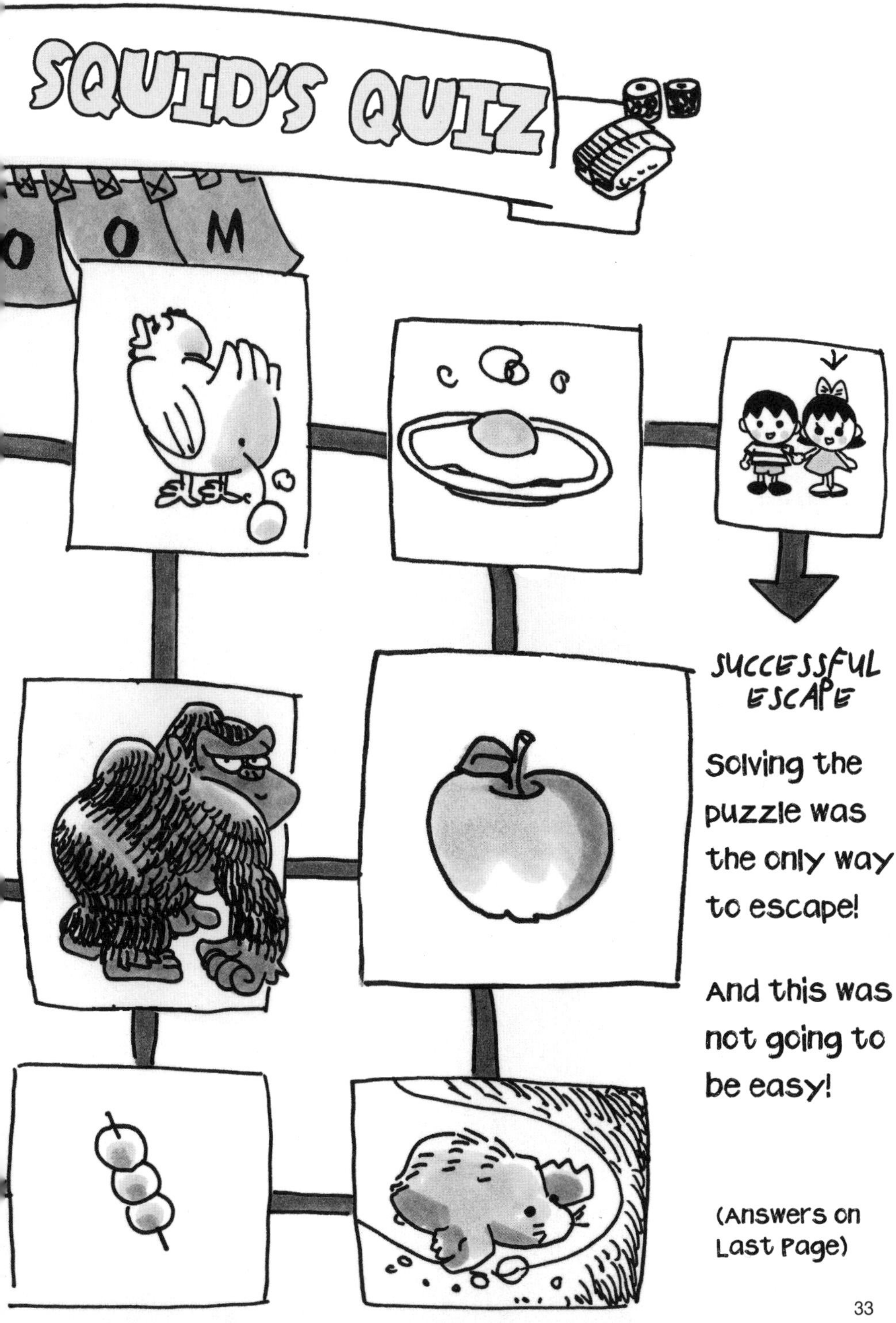
SQUID'S QUIZ
O
O
M
SUCCESSFUL ESCAPE
Solving the puzzle was the only way to escape!
And this was not going to be easy!
(Answers on Last Page)

While Terrie and Hippity solve the puzzle, let's take a tour of Eats Street.

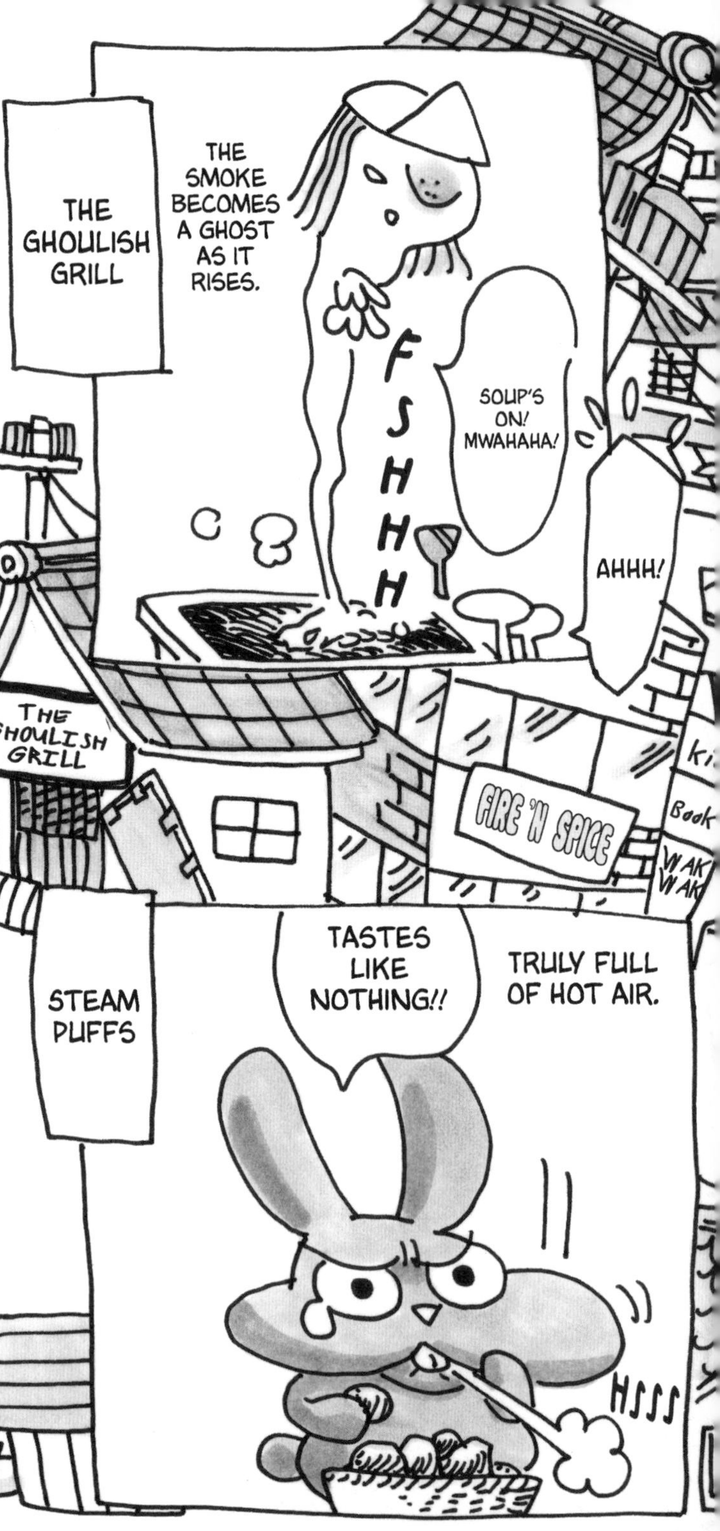
THE GHOULISH GRILL
THE SMOKE BECOMES A GHOST AS IT RISES.
SOUP'S ON! MWAHAHA!
FSHHHH
AHHH!
THE GHOULISH GRILL
FIRE 'N SPICE
Book
WAK WAK
TRULY FULL OF HOT AIR.
TASTES LIKE NOTHING!!
STEAM PUFFS
HSSS

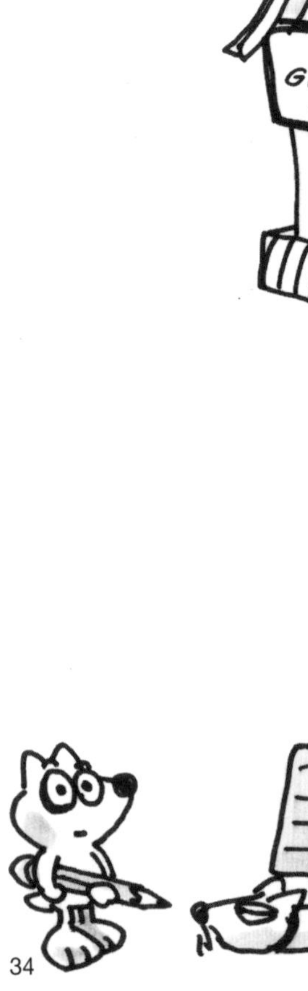

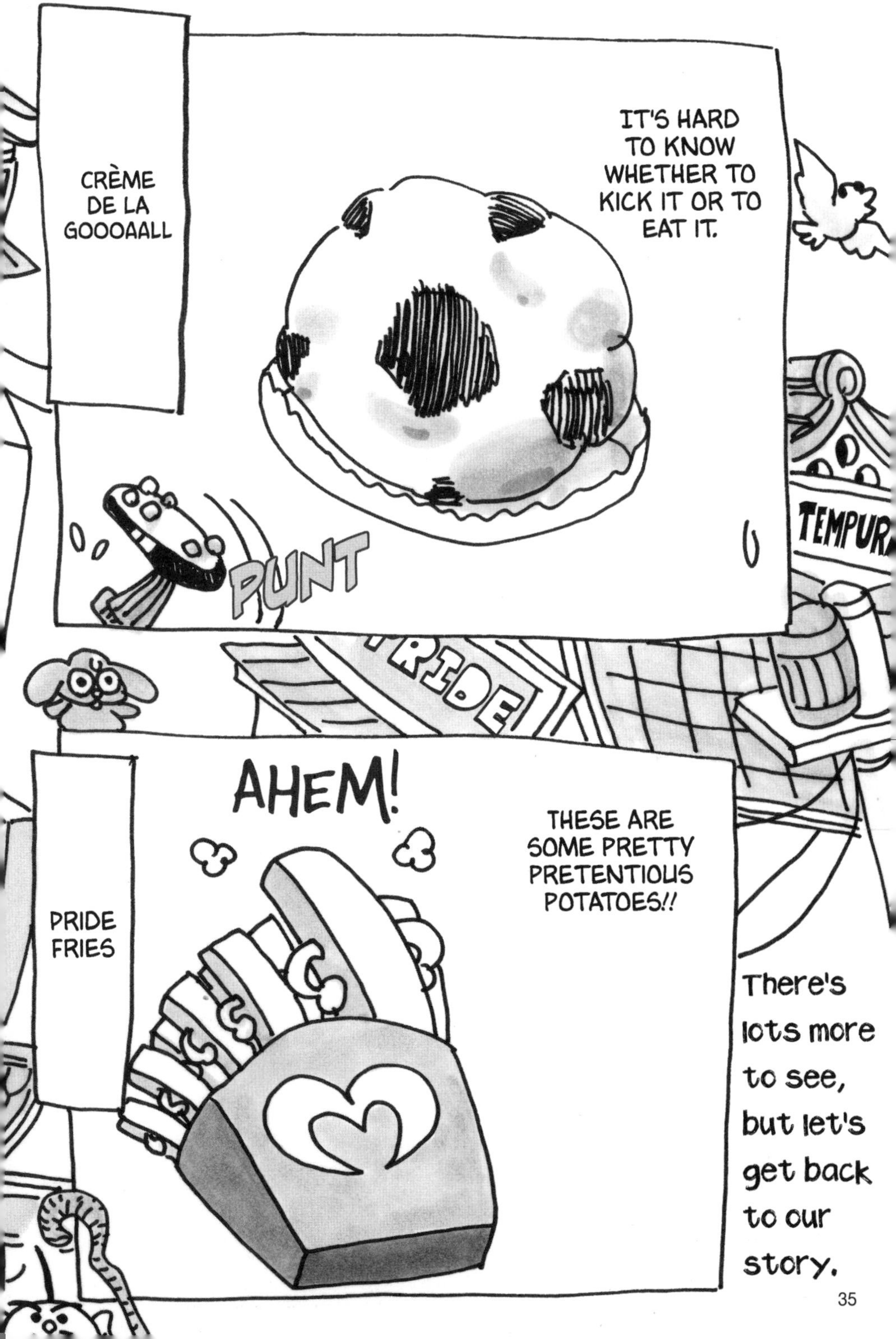
IT'S HARD TO KNOW WHETHER TO KICK IT OR TO EAT IT.
CRÈME DE LA GOOOAALL
PUNT
TEMPURA
PRIDE
AHEM!
THESE ARE SOME PRETTY PRETENTIOUS POTATOES!!
PRIDE FRIES
There's lots more to see, but let's get back to our story.

Terrie and Hippity solved the puzzle and escaped Old Man Squid! From his hiding place, King Crossout saw everything. And he was not pleased.

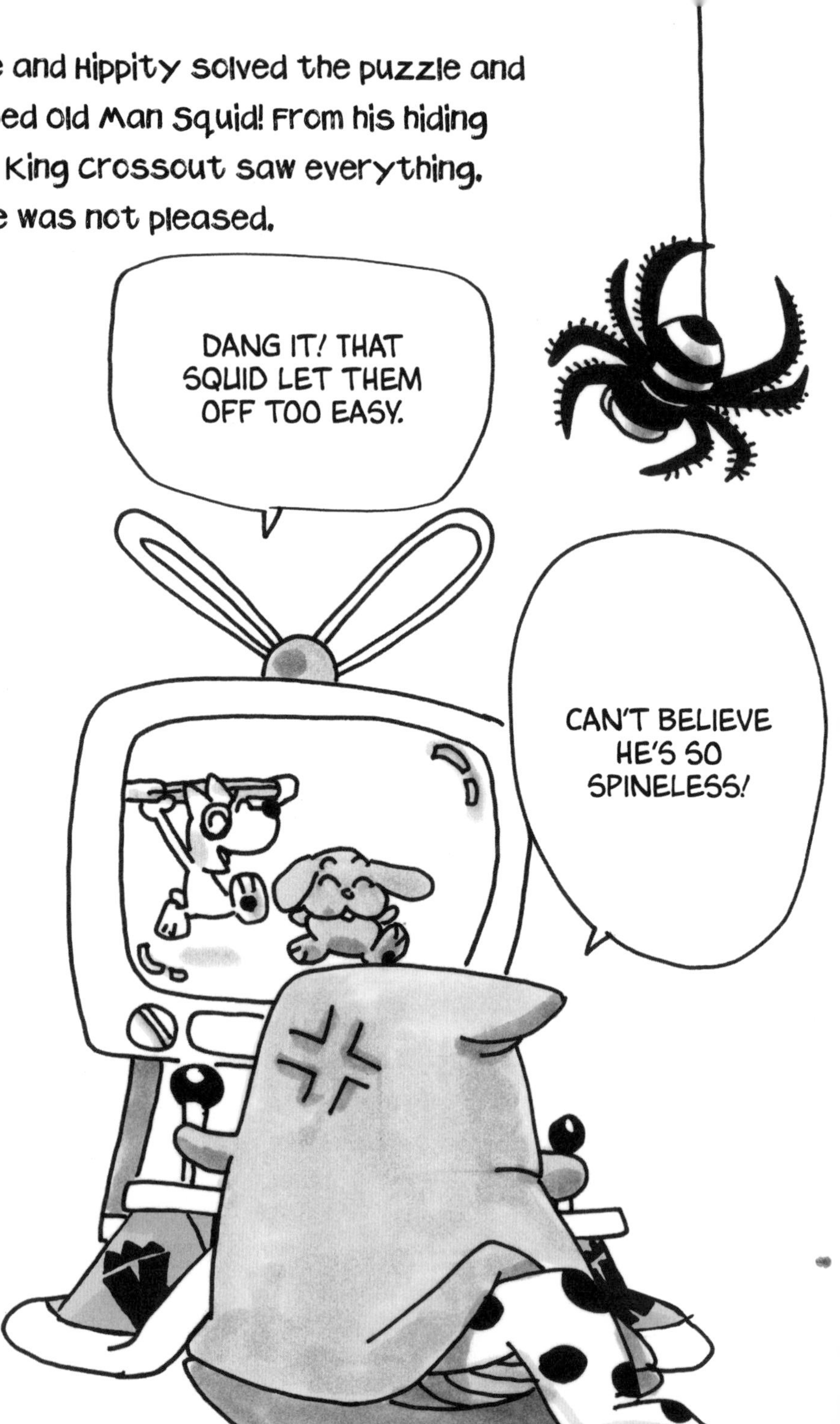
DANG IT! THAT SQUID LET THEM OFF TOO EASY.
CAN'T BELIEVE HE'S SO SPINELESS!

As you've no doubt figured out by now, all of Eats Street was under King Crossout's control.

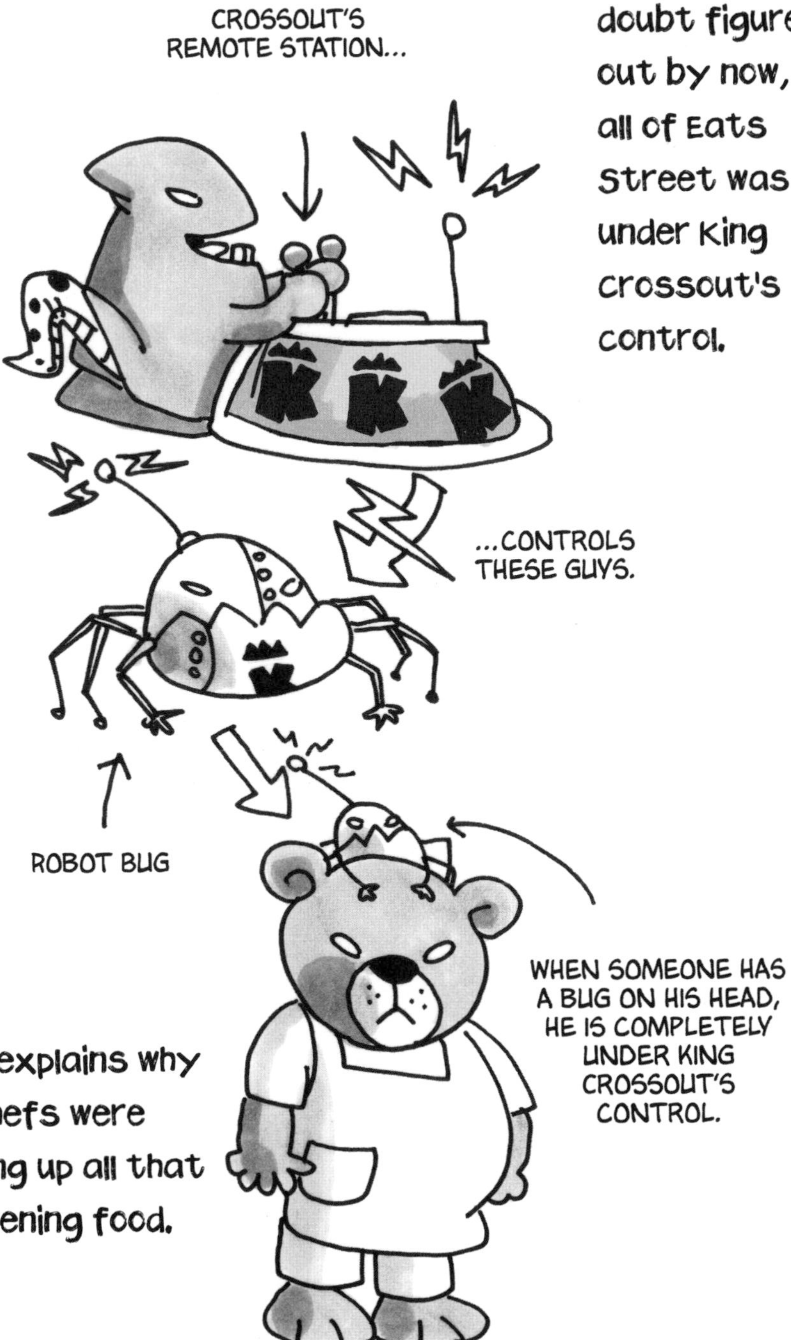
CROSSOUT'S REMOTE STATION...
...CONTROLS THESE GUYS.
ROBOT BUG
WHEN SOMEONE HAS A BUG ON HIS HEAD, HE IS COMPLETELY UNDER KING CROSSOUT'S CONTROL.

Which explains why the chefs were whipping up all that frightening food.

But Terrie and Hippity didn't know that yet. What they did know was that Eats Street needed at least one decent restaurant. Using the Magic Pencil, Terrie drew a small food stand.

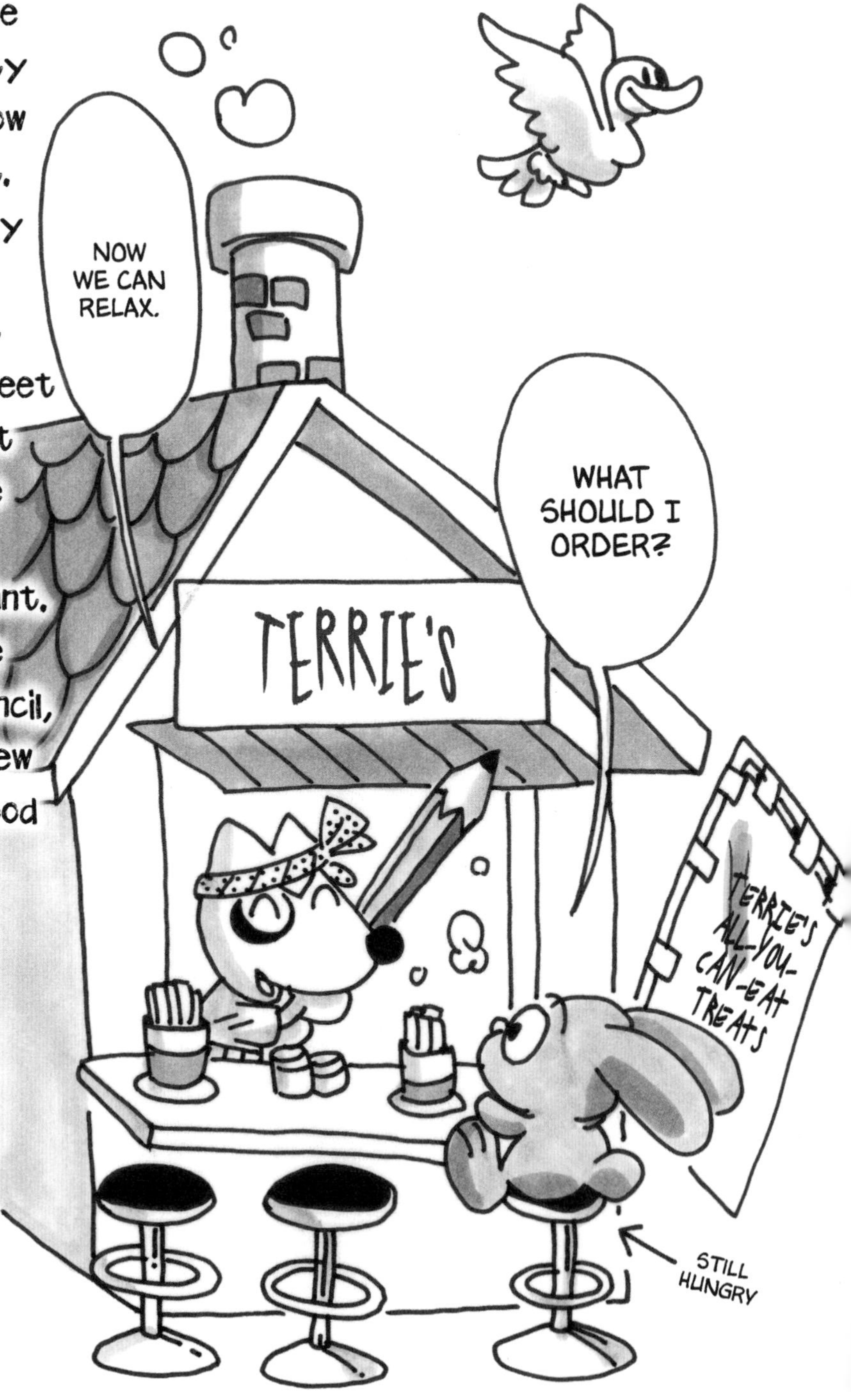
NOW WE CAN RELAX.
WHAT SHOULD I ORDER?
TERRIE'S
TERRIE'S ALL-YOU-CAN-EAT TREATS
STILL HUNGRY

Terrie handed Hippity a menu. Here's how it works:

First choose a number. Then follow the vertical line down until you get to a line that goes across. You have to take the first one you come to! Follow that line up, down, round-and-round until it takes you to another vertical line. Take that line down until you get to another line that goes across. Keep doing this until you get to one of the letters at the bottom.

ALL-YOU-CAN-EAT MENU

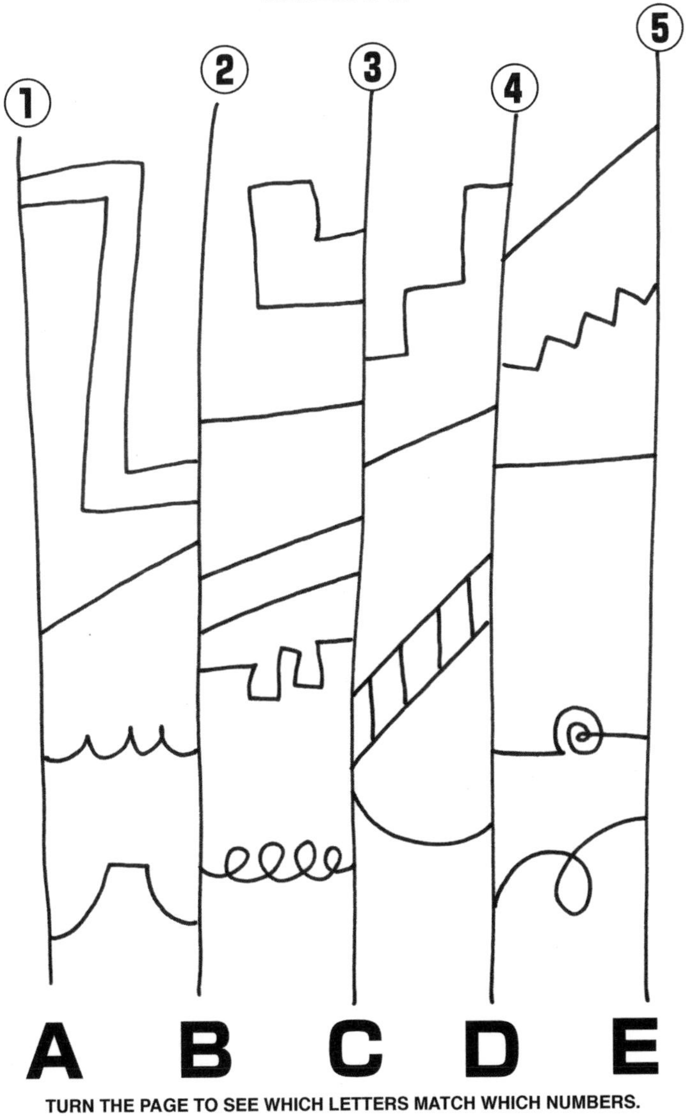

1
2
3
4
5
A
B
C
D
E

TURN THE PAGE TO SEE WHICH LETTERS MATCH WHICH NUMBERS.

Here's what's on the menu:

① - A = hamburger steak

② - E = rice ball

③ - B = pork on rice

④ - C = ramen

⑤ - D = stir-fry

What did you end up ordering?

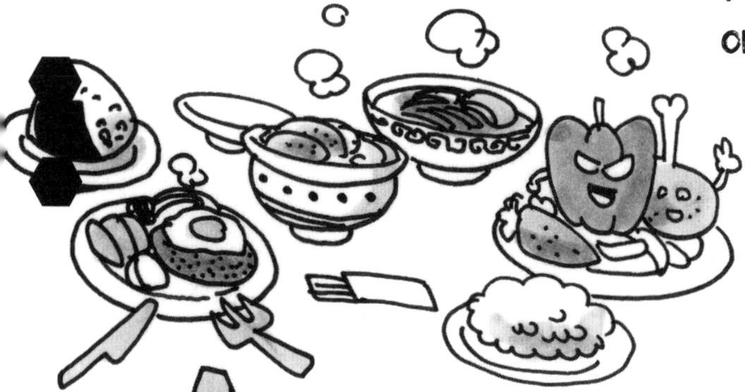

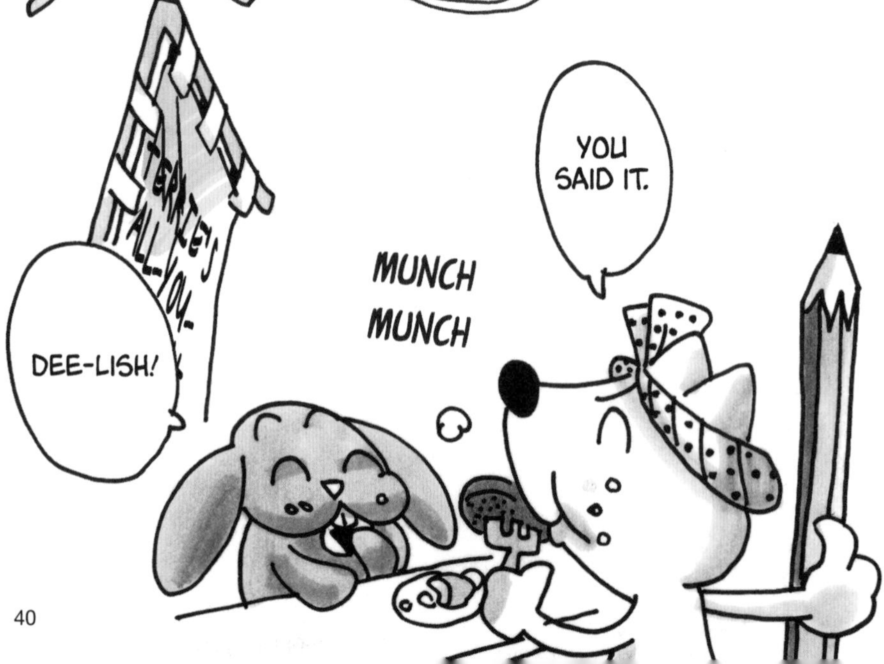
DEE-LISH!
MUNCH MUNCH
YOU SAID IT.

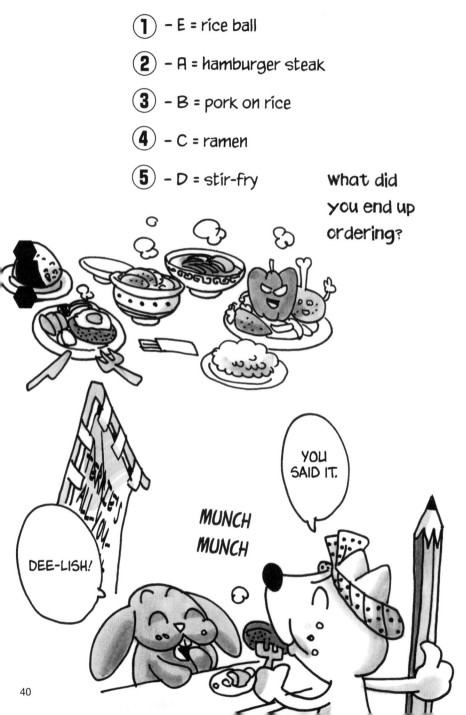

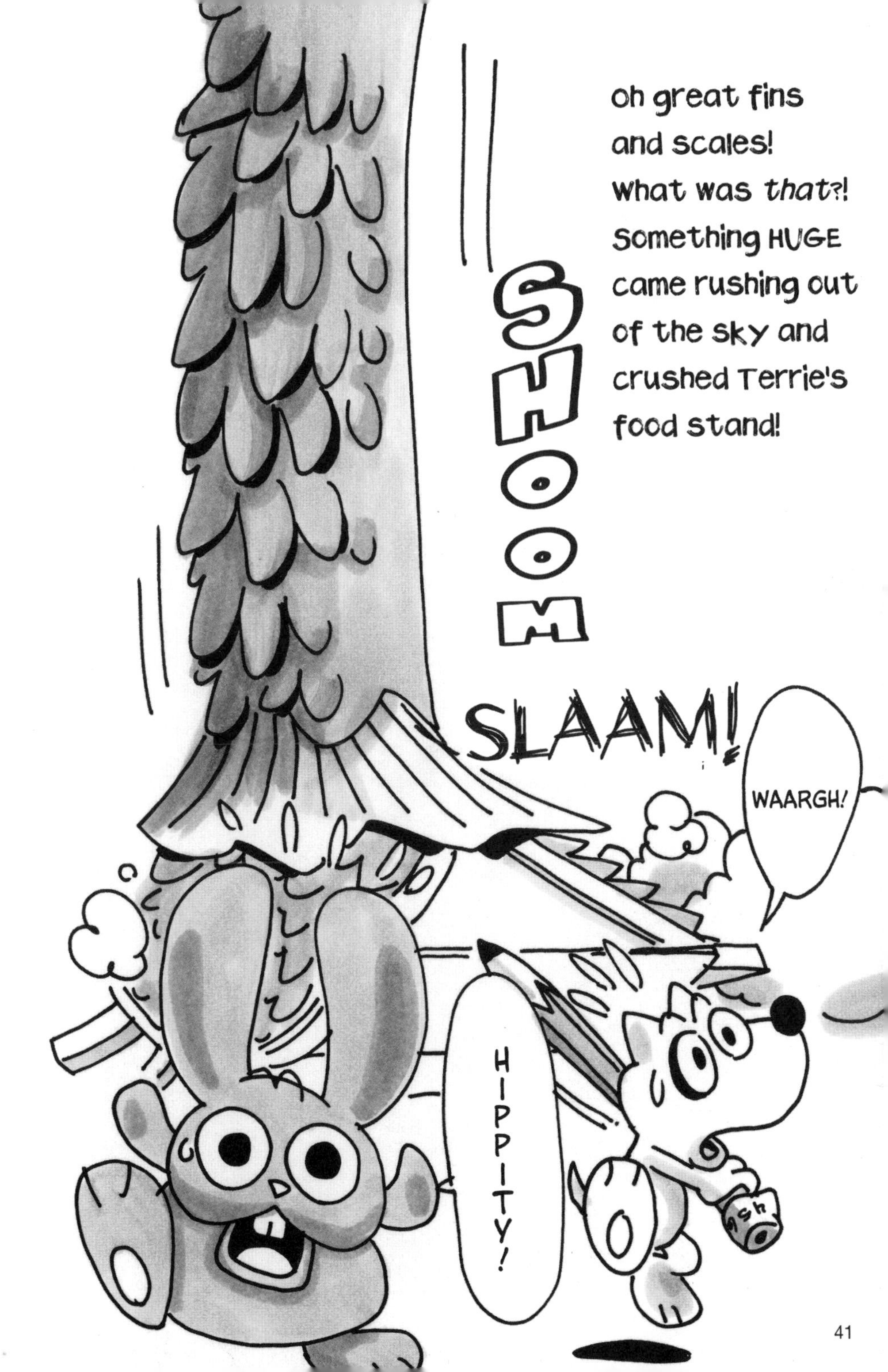
oh great fins and scales! What was *that*?! Something HUGE came rushing out of the sky and crushed Terrie's food stand!
SHOOOM
SLAAM!
WAARGH!
HIPPITY!

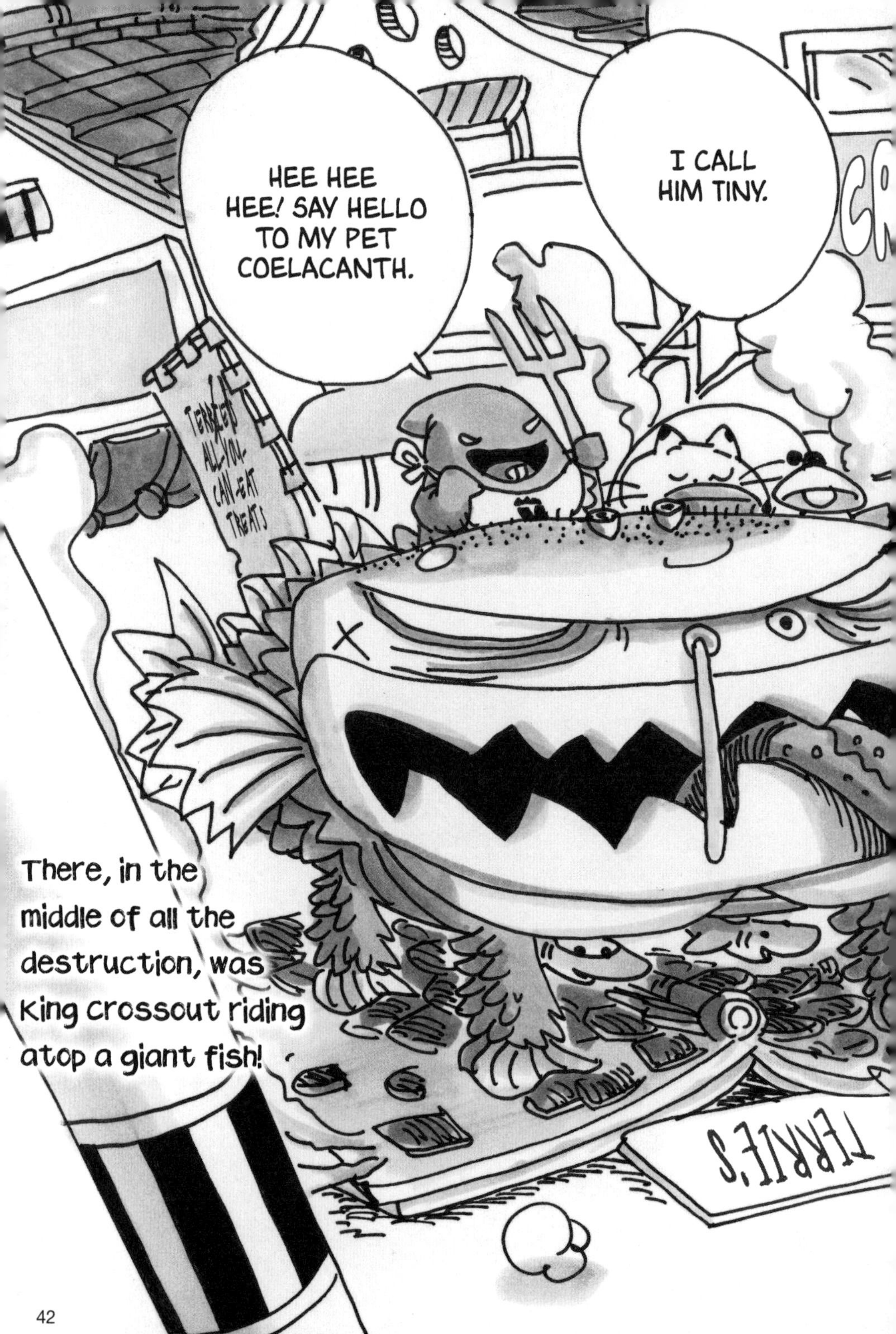
HEE HEE HEE! SAY HELLO TO MY PET COELACANTH.
I CALL HIM TINY.
TERRIE'S ALL-YOU-CAN-EAT TREATS
There, in the middle of all the destruction, was King Crossout riding atop a giant fish!

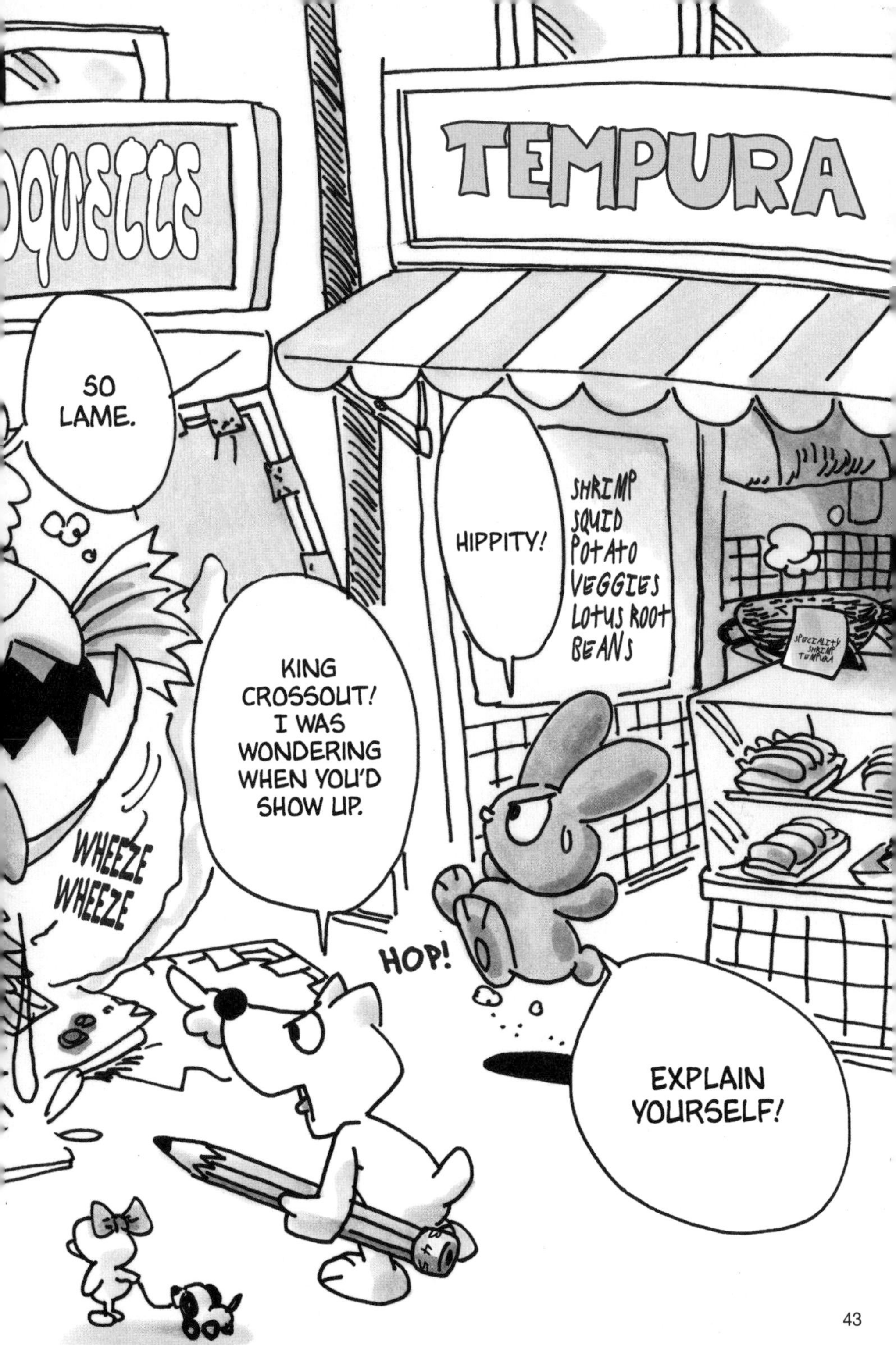
TEMPURA
HIPPITY!
SHRIMP
SQUID
POTATO
VEGGIES
LOTUS ROOT
BEANS
SPECIALITY SHRIMP TEMPURA
SO LAME.
KING CROSSOUT! I WAS WONDERING WHEN YOU'D SHOW UP.
HOP!
EXPLAIN YOURSELF!
WHEEZE WHEEZE

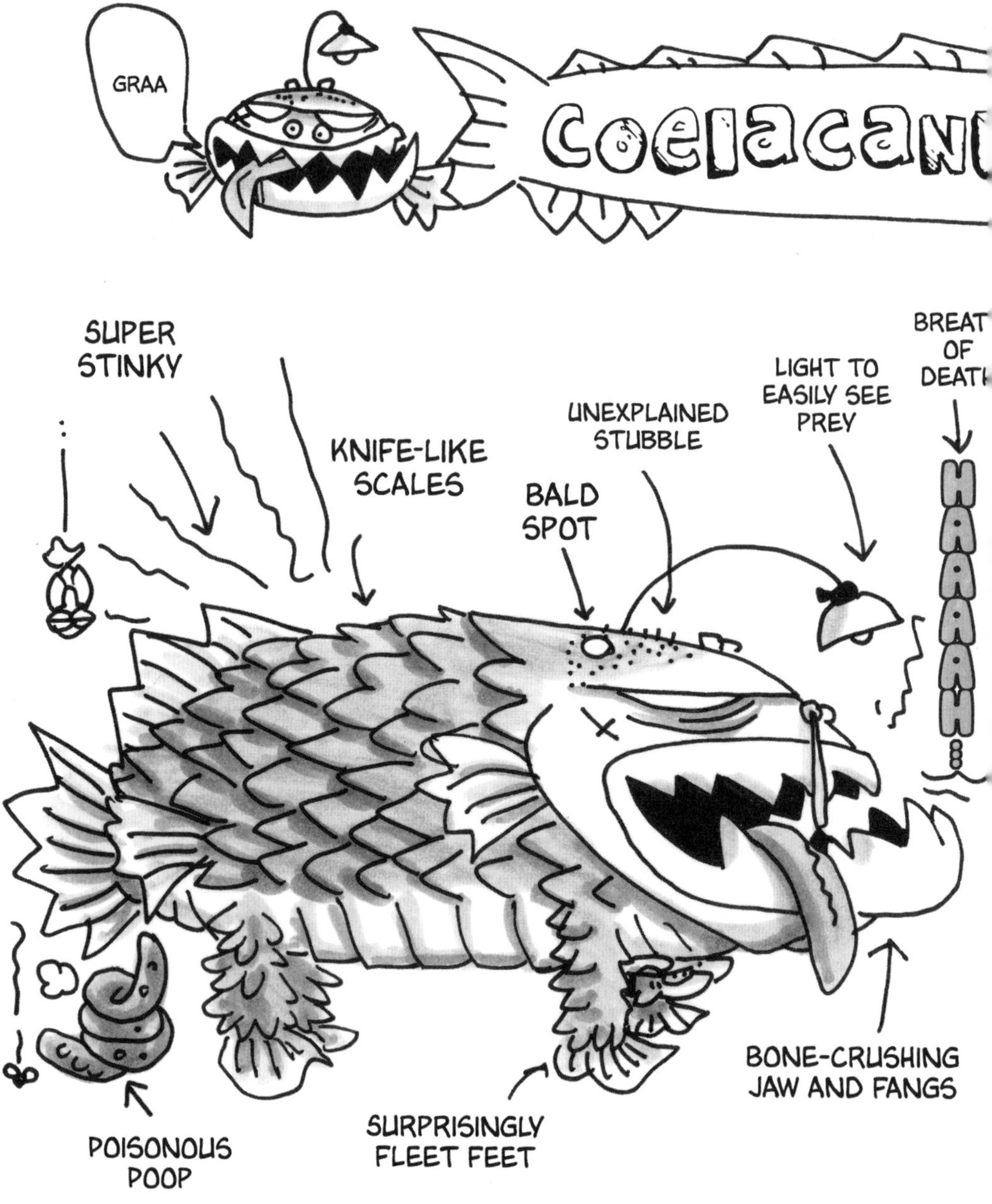
GRAA
Coelacan
SUPER STINKY
KNIFE-LIKE SCALES
BALD SPOT
UNEXPLAINED STUBBLE
LIGHT TO EASILY SEE PREY
BREAT OF DEAT
HAAAAH...
BONE-CRUSHING JAW AND FANGS
SURPRISINGLY FLEET FEET
POISONOUS POOP

LENGTH	16 FEET
WEIGHT	2 TONS

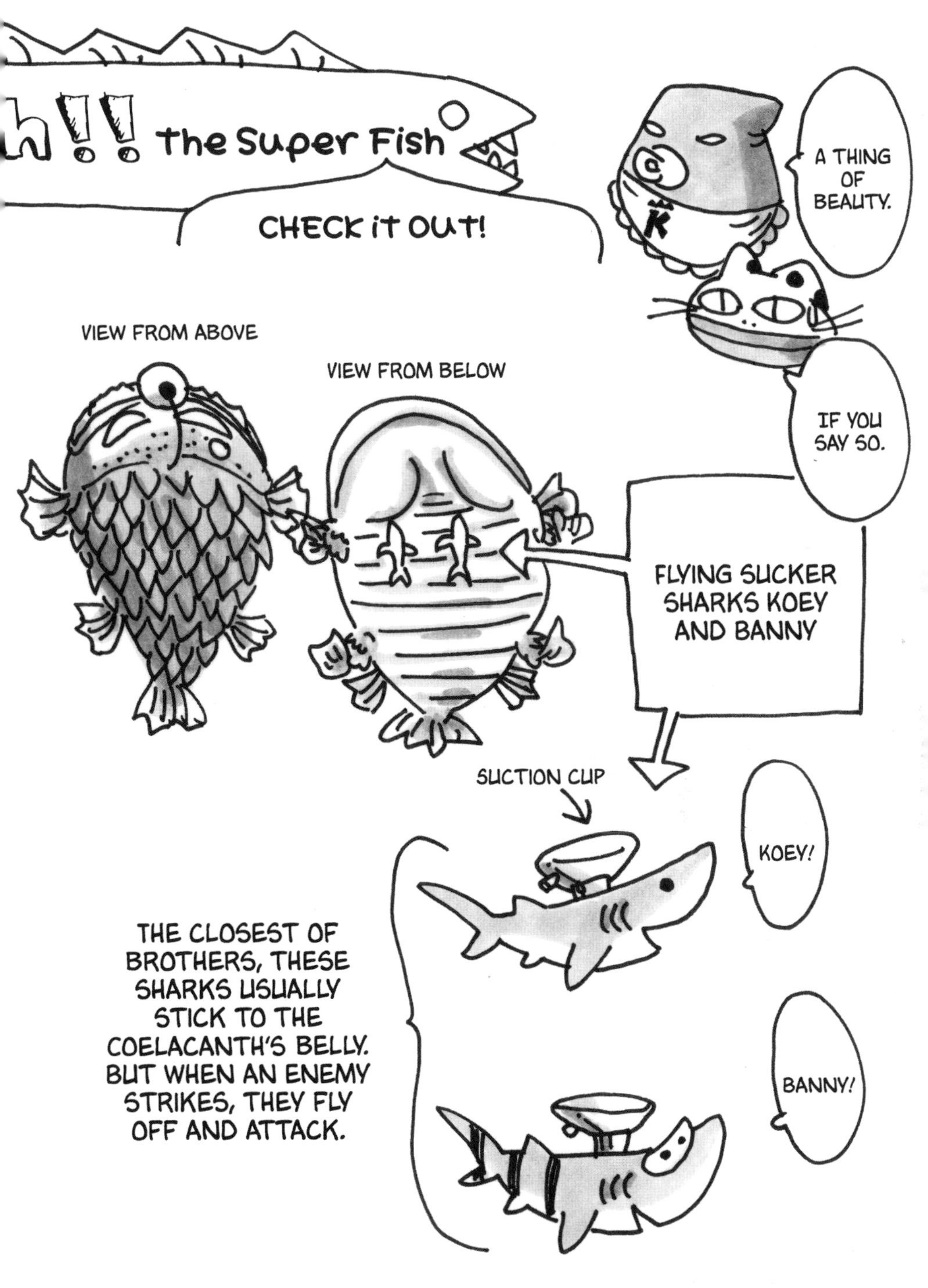
h!! the Super Fish
CHECK it OUT!
A THING OF BEAUTY.
IF YOU SAY SO.
VIEW FROM ABOVE
VIEW FROM BELOW
FLYING SUCKER SHARKS KOEY AND BANNY
SUCTION CUP
KOEY!
BANNY!
THE CLOSEST OF BROTHERS, THESE SHARKS USUALLY STICK TO THE COELACANTH'S BELLY. BUT WHEN AN ENEMY STRIKES, THEY FLY OFF AND ATTACK.

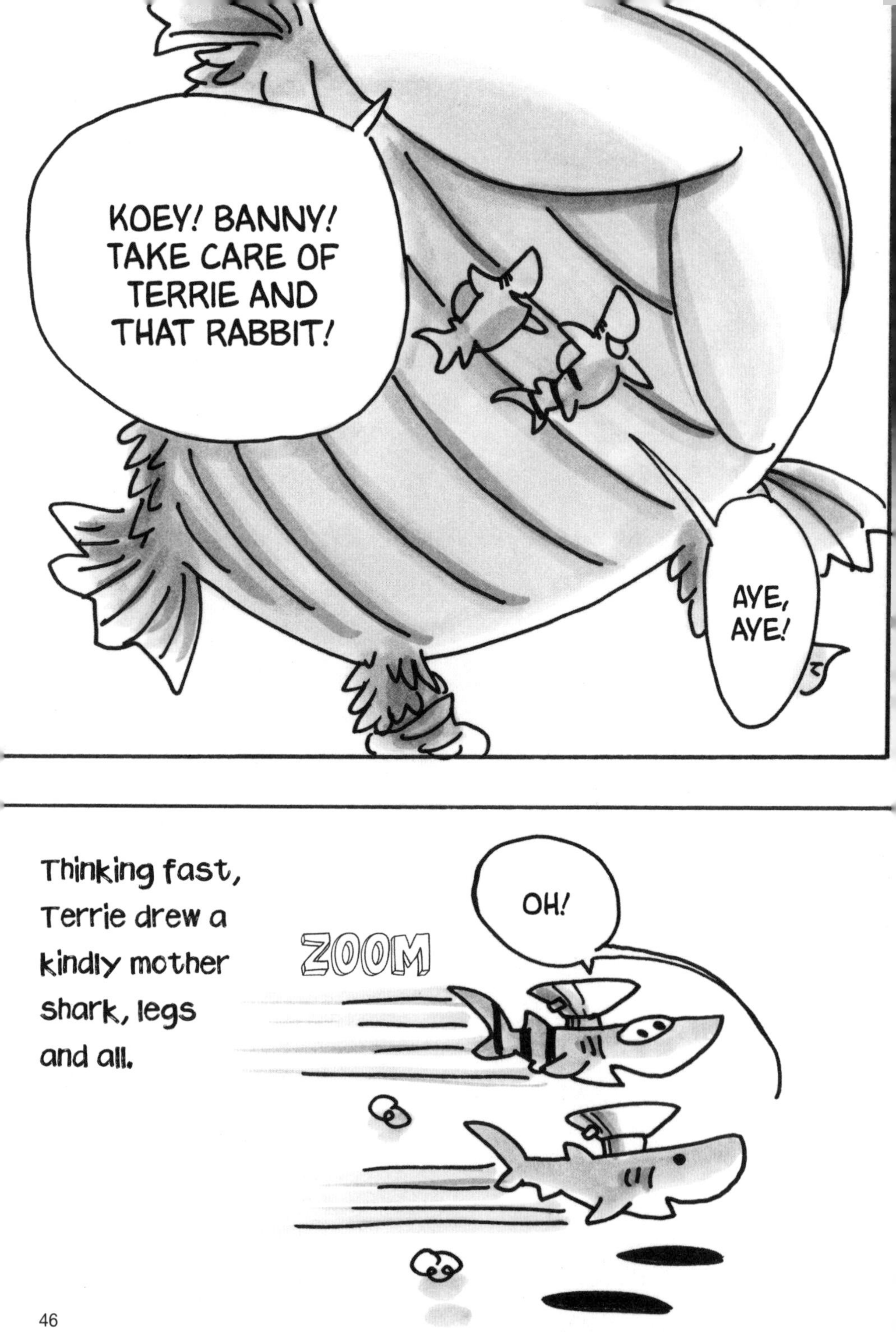
KOEY! BANNY! TAKE CARE OF TERRIE AND THAT RABBIT!
AYE, AYE!
Thinking fast, Terrie drew a kindly mother shark, legs and all.
ZOOM
OH!

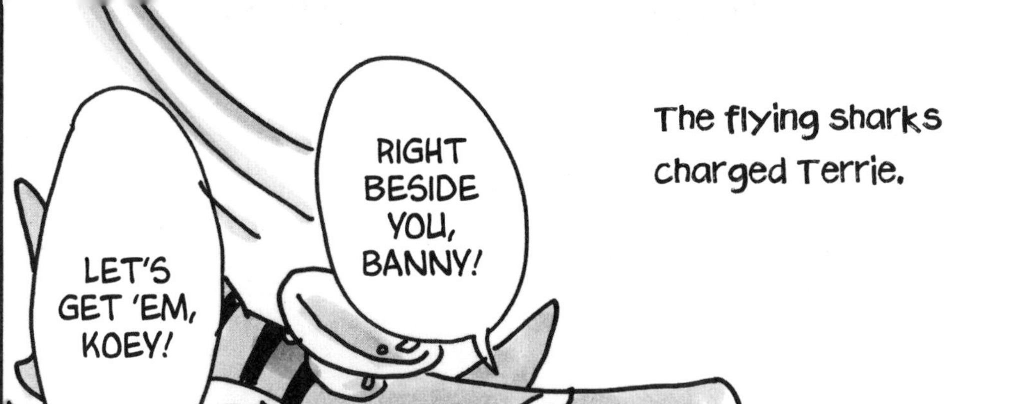
The flying sharks charged Terrie.
LET'S GET 'EM, KOEY!
RIGHT BESIDE YOU, BANNY!
WHOOSH

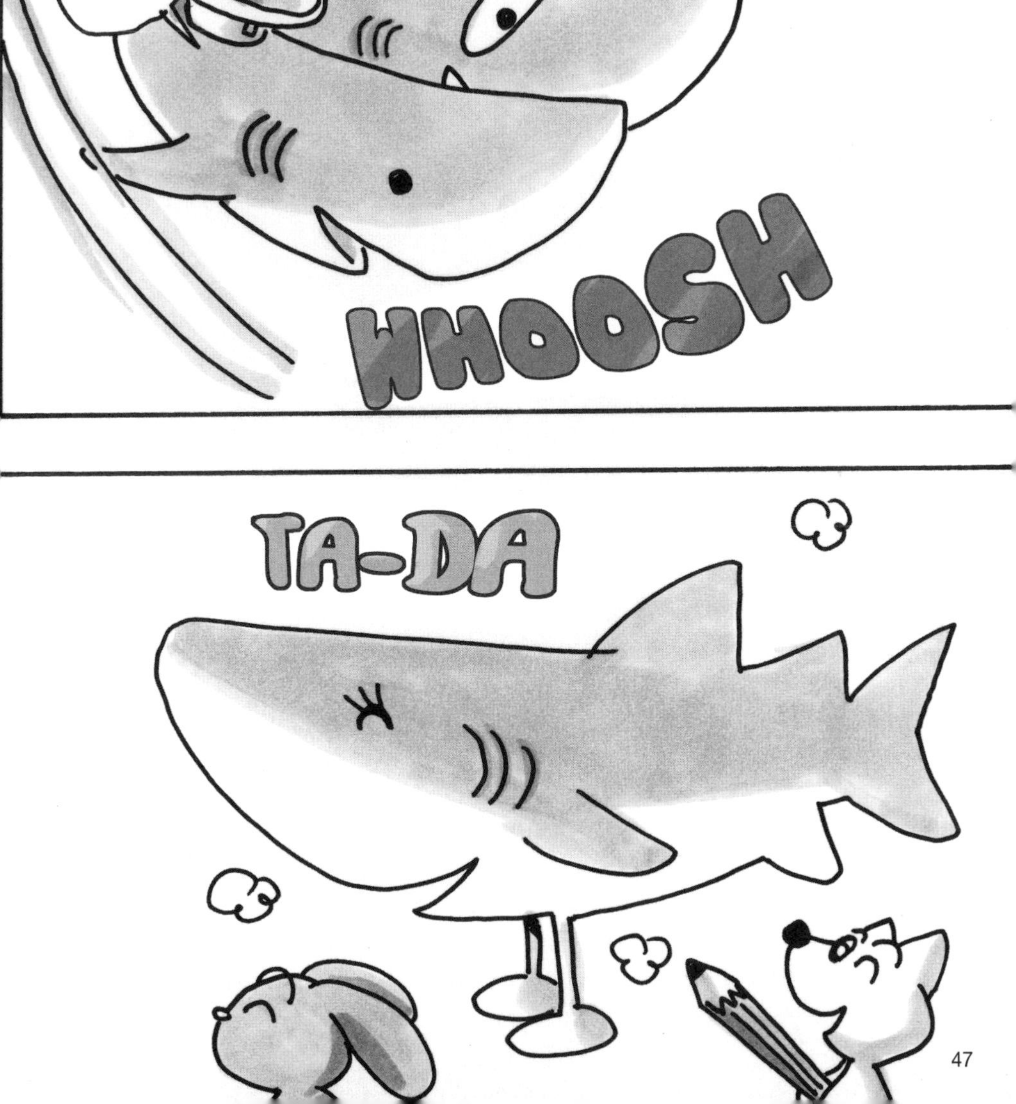
TA-DA

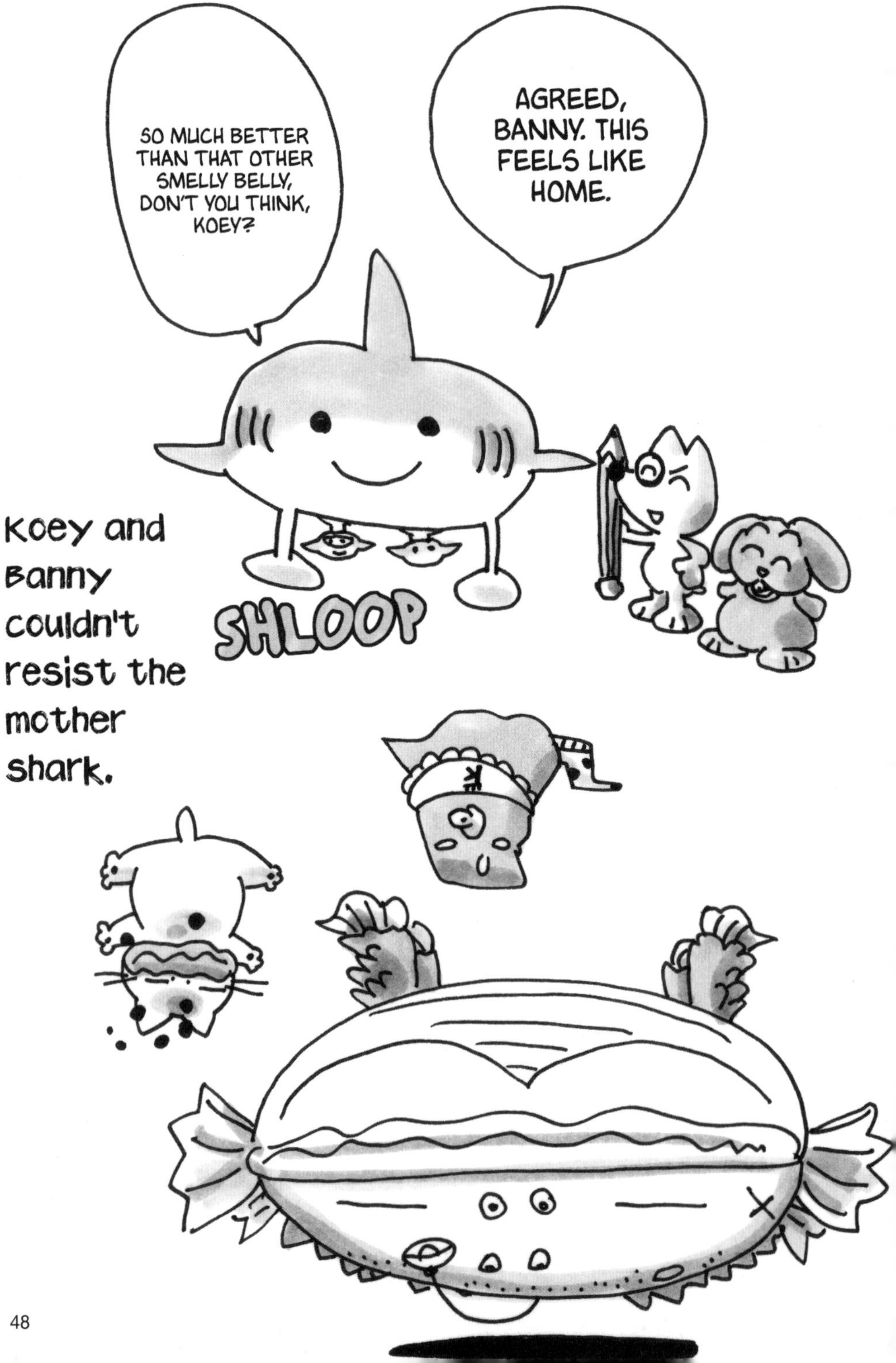
SO MUCH BETTER THAN THAT OTHER SMELLY BELLY, DON'T YOU THINK, KOEY?
AGREED, BANNY. THIS FEELS LIKE HOME.
SHLOOP
Koey and Banny couldn't resist the mother shark.

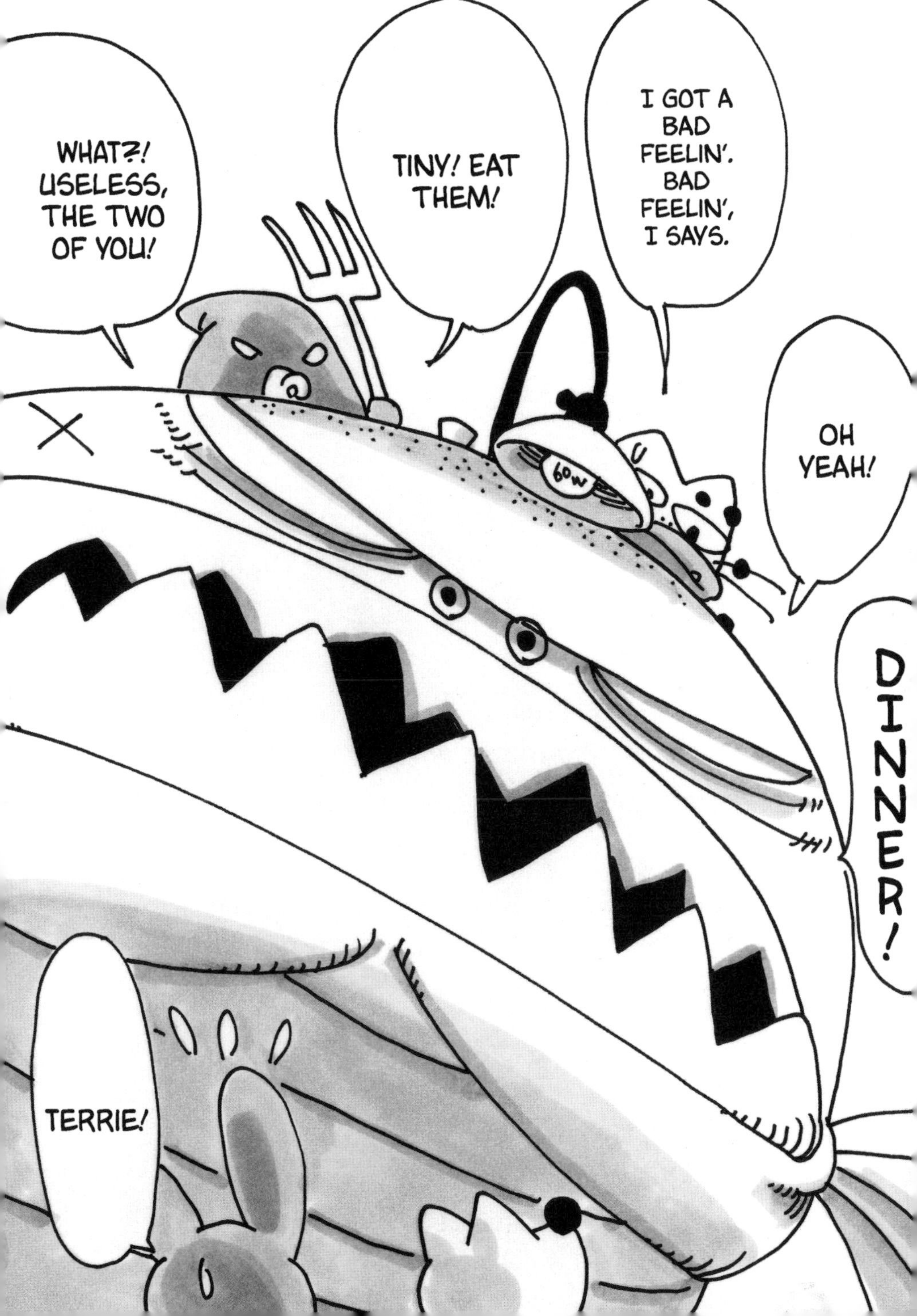
WHAT?! USELESS, THE TWO OF YOU!
TINY! EAT THEM!
I GOT A BAD FEELIN'. BAD FEELIN', I SAYS.
OH YEAH!
DINNER!
TERRIE!

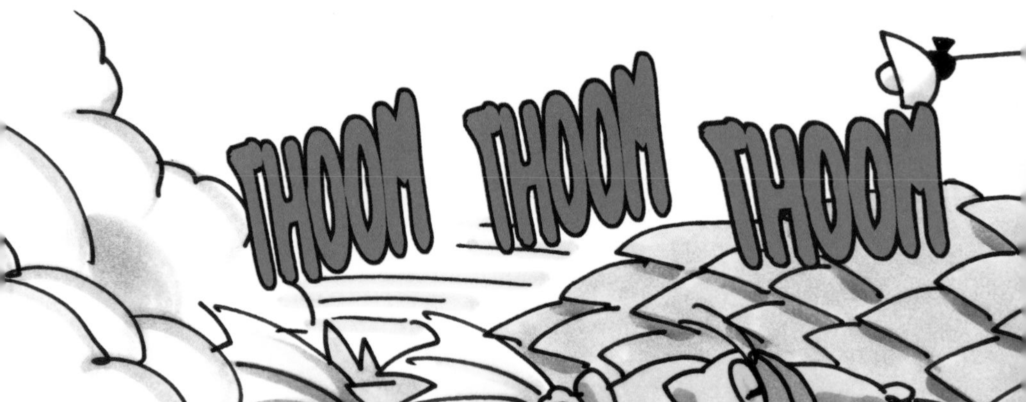
THOOM THOOM THOOM
The coelacanth rushed at Terrie and Hippity with the force of a locomotive.

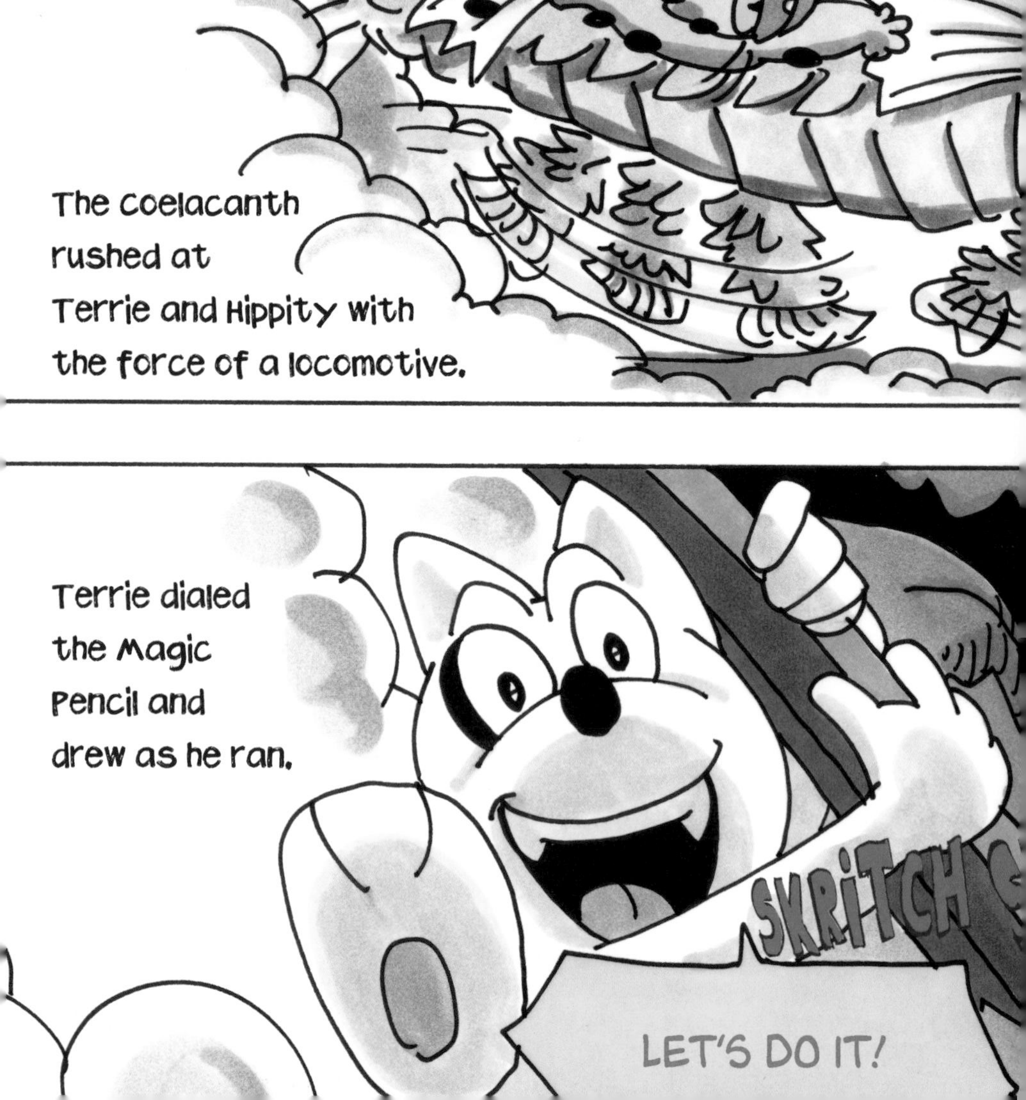
Terrie dialed the Magic Pencil and drew as he ran.
SKRITCH
LET'S DO IT!

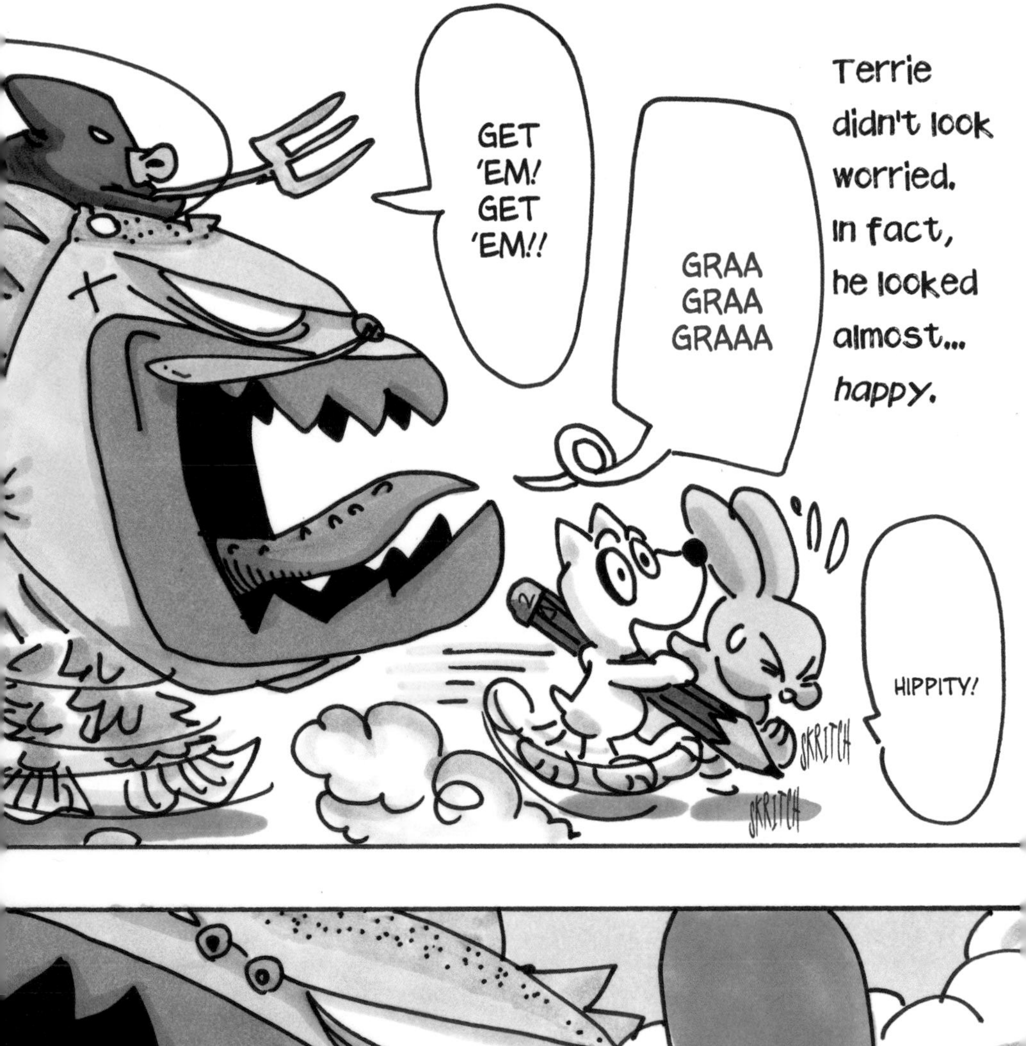
Terrie didn't look worried. In fact, he looked almost... *happy*.
GRAA GRAA GRAAA
GET 'EM! GET 'EM!!
HIPPITY!
SKRITCH
SKRITCH
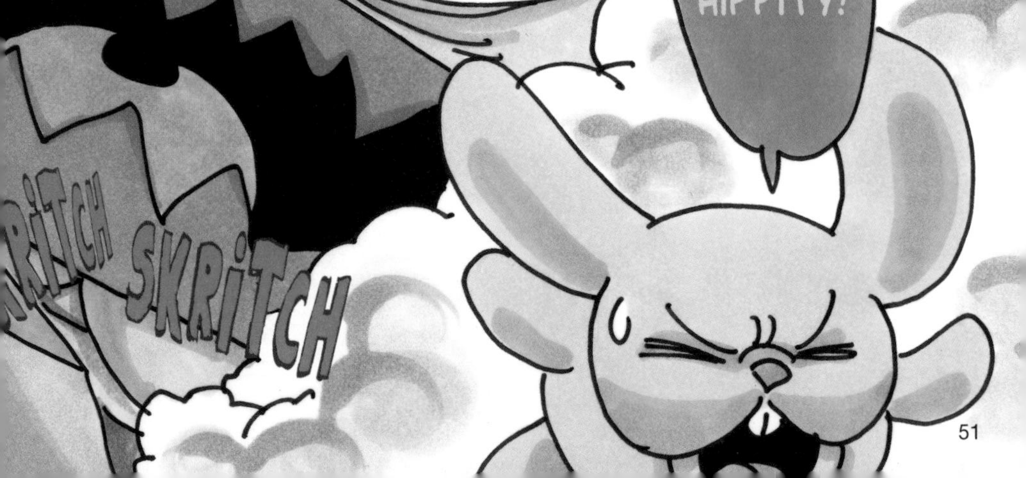
HIPPITY!
SKRITCH SKRITCH SKRITCH

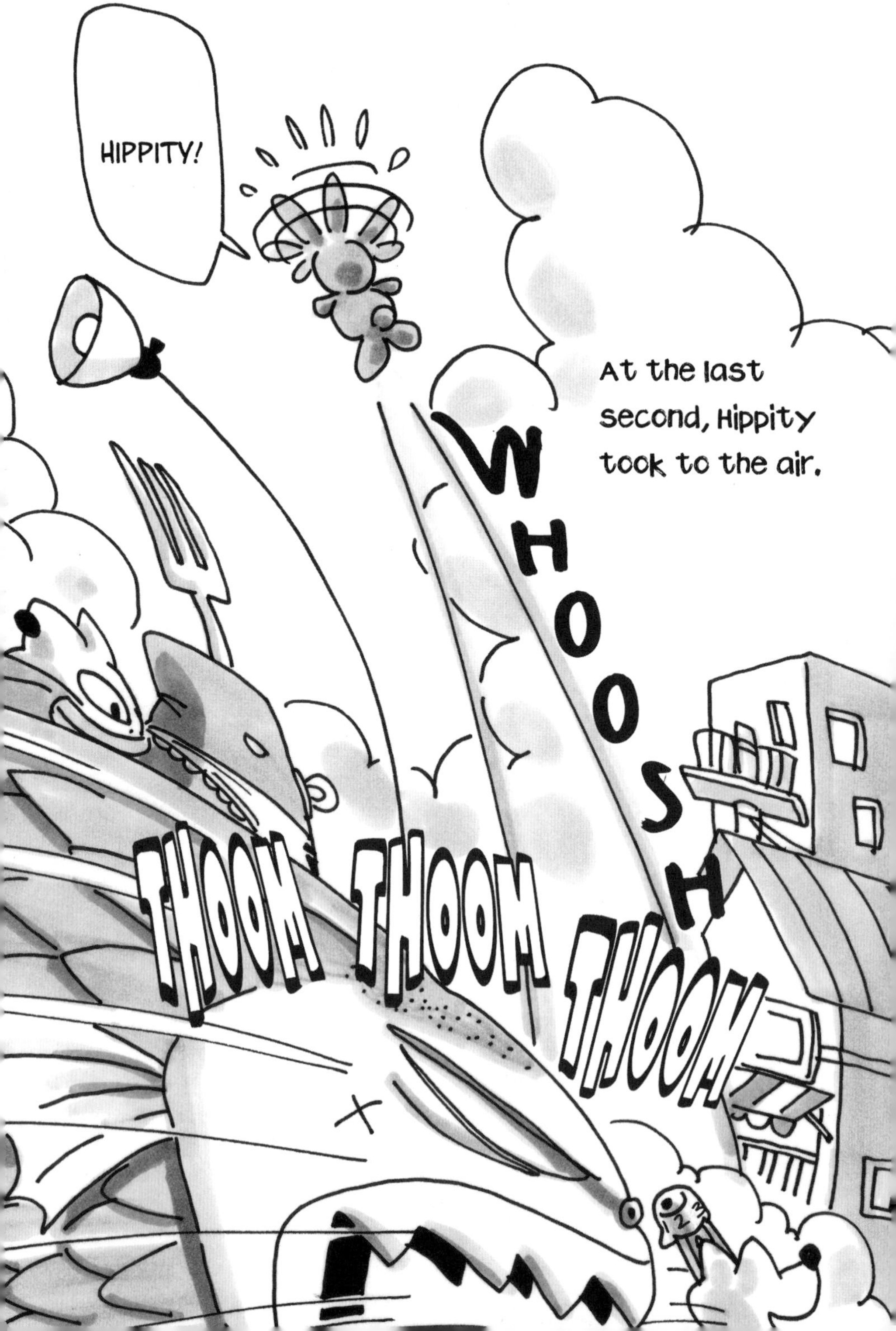
HIPPITY!
At the last second, Hippity took to the air.
WHOOSH
THOOM THOOM THOOM

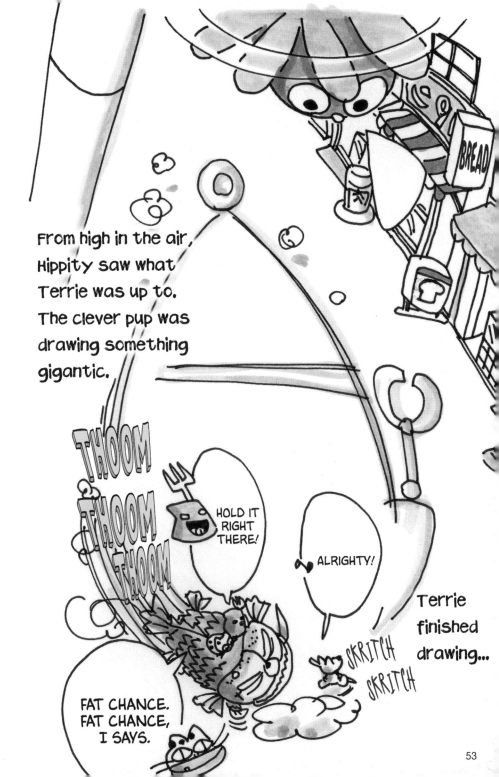

From high in the air, Hippity saw what Terrie was up to. The clever pup was drawing something gigantic.

THOOM THOOM THOOM

HOLD IT RIGHT THERE!

ALRIGHTY!

Terrie finished drawing...

SKRITCH SKRITCH

FAT CHANCE. FAT CHANCE, I SAYS.

BREAD!

...and there, looming over everyone, stood a humongous robot!

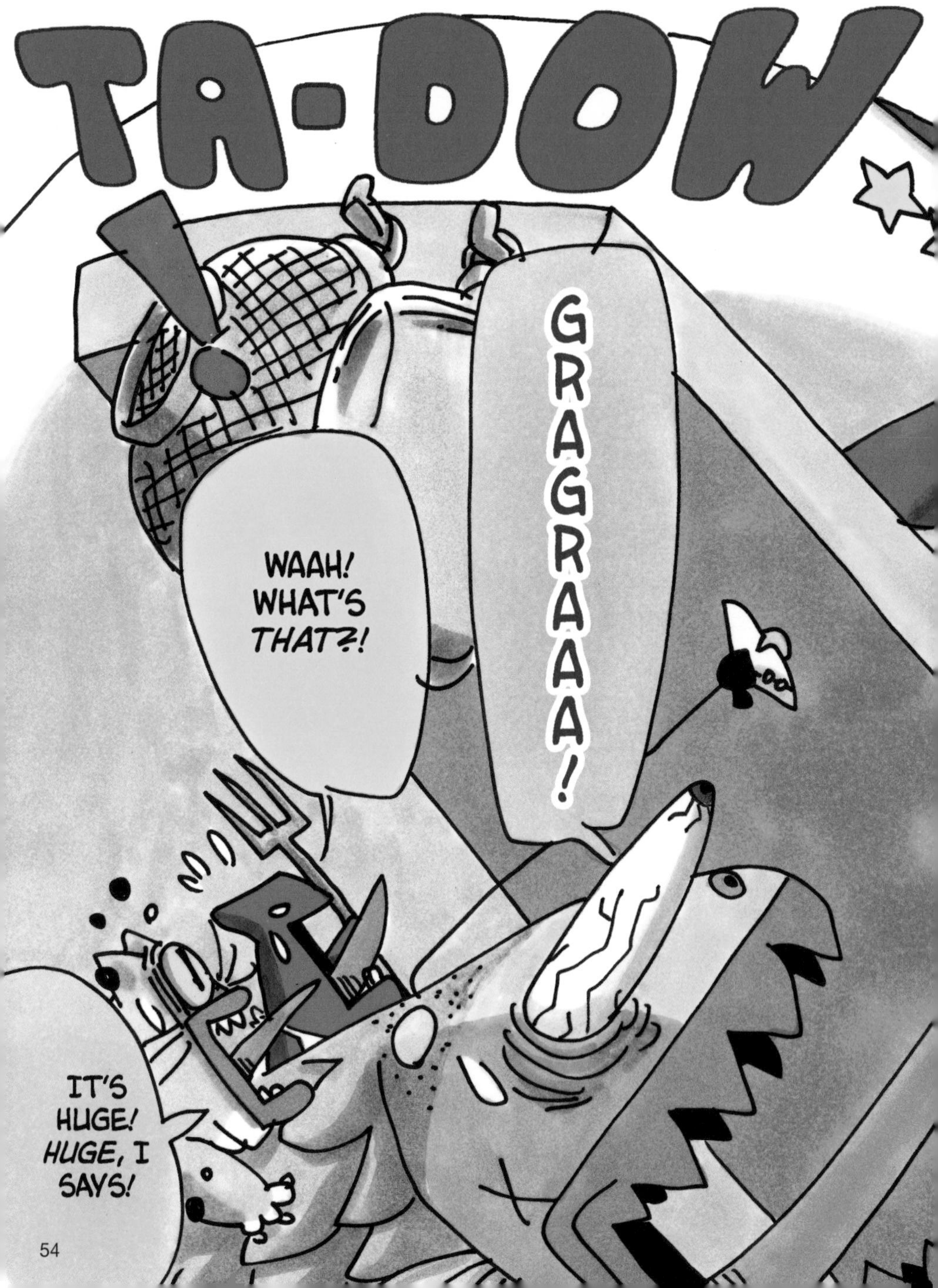
TA-DOW
GRAGRAAAA!
WAAH! WHAT'S *THAT?!*
IT'S HUGE! *HUGE,* I SAYS!

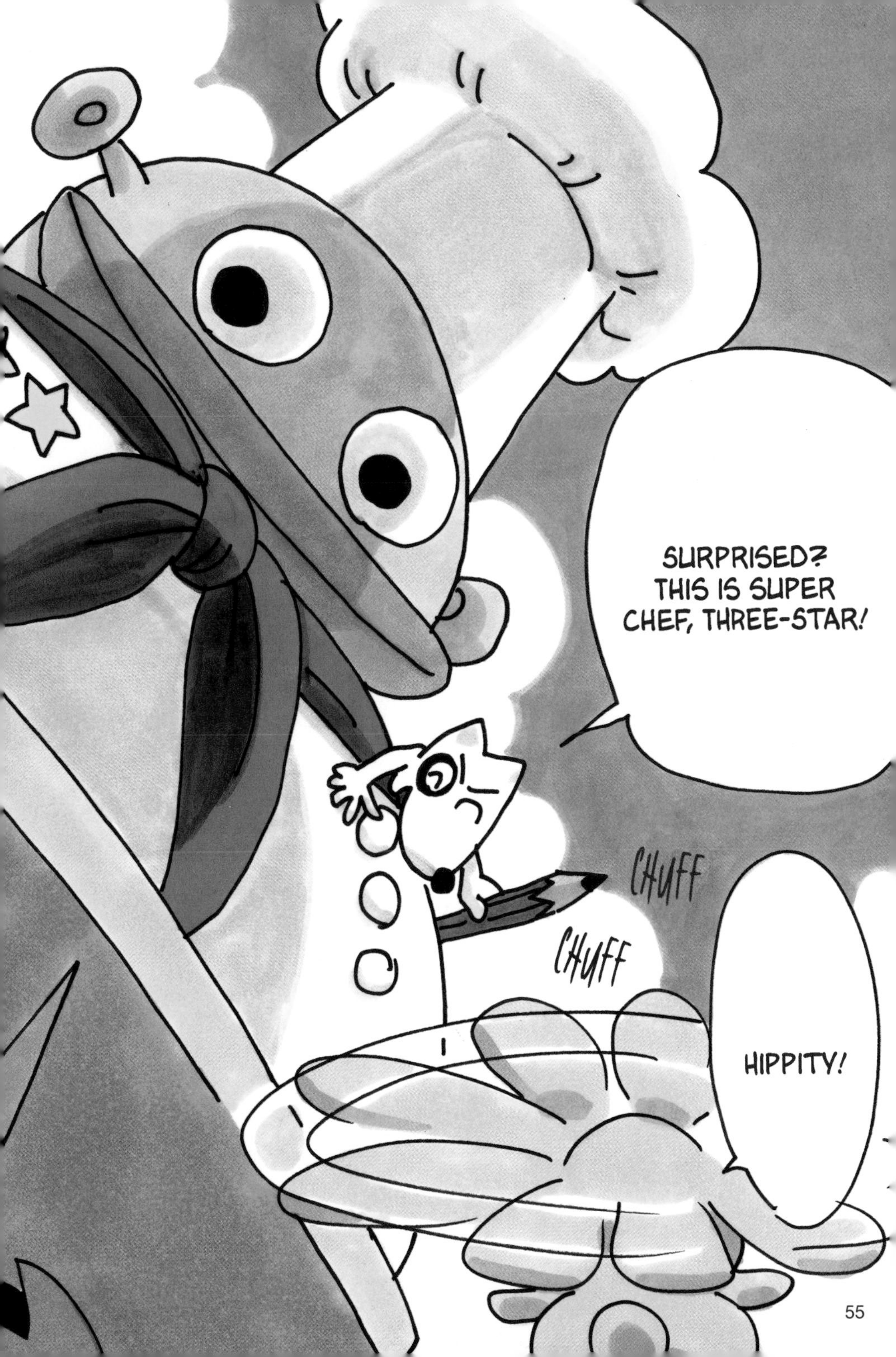
SURPRISED? THIS IS SUPER CHEF, THREE-STAR!
CHUFF
CHUFF
HIPPITY!

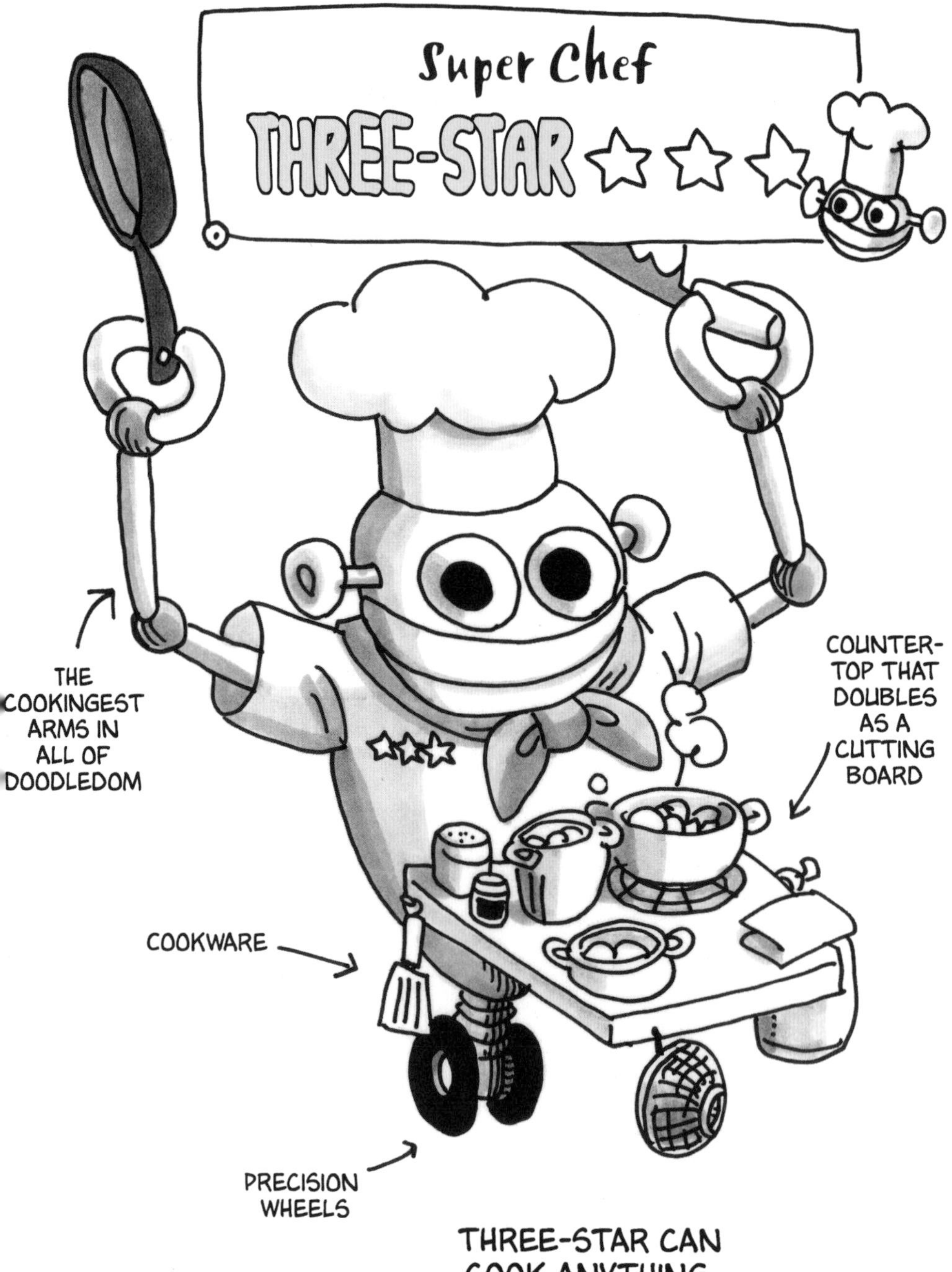
Super Chef
THREE-STAR
THE COOKINGEST ARMS IN ALL OF DOODLEDOM
COUNTER-TOP THAT DOUBLES AS A CUTTING BOARD
COOKWARE
PRECISION WHEELS
THREE-STAR CAN COOK ANYTHING.

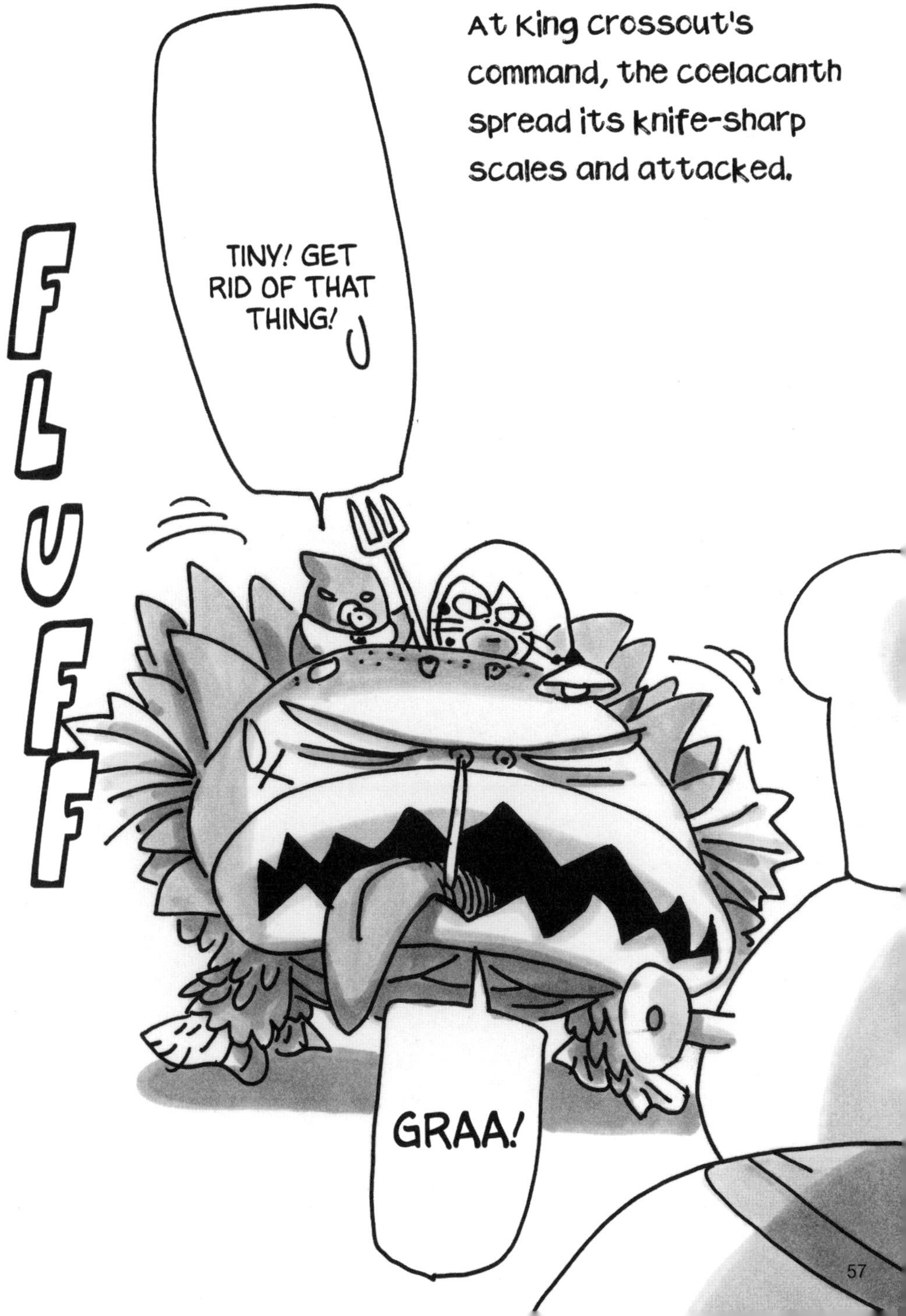
At King crossout's command, the coelacanth spread its knife-sharp scales and attacked.
TINY! GET RID OF THAT THING!
FLUFF
GRAA!

But Three-Star was not afraid. When the coelacanth was close enough, Three-Star used its scales to grate a big fat radish.

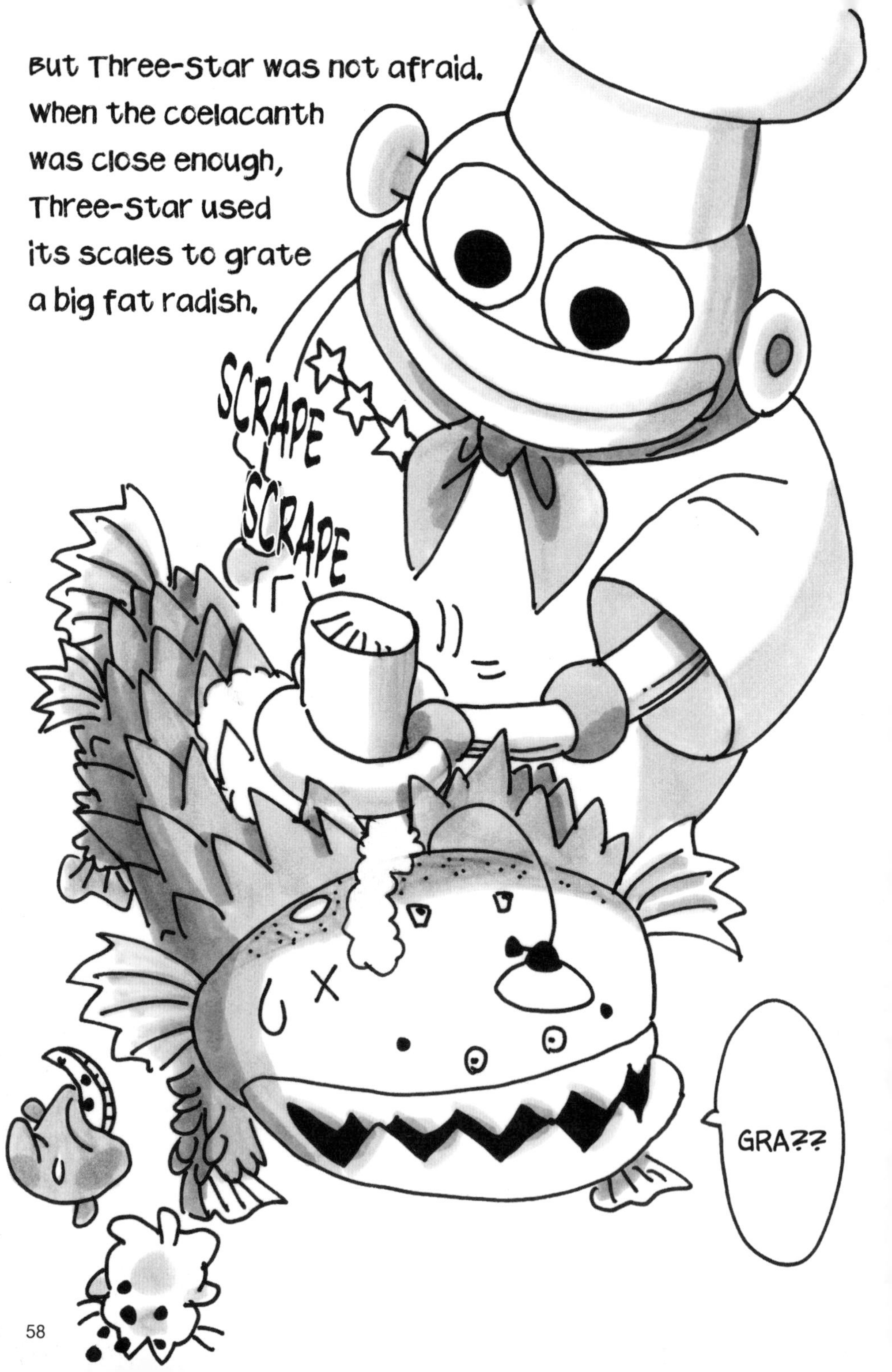
SCRAPE
SCRAPE
SCRAPE
GRA??

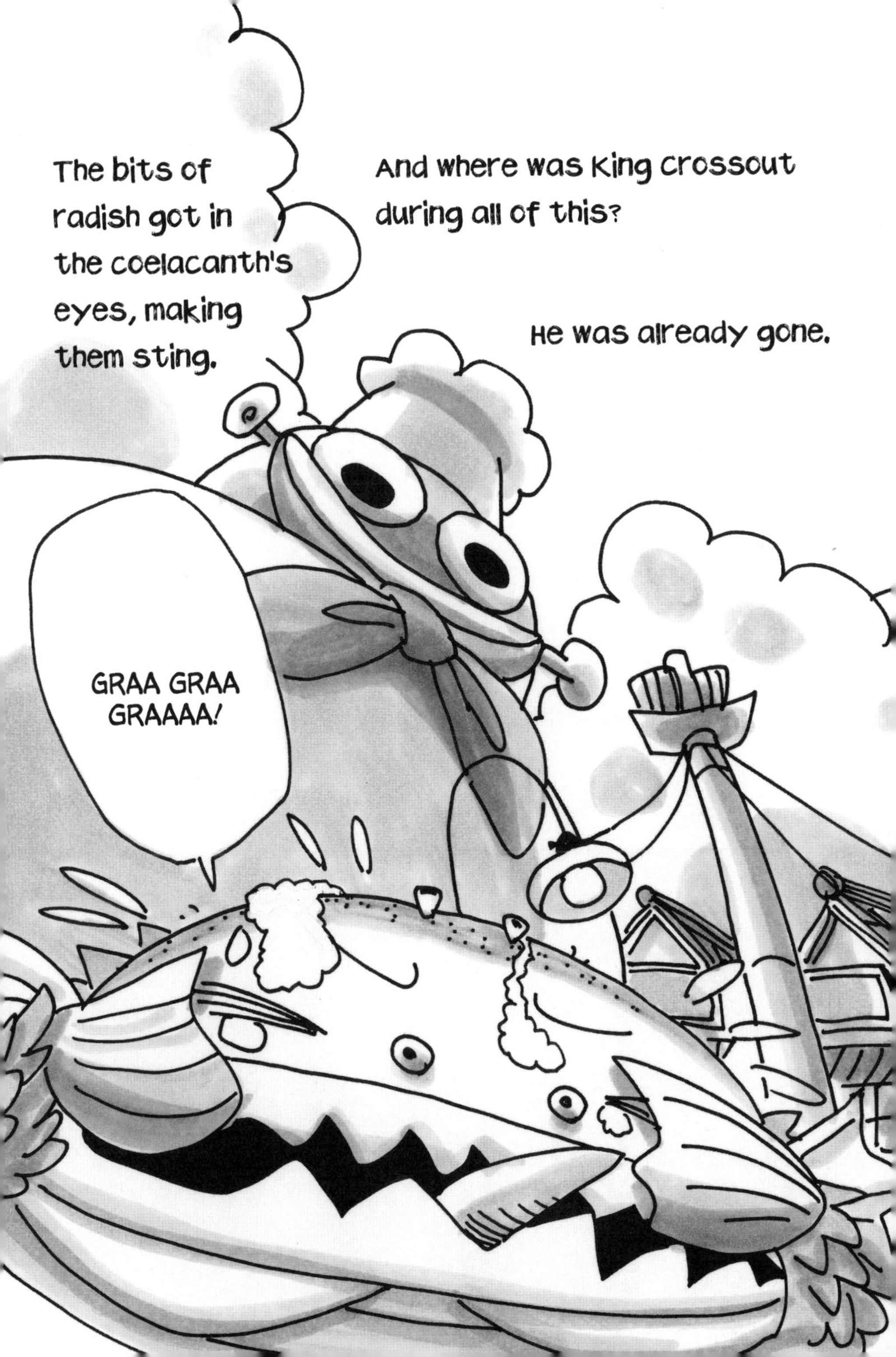

The bits of radish got in the coelacanth's eyes, making them sting.
And where was King crossout during all of this?
He was already gone.
GRAA GRAA GRAAAA!

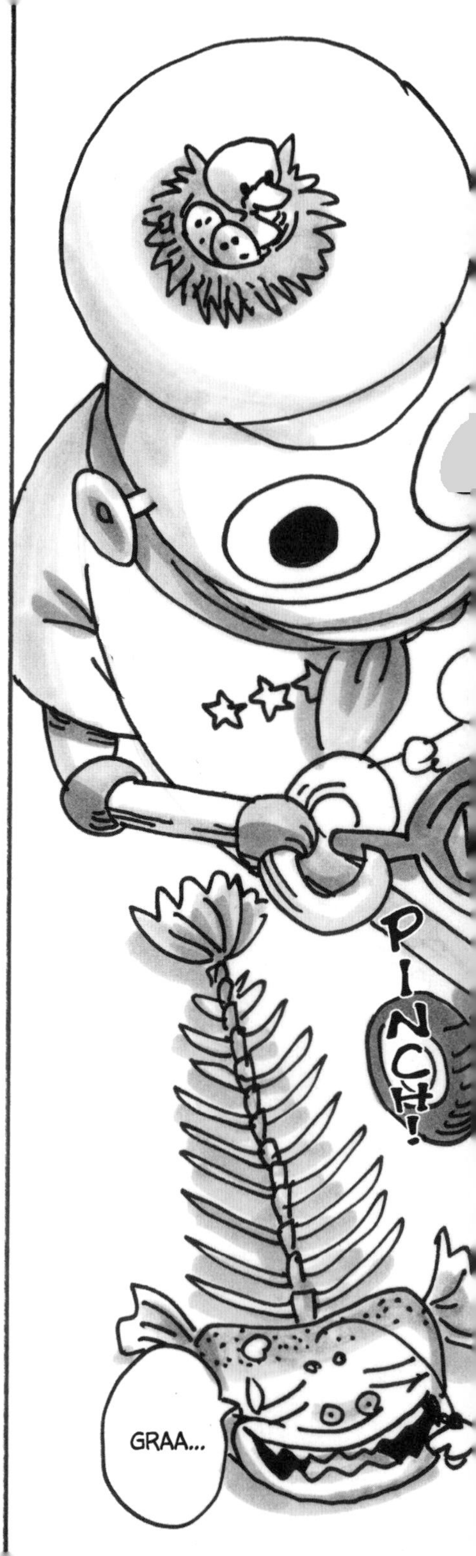
PINCH!
GRAA...
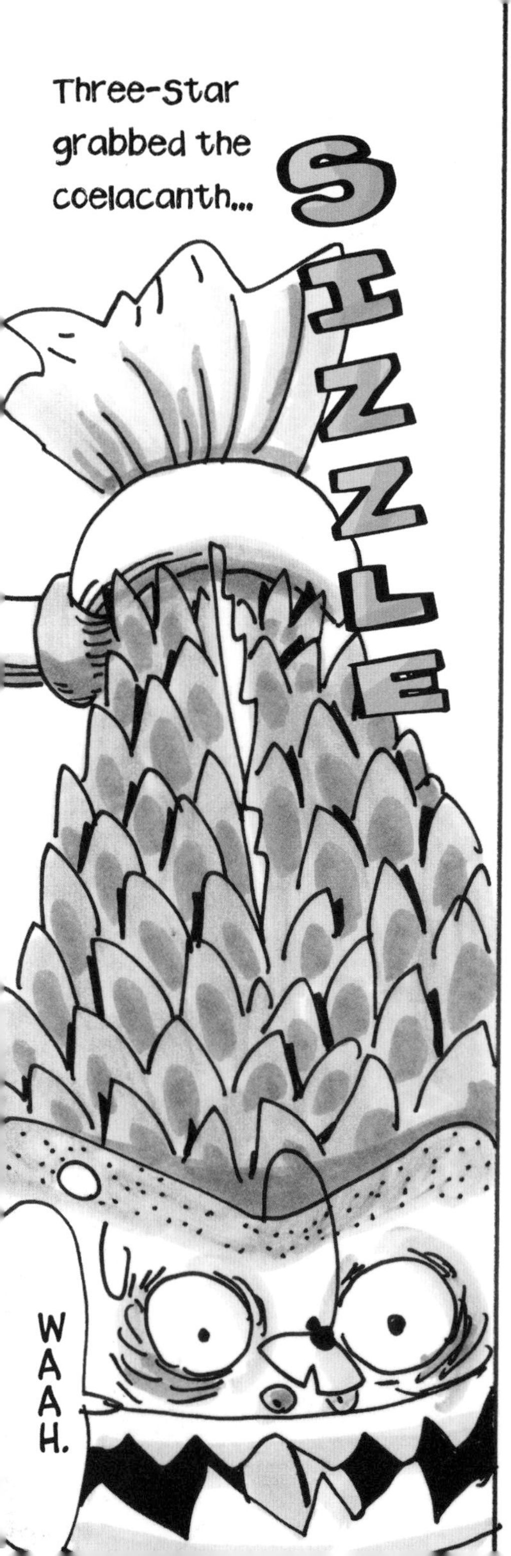
Three-Star grabbed the coelacanth...
SIZZLE
WAAH.

...and cooked him up, lickety-split. The air filled with the delicious smell of cooking fish. Three-Star made quite a meal.

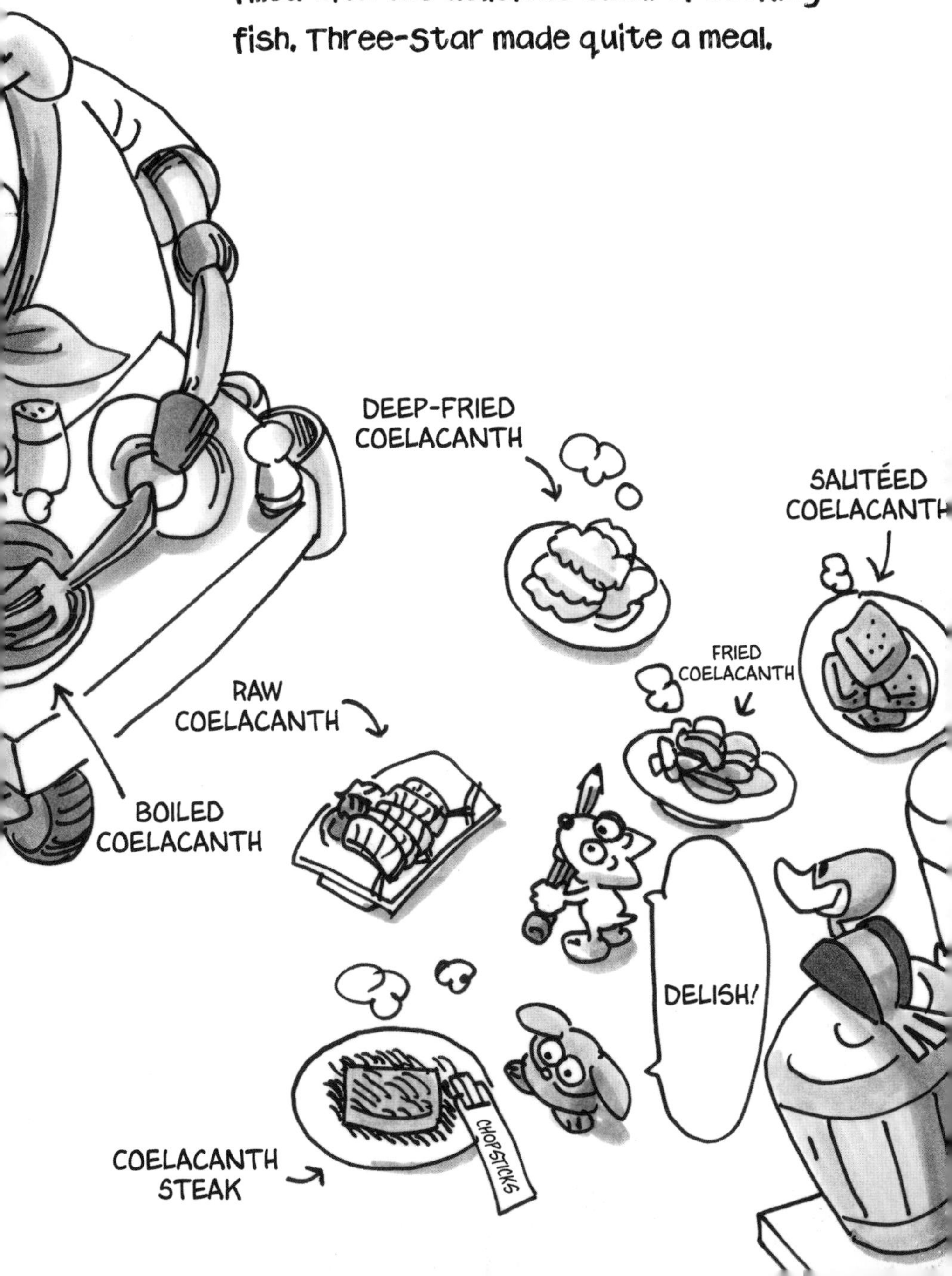
DEEP-FRIED COELACANTH
SAUTÉED COELACANTH
FRIED COELACANTH
RAW COELACANTH
BOILED COELACANTH
DELISH!
CHOPSTICKS
COELACANTH STEAK

Just as Terrie was about to take a bite, he noticed something strange about Three-Star.

Three-Star's head had disappeared!

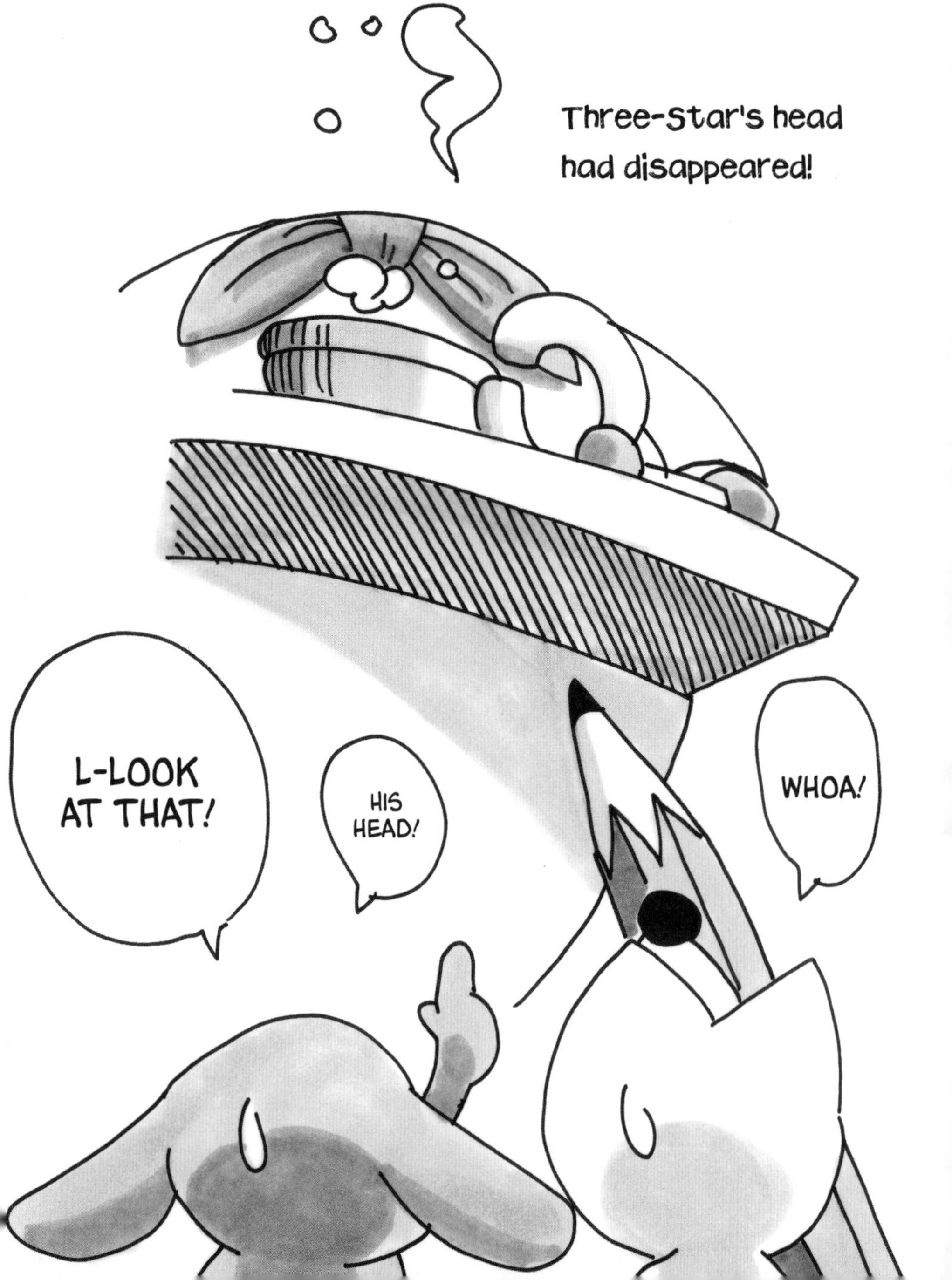
WHOA!
HIS HEAD!
L-LOOK AT THAT!

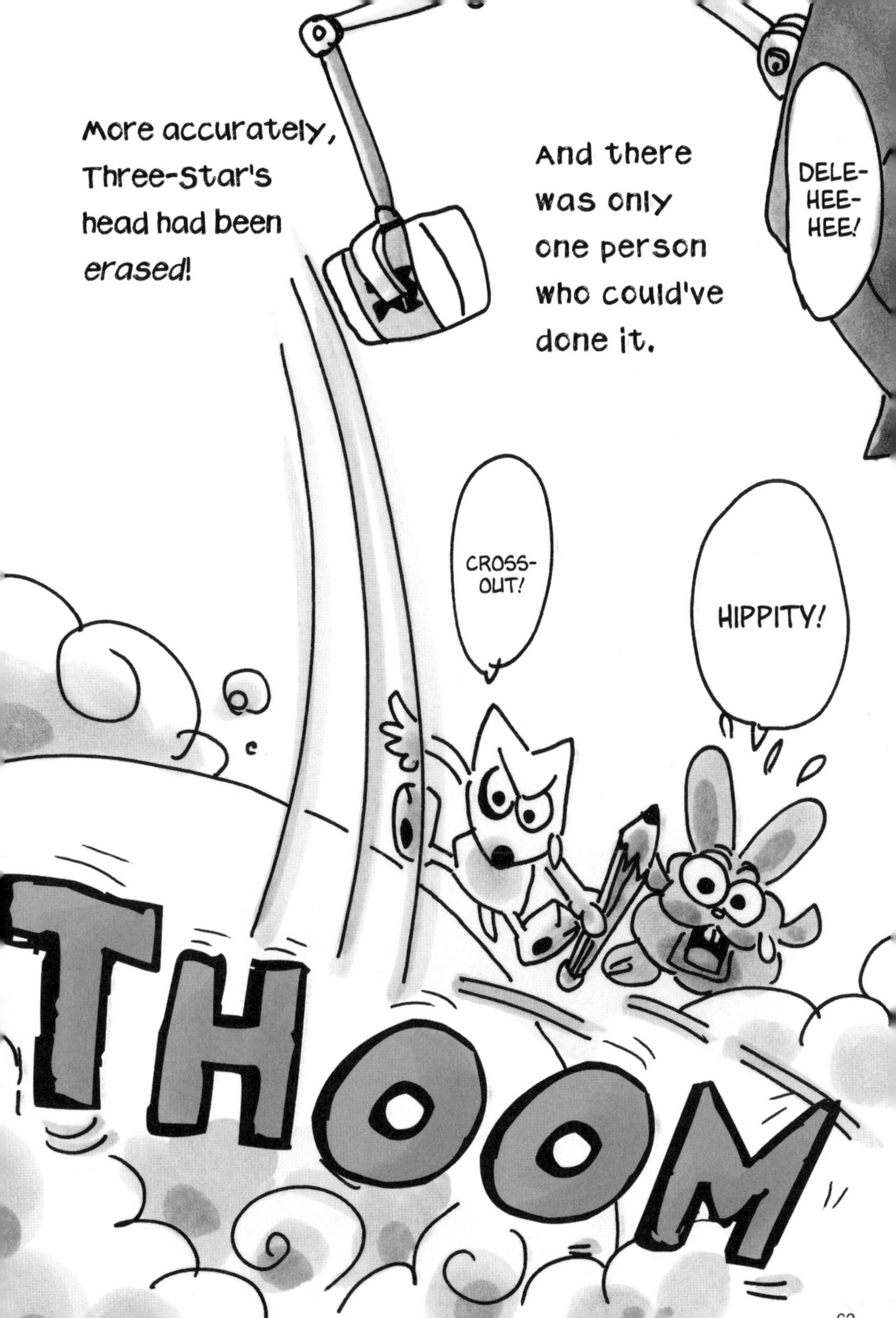

DELE-HEE-HEE!
And there was only one person who could've done it.
More accurately, Three-Star's head had been *erased*!
HIPPITY!
CROSS-OUT!
THOOM

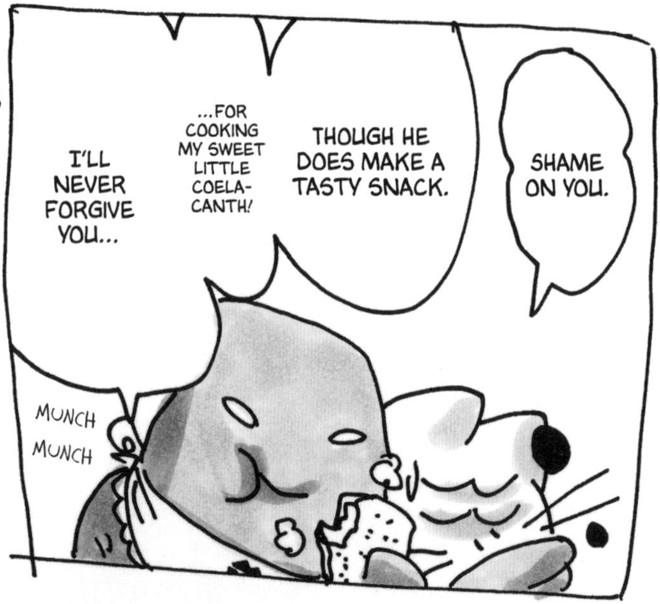
SHAME ON YOU.
THOUGH HE DOES MAKE A TASTY SNACK.
I'LL NEVER FORGIVE YOU...
...FOR COOKING MY SWEET LITTLE COELA-CANTH!
MUNCH
MUNCH

King crossout's Eraser-o-Doom was back!

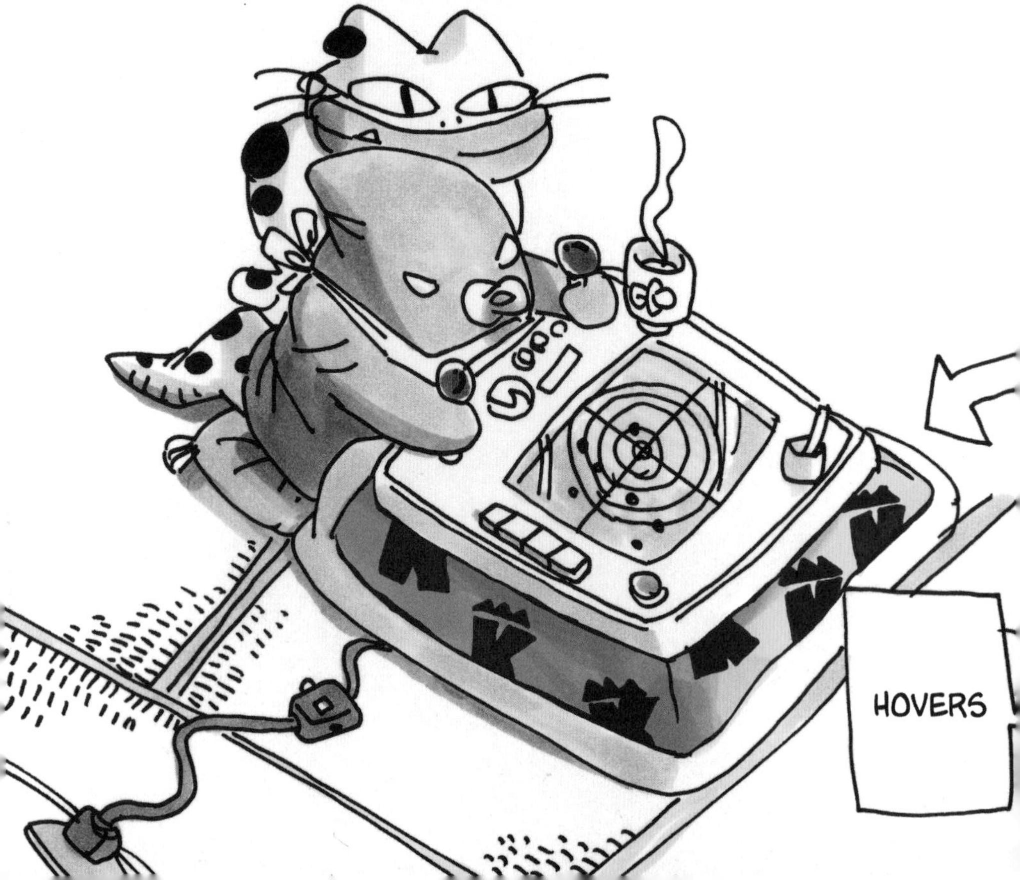
HOVERS

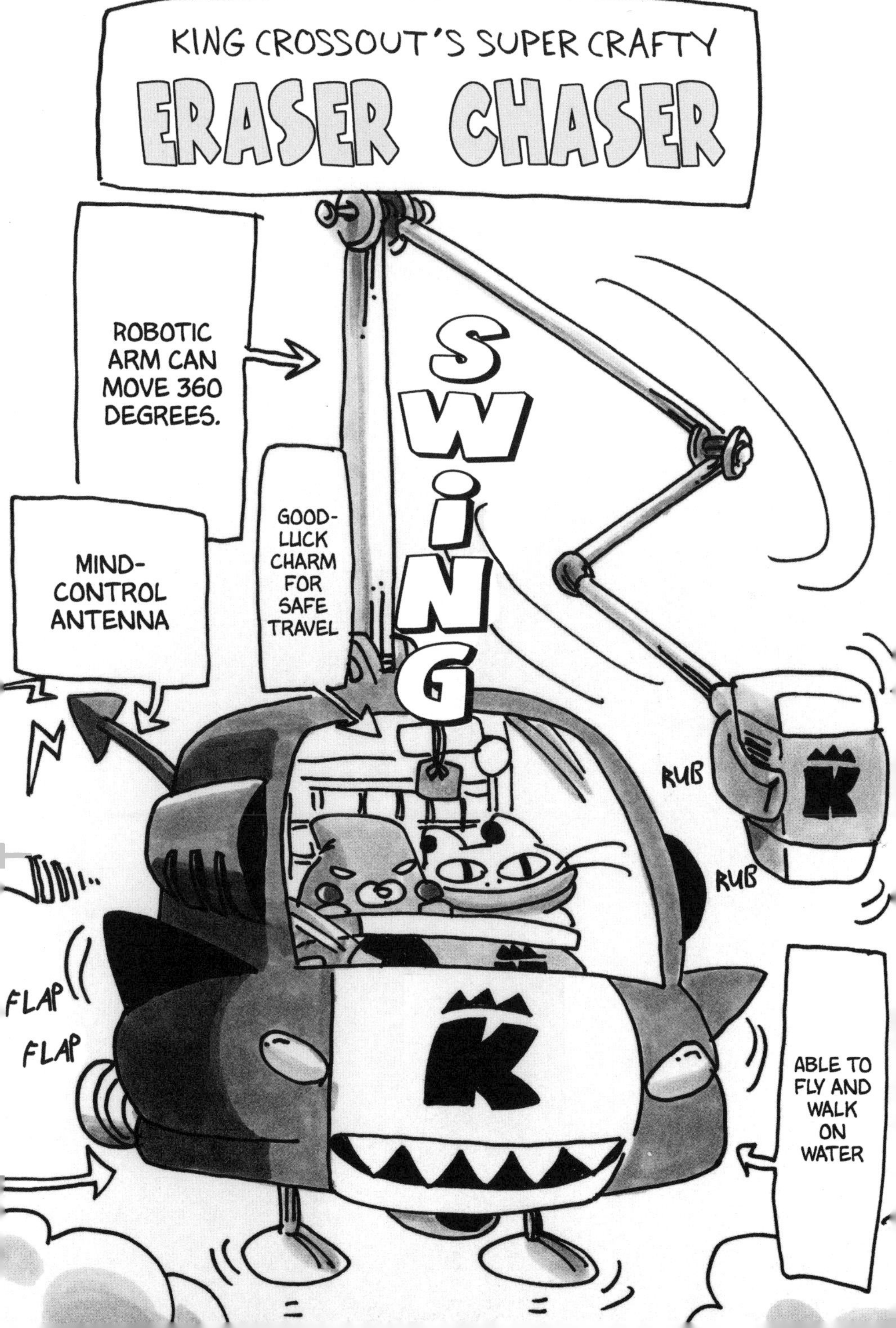
KING CROSSOUT'S SUPER CRAFTY
ERASER CHASER
ROBOTIC ARM CAN MOVE 360 DEGREES.
SWING
GOOD-LUCK CHARM FOR SAFE TRAVEL
MIND-CONTROL ANTENNA
RUB
RUB
FLAP
FLAP
ABLE TO FLY AND WALK ON WATER

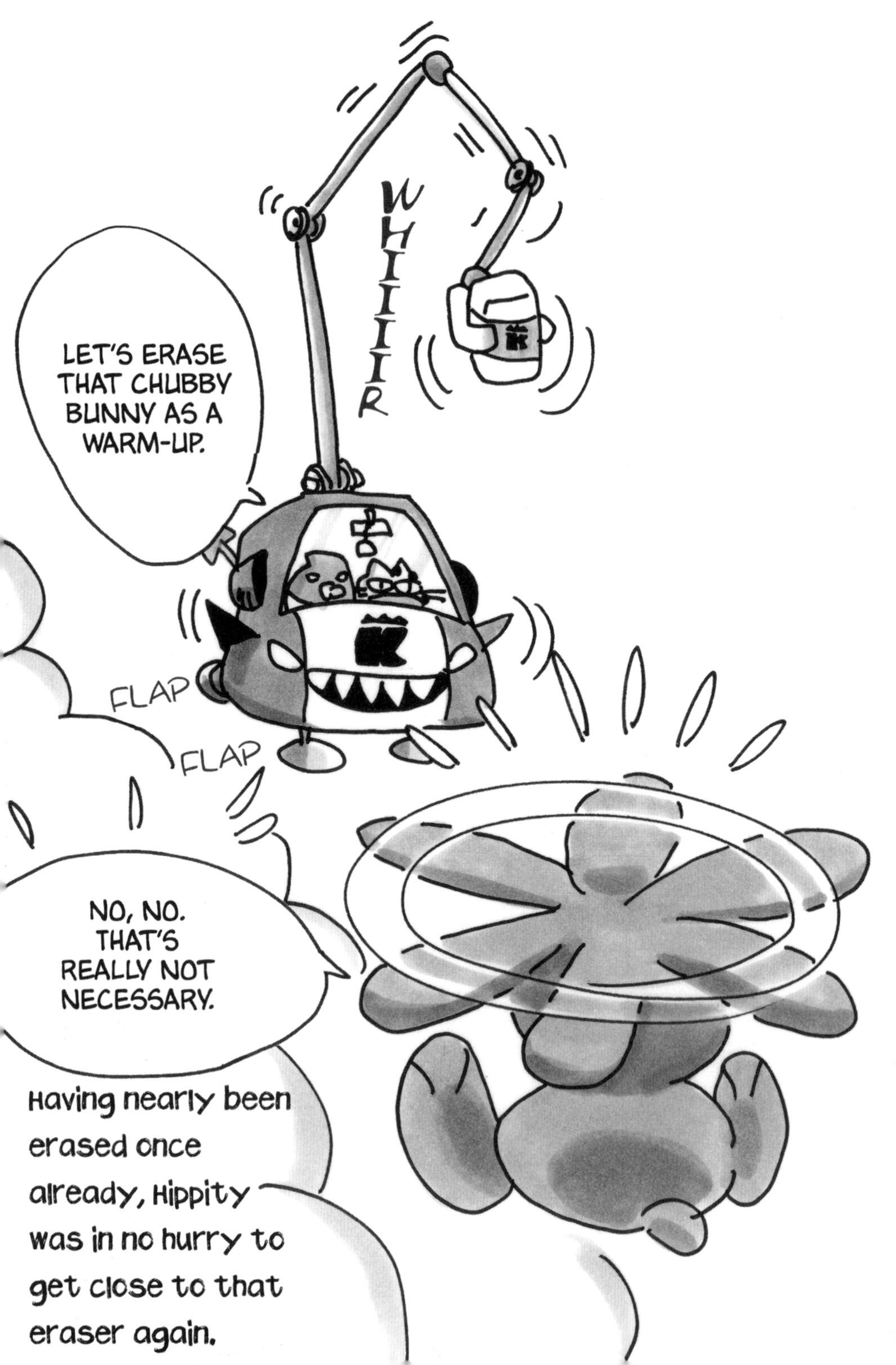
WHIIIIIR
LET'S ERASE THAT CHUBBY BUNNY AS A WARM-UP.
FLAP
FLAP
NO, NO. THAT'S REALLY NOT NECESSARY.
Having nearly been erased once already, Hippity was in no hurry to get close to that eraser again.

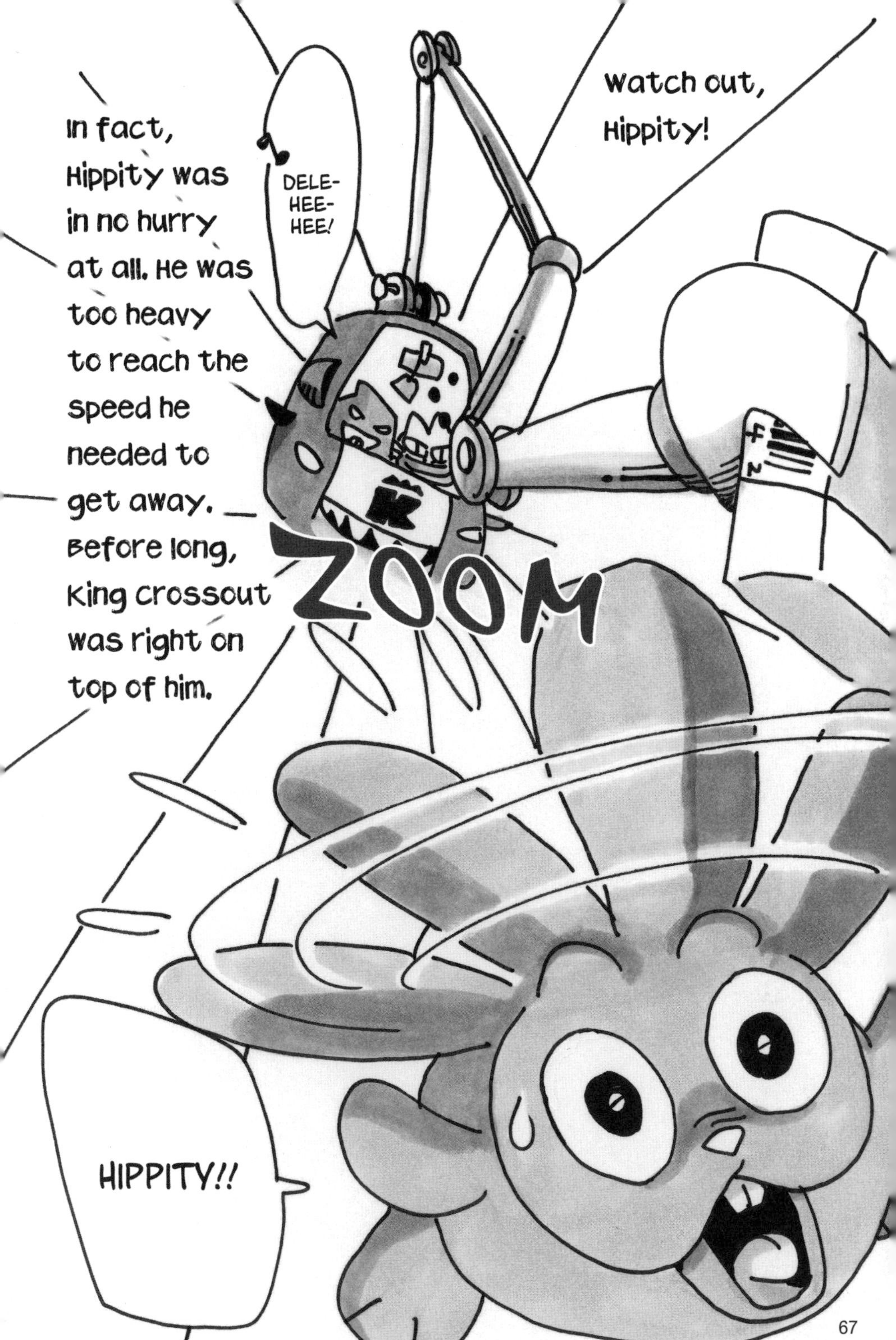

Watch out, Hippity!
DELE-HEE-HEE!
In fact, Hippity was in no hurry at all. He was too heavy to reach the speed he needed to get away. Before long, King Crossout was right on top of him.
ZOOM
HIPPITY!!

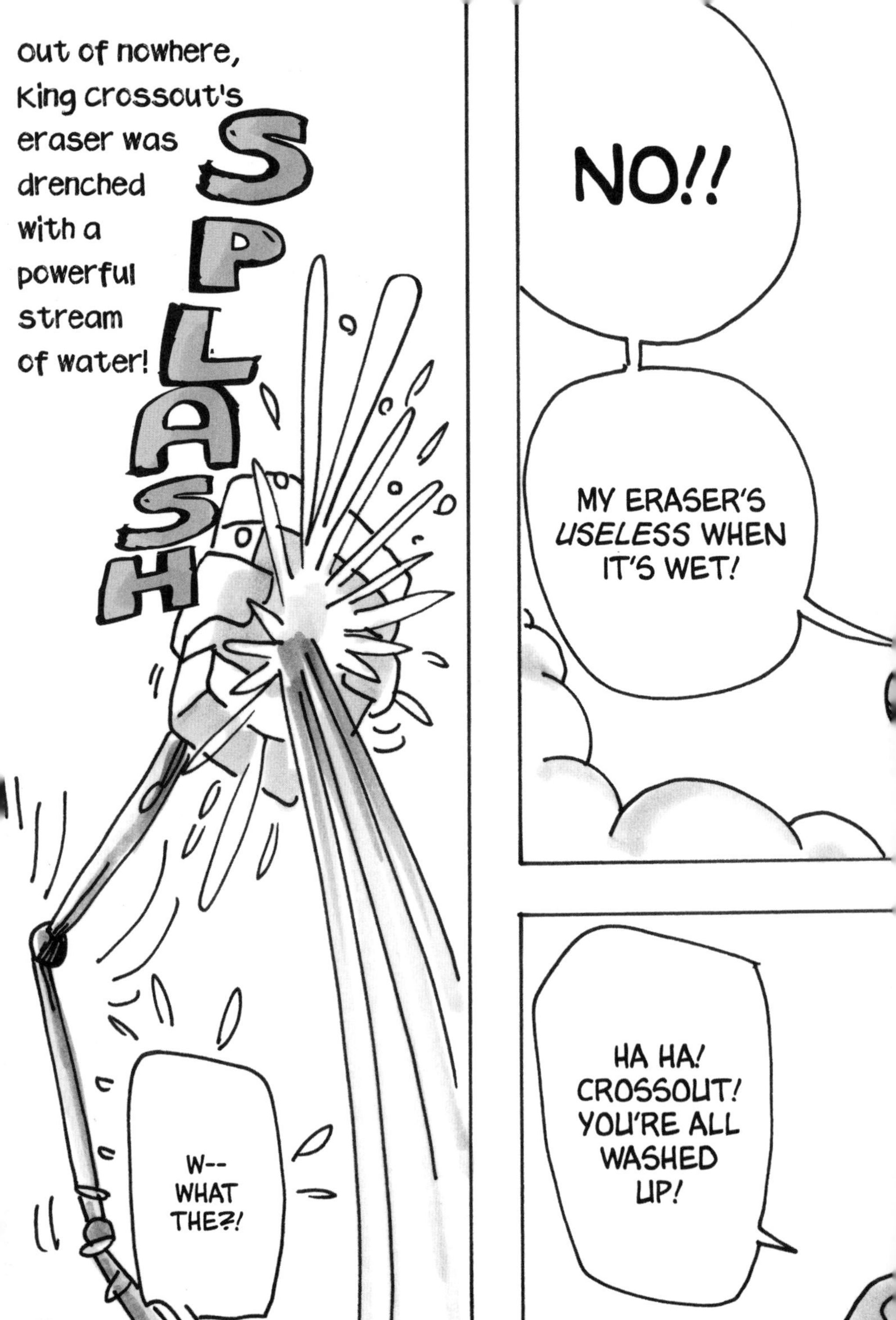
out of nowhere, King Crossout's eraser was drenched with a powerful stream of water!
SPLASH
W-- WHAT THE?!
NO!!
MY ERASER'S *USELESS* WHEN IT'S WET!
HA HA! CROSSOUT! YOU'RE ALL WASHED UP!

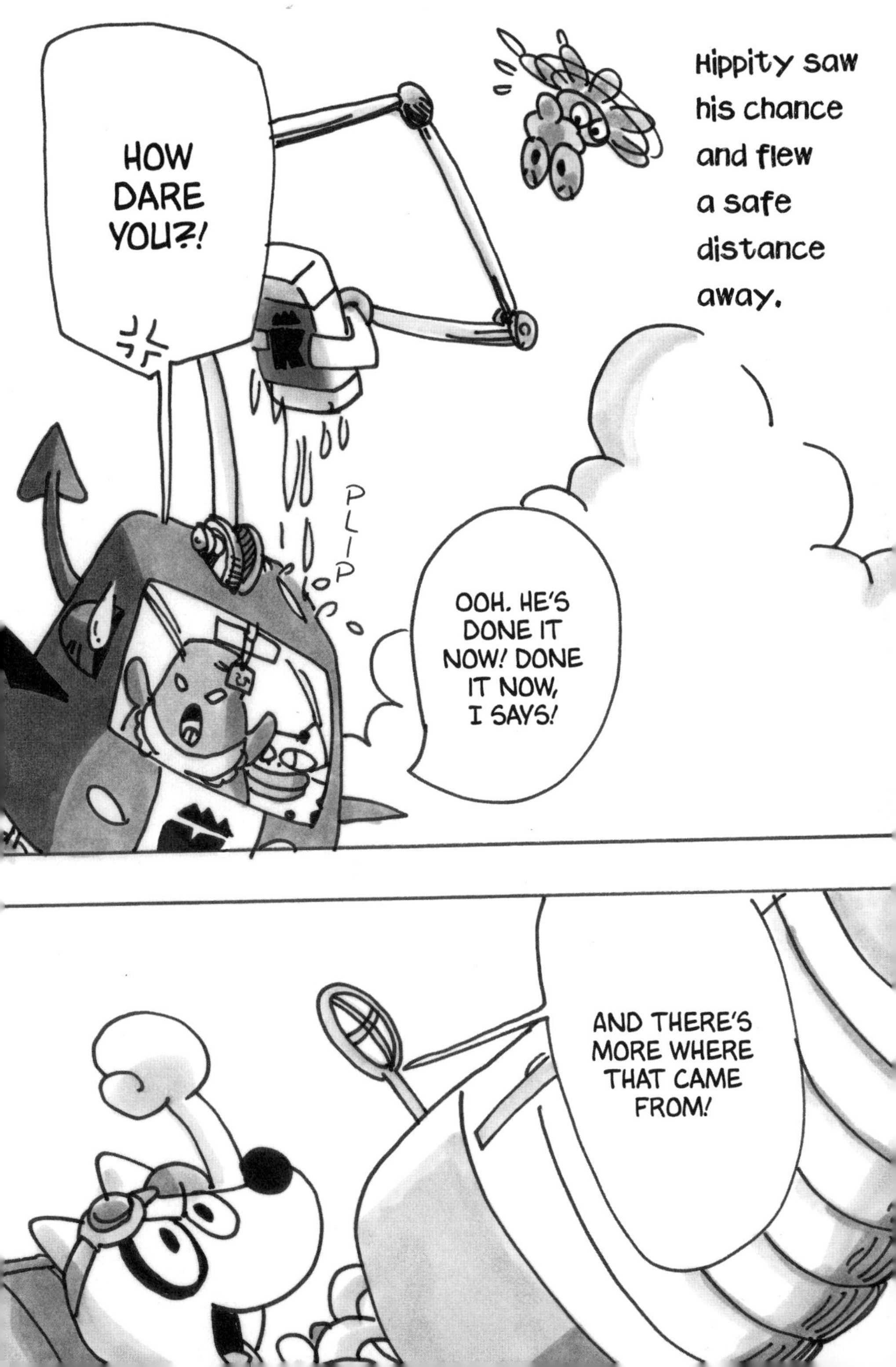
Hippity saw his chance and flew a safe distance away.
HOW DARE YOU?!
PLIP
OOH. HE'S DONE IT NOW! DONE IT NOW, I SAYS!
AND THERE'S MORE WHERE THAT CAME FROM!

Terrie sprayed the king with a powerful water cannon he'd drawn with the Magic Pencil.

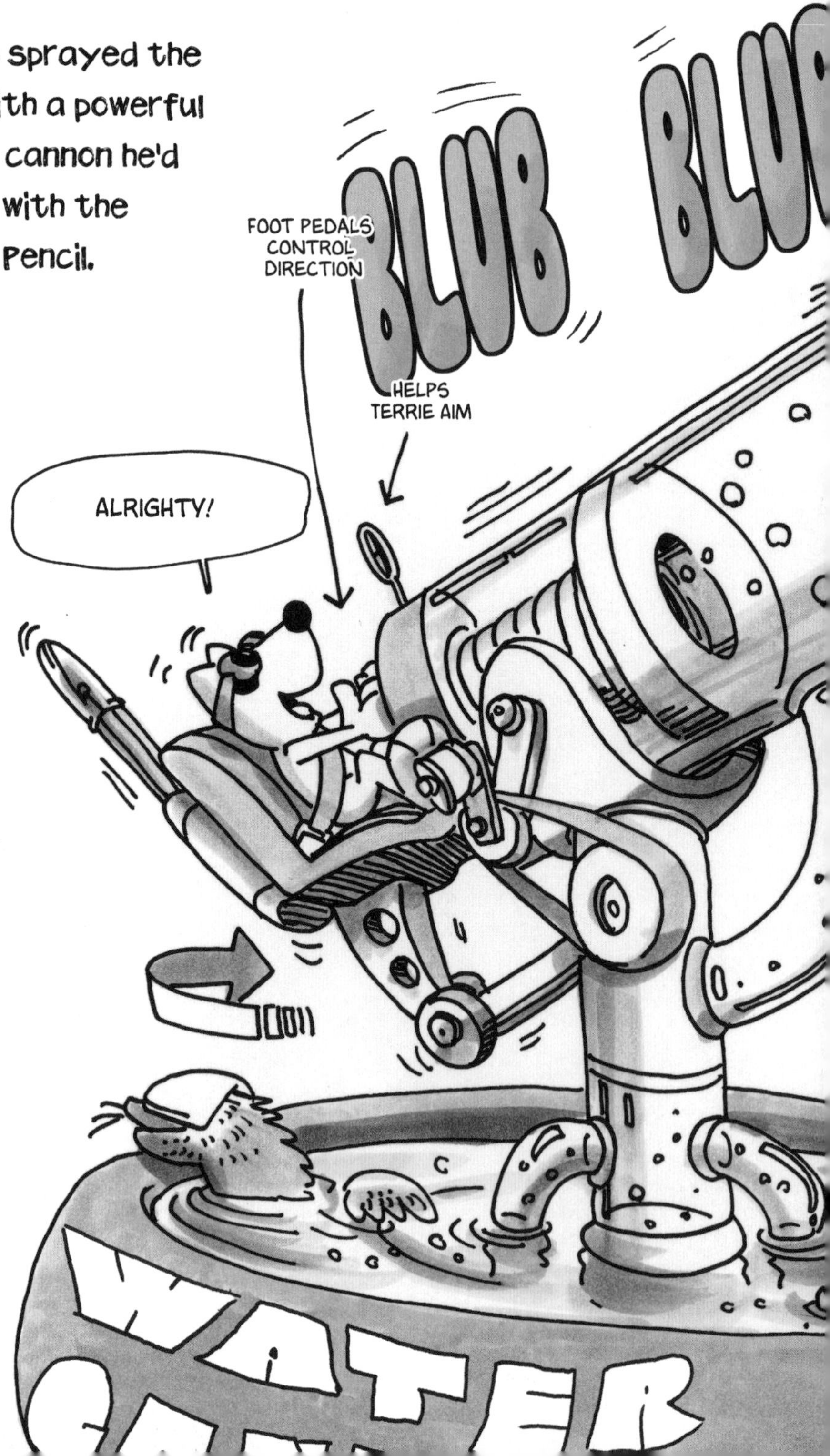
BLUB BLUB
FOOT PEDALS CONTROL DIRECTION
HELPS TERRIE AIM
ALRIGHTY!

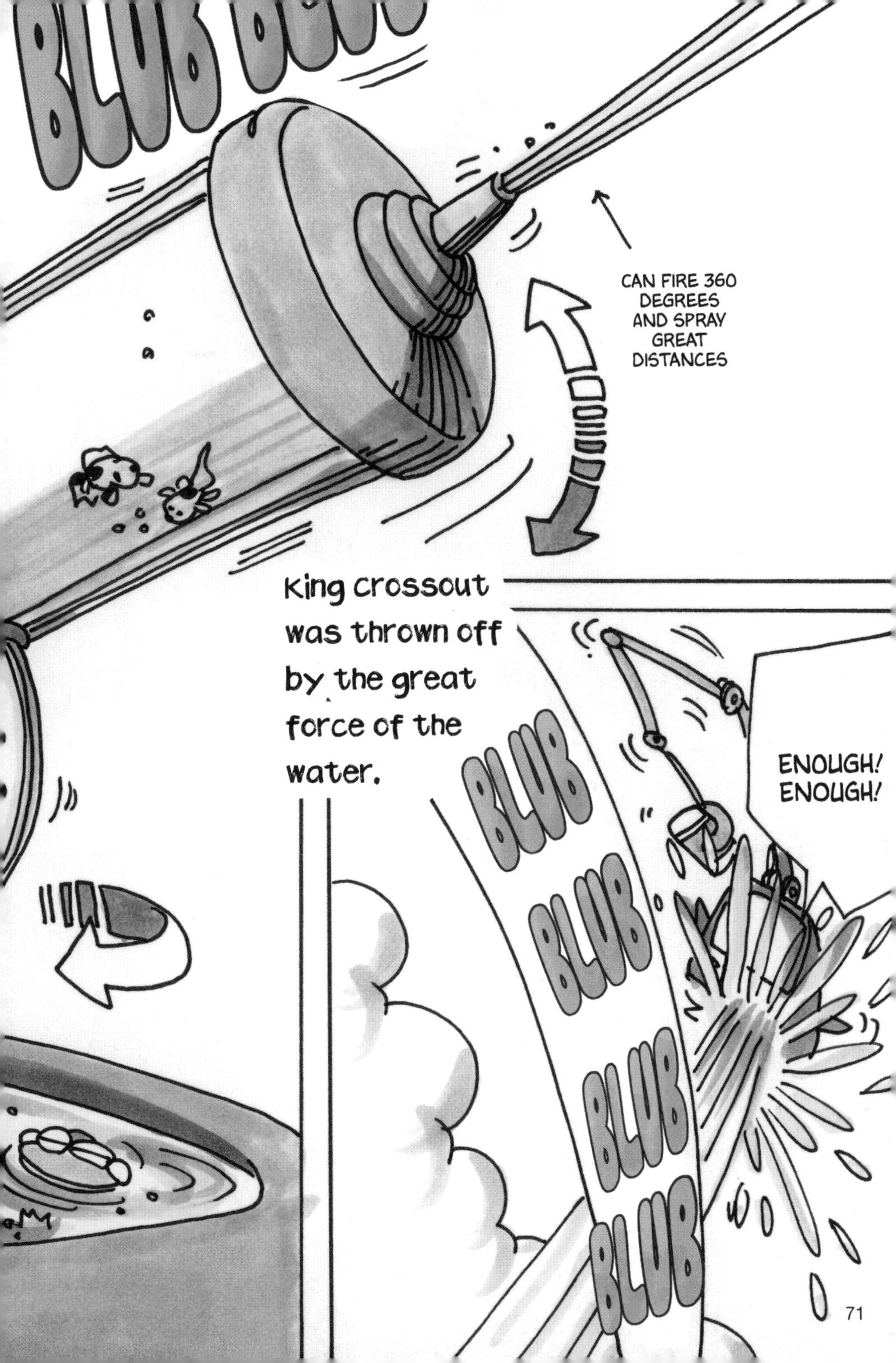
BLUB BLUB
CAN FIRE 360 DEGREES AND SPRAY GREAT DISTANCES
King crossout was thrown off by the great force of the water.
ENOUGH! ENOUGH!
BLUB BLUB BLUB BLUB

As if on the king's command, the cannon stopped pumping water.

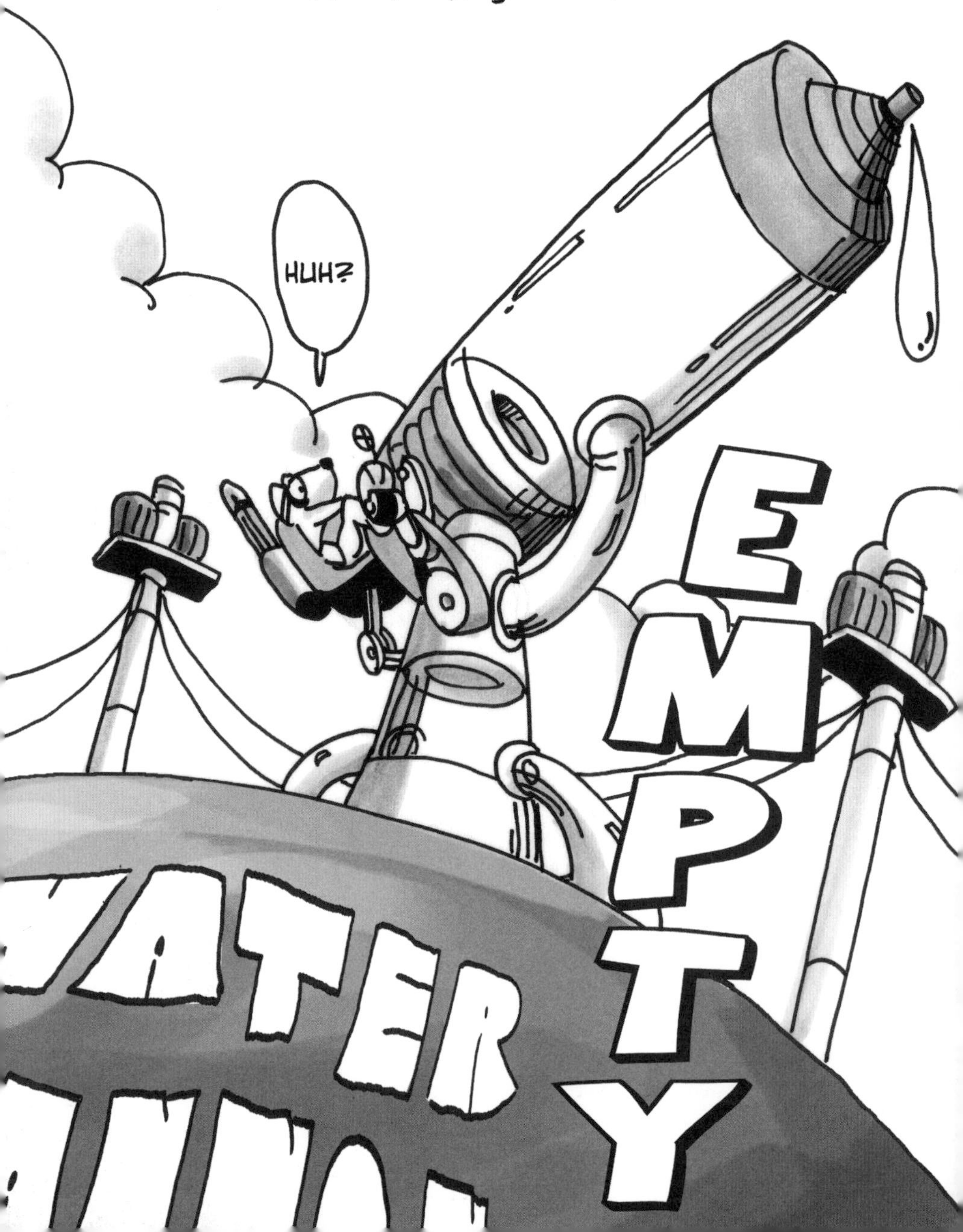
HUH?
EMPTY
WATER

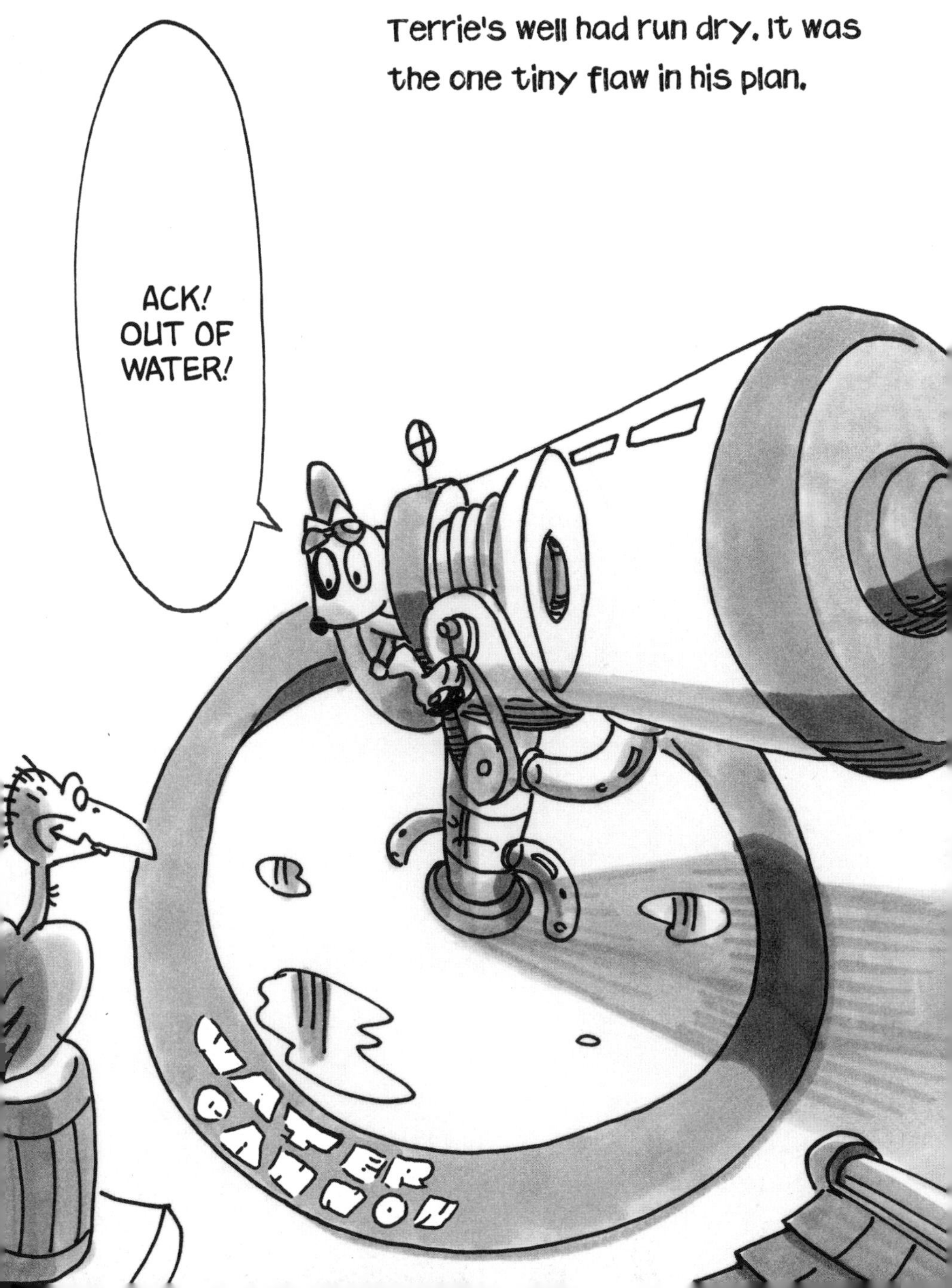
Terrie's well had run dry. It was the one tiny flaw in his plan.
ACK! OUT OF WATER!
WATER CANNON

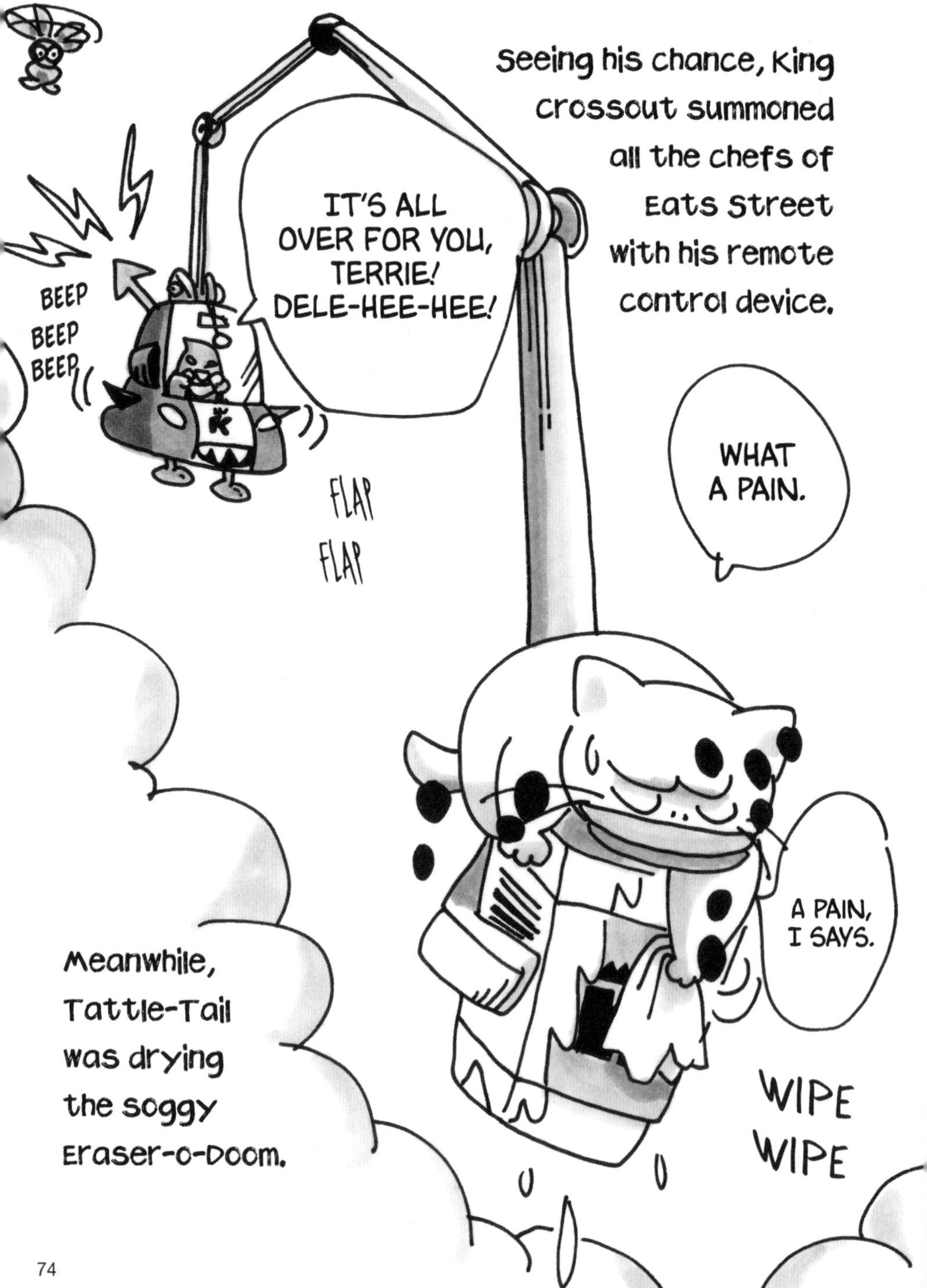

Seeing his chance, King Crossout summoned all the chefs of Eats Street with his remote control device.
IT'S ALL OVER FOR YOU, TERRIE! DELE-HEE-HEE!
BEEP BEEP BEEP
FLAP FLAP
WHAT A PAIN.
A PAIN, I SAYS.
Meanwhile, Tattle-Tail was drying the soggy Eraser-o-Doom.
WIPE WIPE

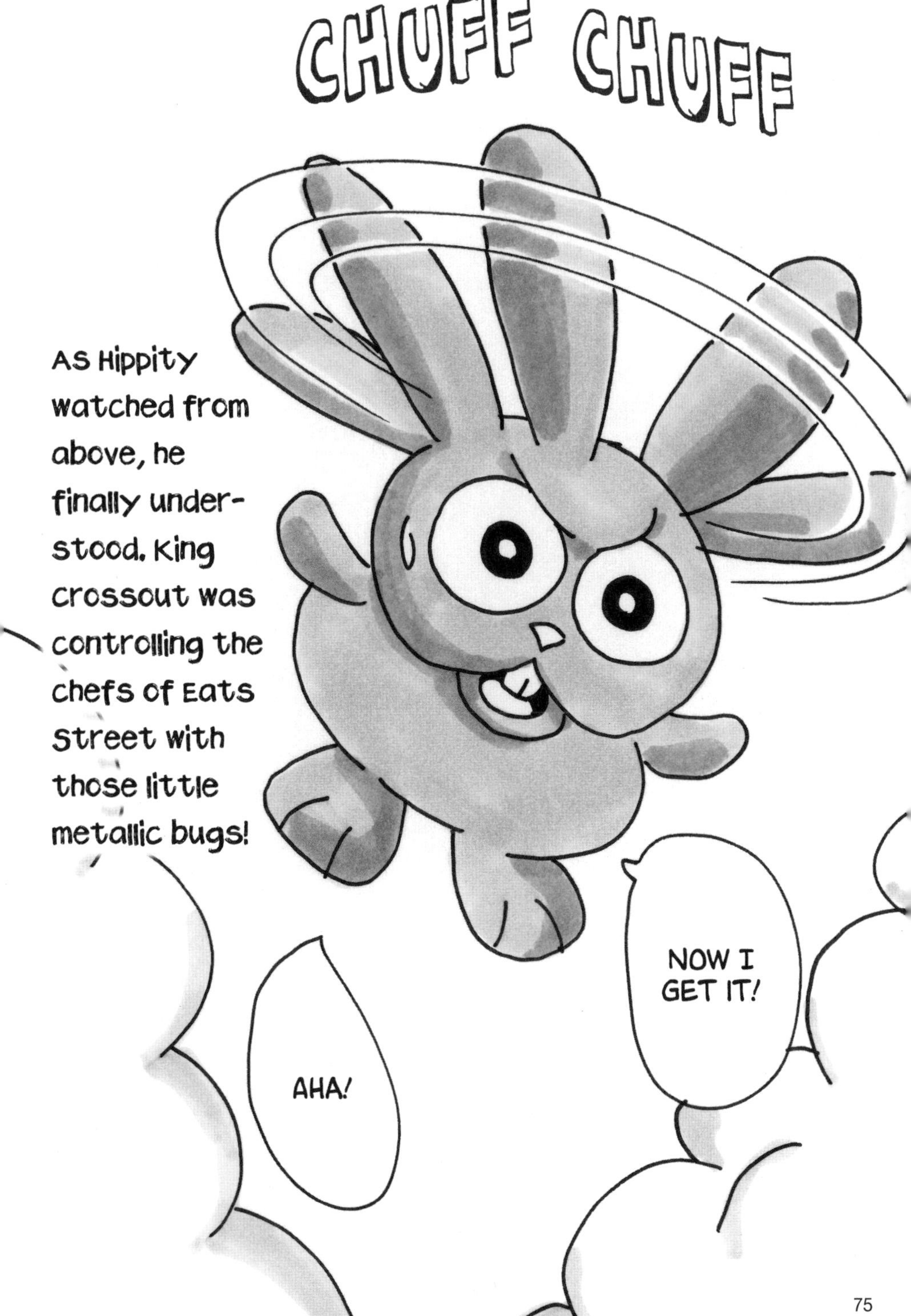
CHUFF CHUFF
As Hippity watched from above, he finally understood. King Crossout was controlling the chefs of Eats Street with those little metallic bugs!
NOW I GET IT!
AHA!

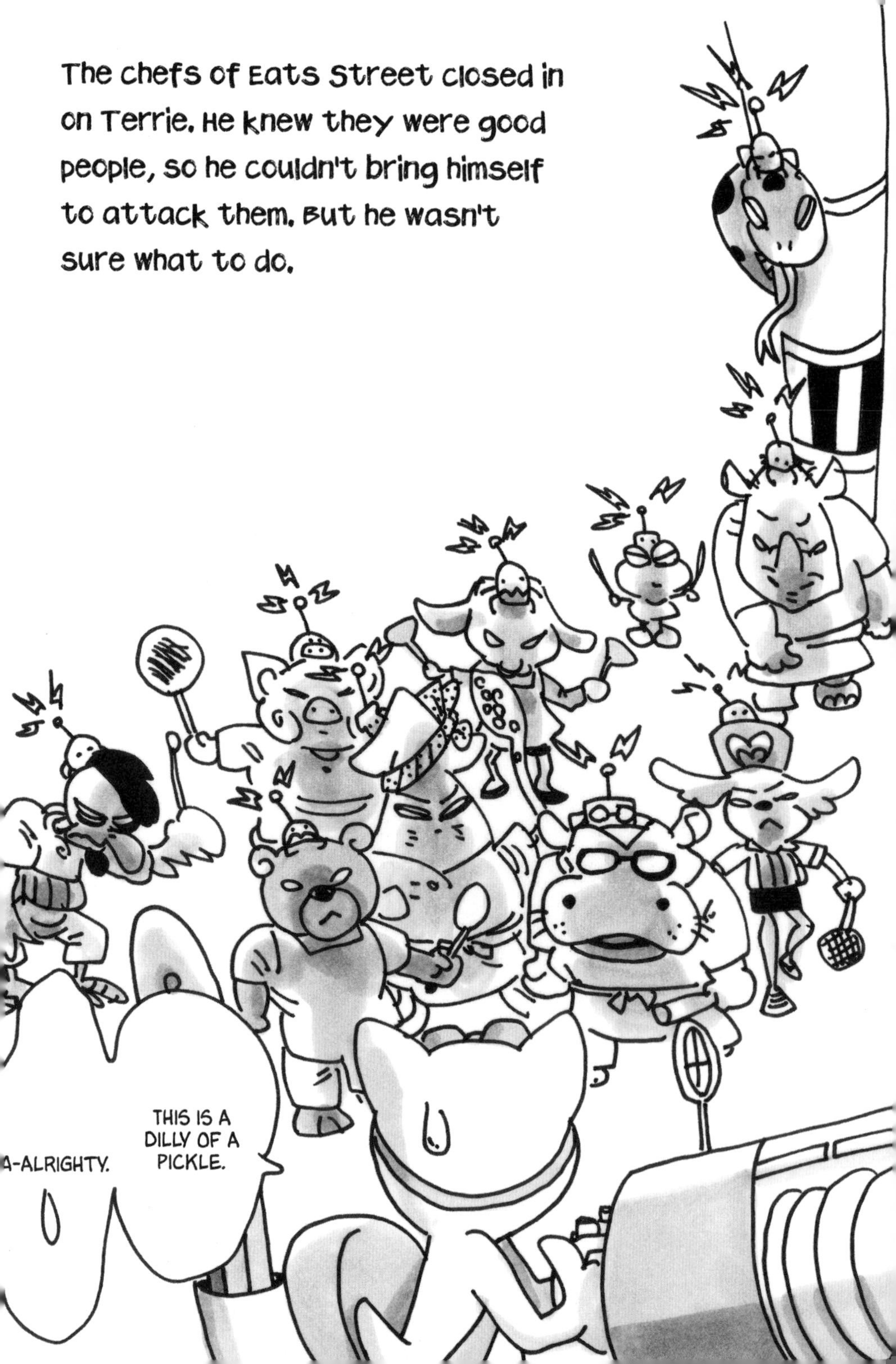
The chefs of Eats Street closed in on Terrie. He knew they were good people, so he couldn't bring himself to attack them. But he wasn't sure what to do.
A-ALRIGHTY.
THIS IS A DILLY OF A PICKLE.

Hippity, on the other hand, knew just what to do. He snuck up behind King Crossout and snapped the mind control antenna clean in half. The chefs of Eats Street were no longer under King Crossout's control.

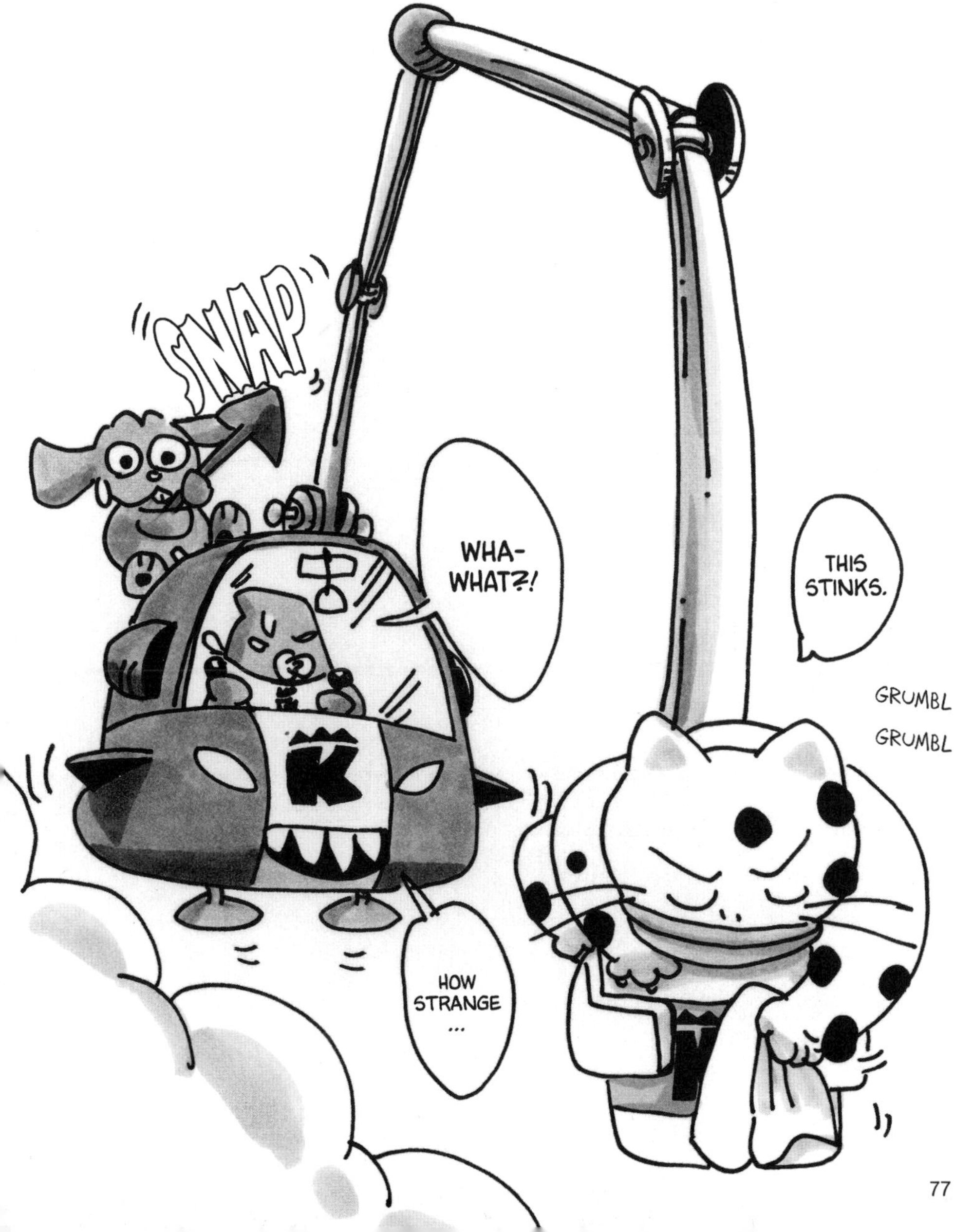
SNAP
THIS STINKS.
WHA-WHAT?!
GRUMBL
GRUMBL
HOW STRANGE ...

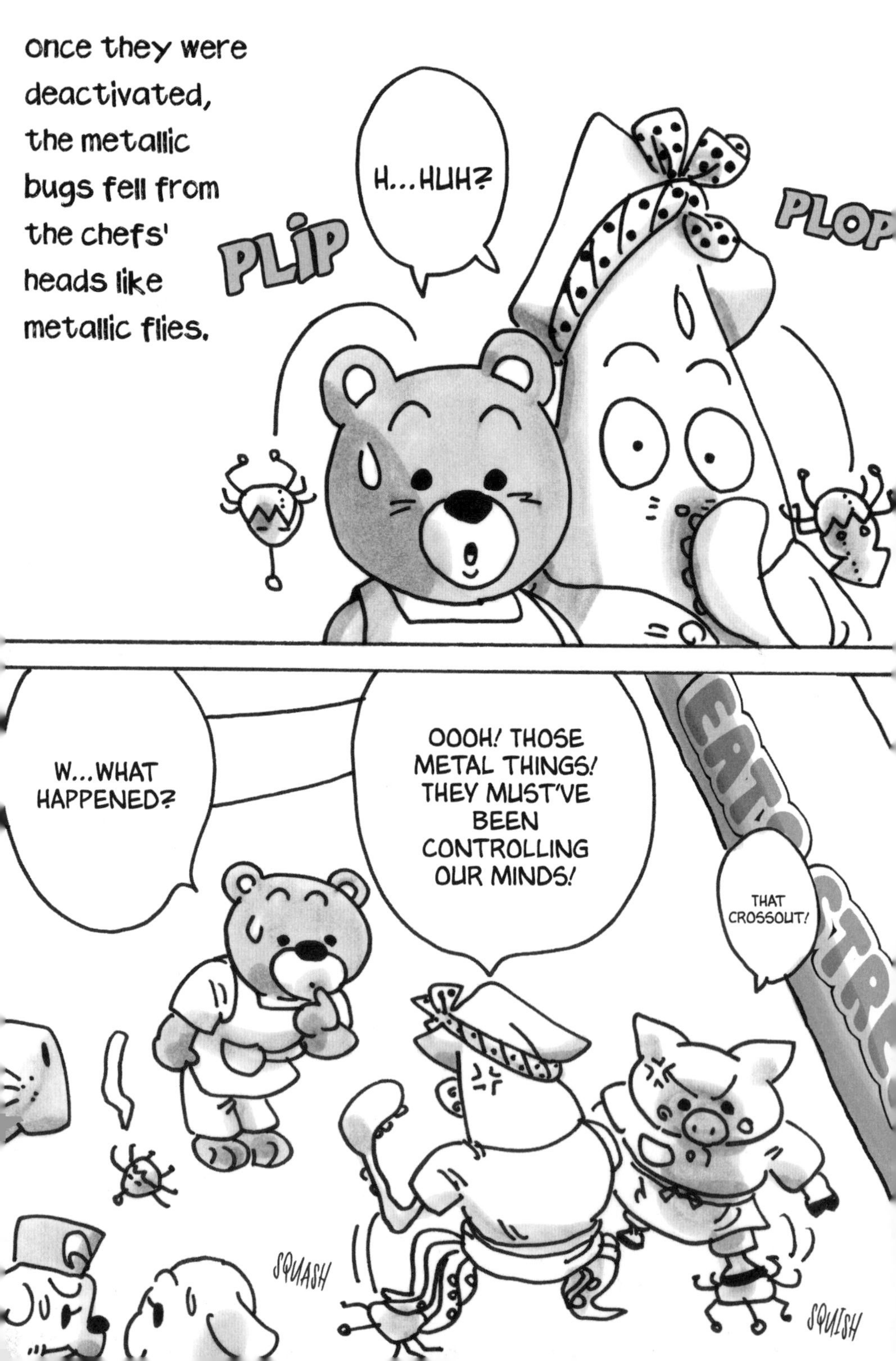
once they were deactivated, the metallic bugs fell from the chefs' heads like metallic flies.
PLIP
H...HUH?
PLOP
W...WHAT HAPPENED?
OOOH! THOSE METAL THINGS! THEY MUST'VE BEEN CONTROLLING OUR MINDS!
THAT CROSSOUT!
SQUASH
SQUISH

All the chefs of Eats Street were back to their old selves. And they vowed to band together to defeat King Crossout once and for all.

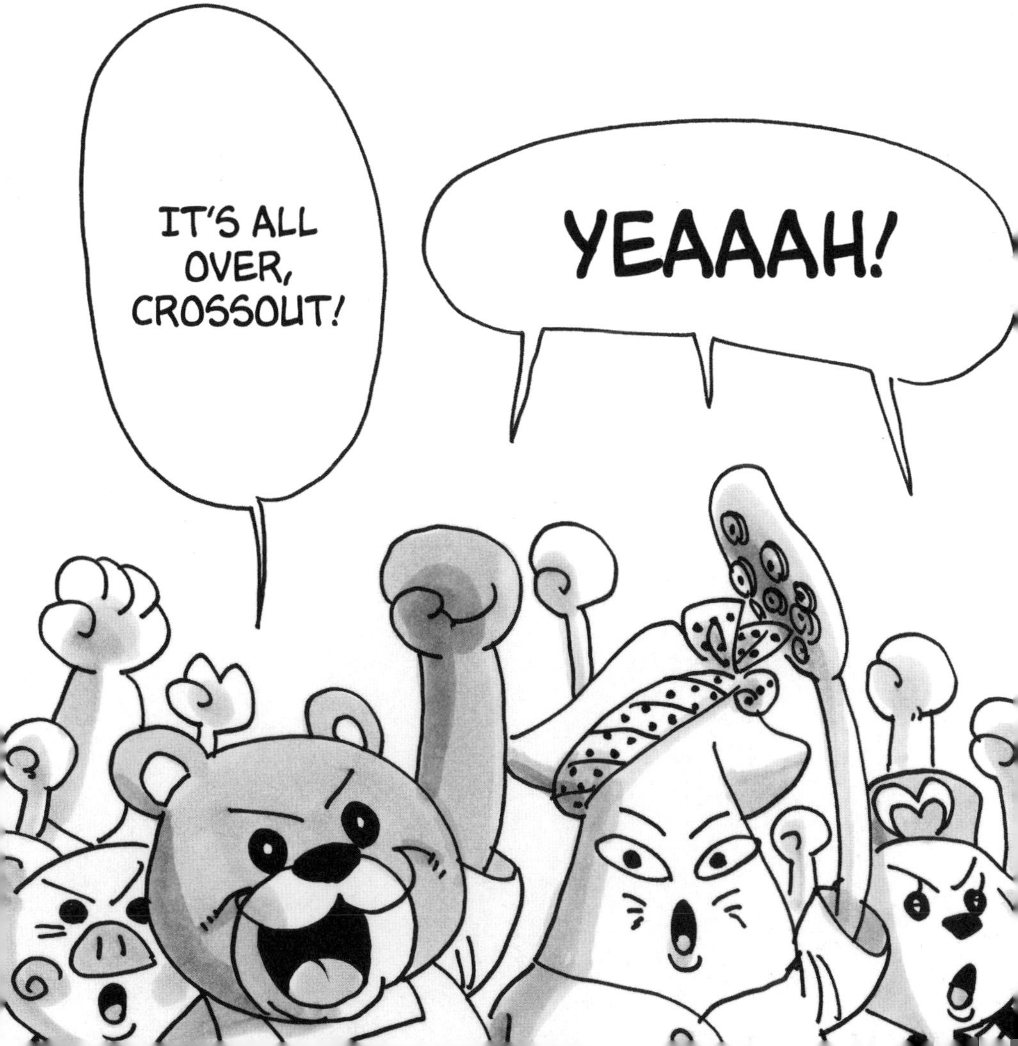
IT'S ALL OVER, CROSSOUT!
YEAAAH!

The chefs dragged the hoses from their shops and filled the tank of Terrie's water cannon.

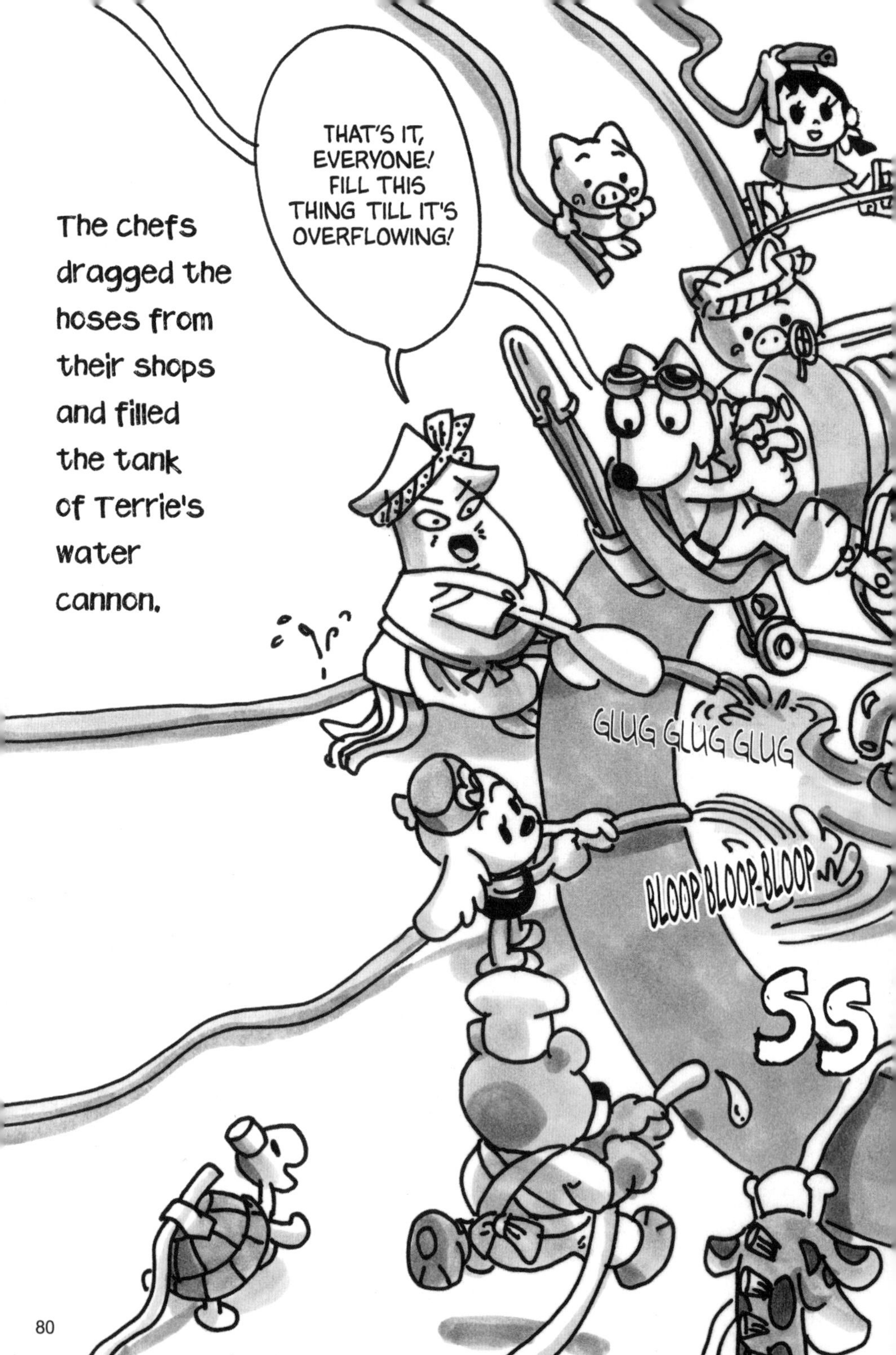

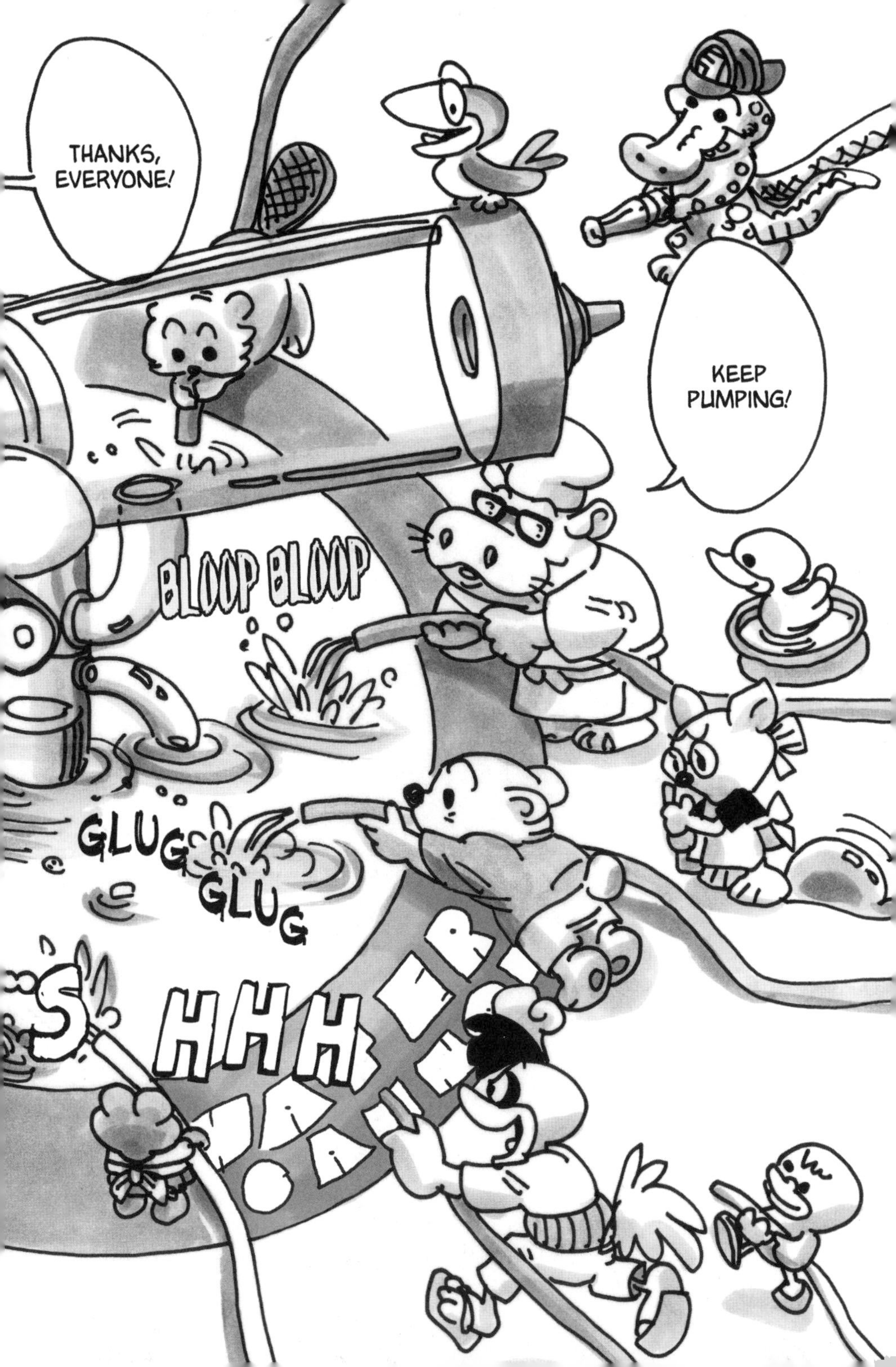
KEEP PUMPING!
THANKS, EVERYONE!
BLOOP BLOOP
GLUG GLUG
SHHH

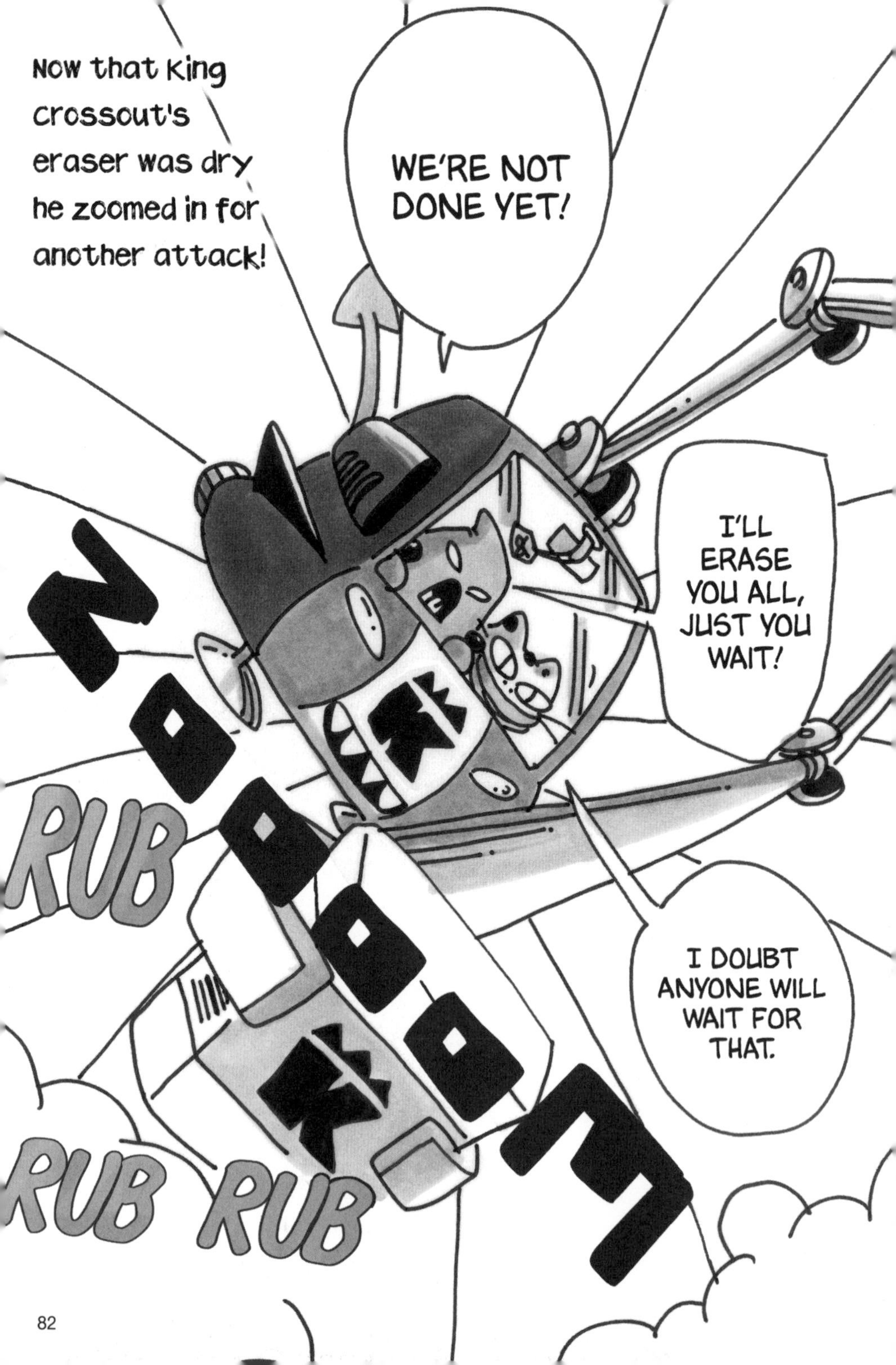
Now that King crossout's eraser was dry he zoomed in for another attack!
WE'RE NOT DONE YET!
I'LL ERASE YOU ALL, JUST YOU WAIT!
I DOUBT ANYONE WILL WAIT FOR THAT.
ZOOOOM
RUB
RUB RUB

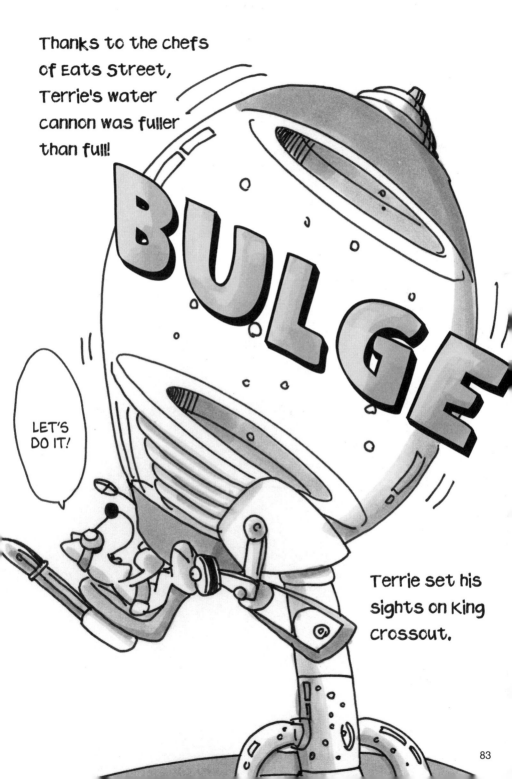

Thanks to the chefs of Eats Street, Terrie's water cannon was fuller than full!

LET'S DO IT!

Terrie set his sights on King Crossout.

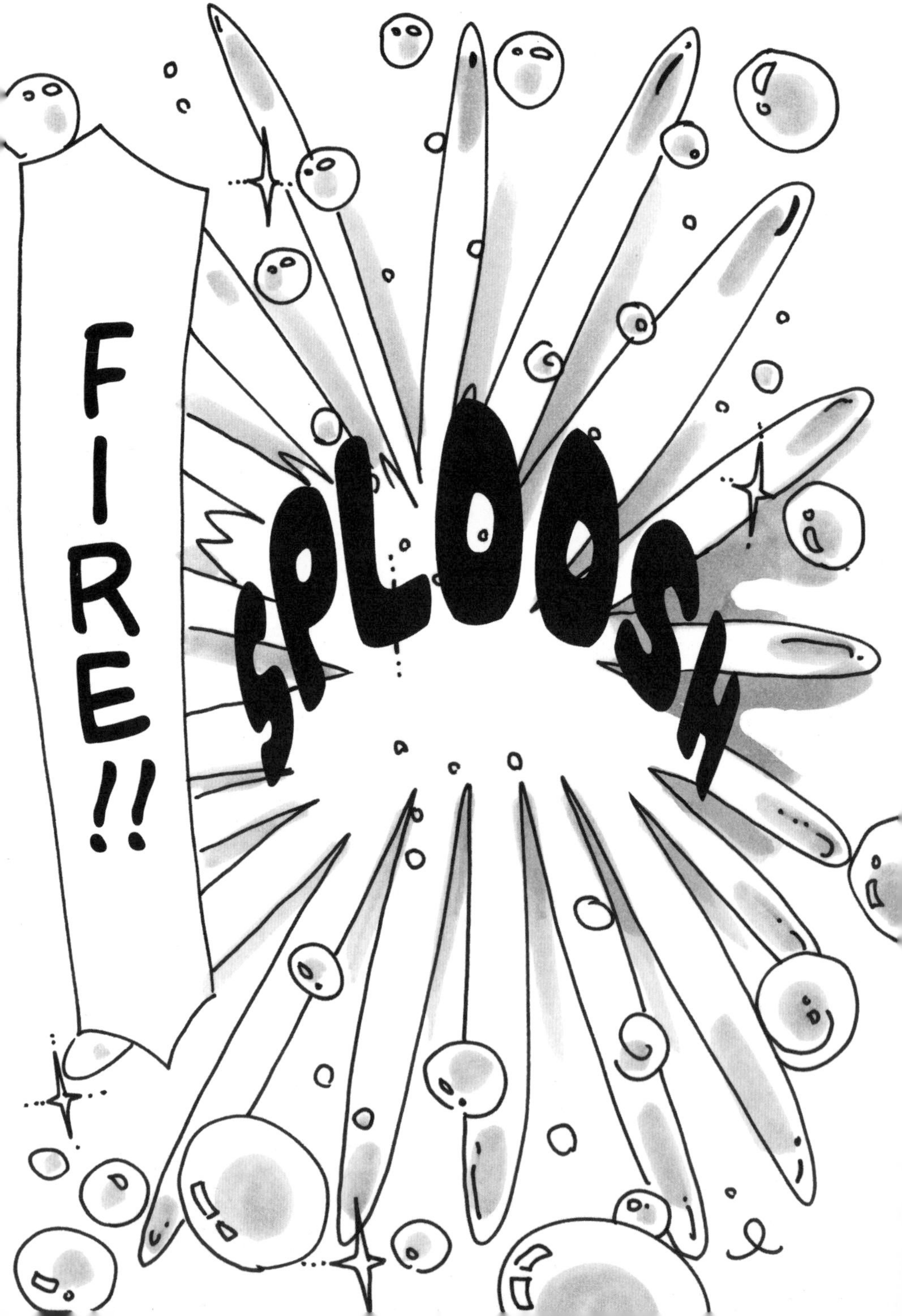
FIRE!!
SPLOOSH

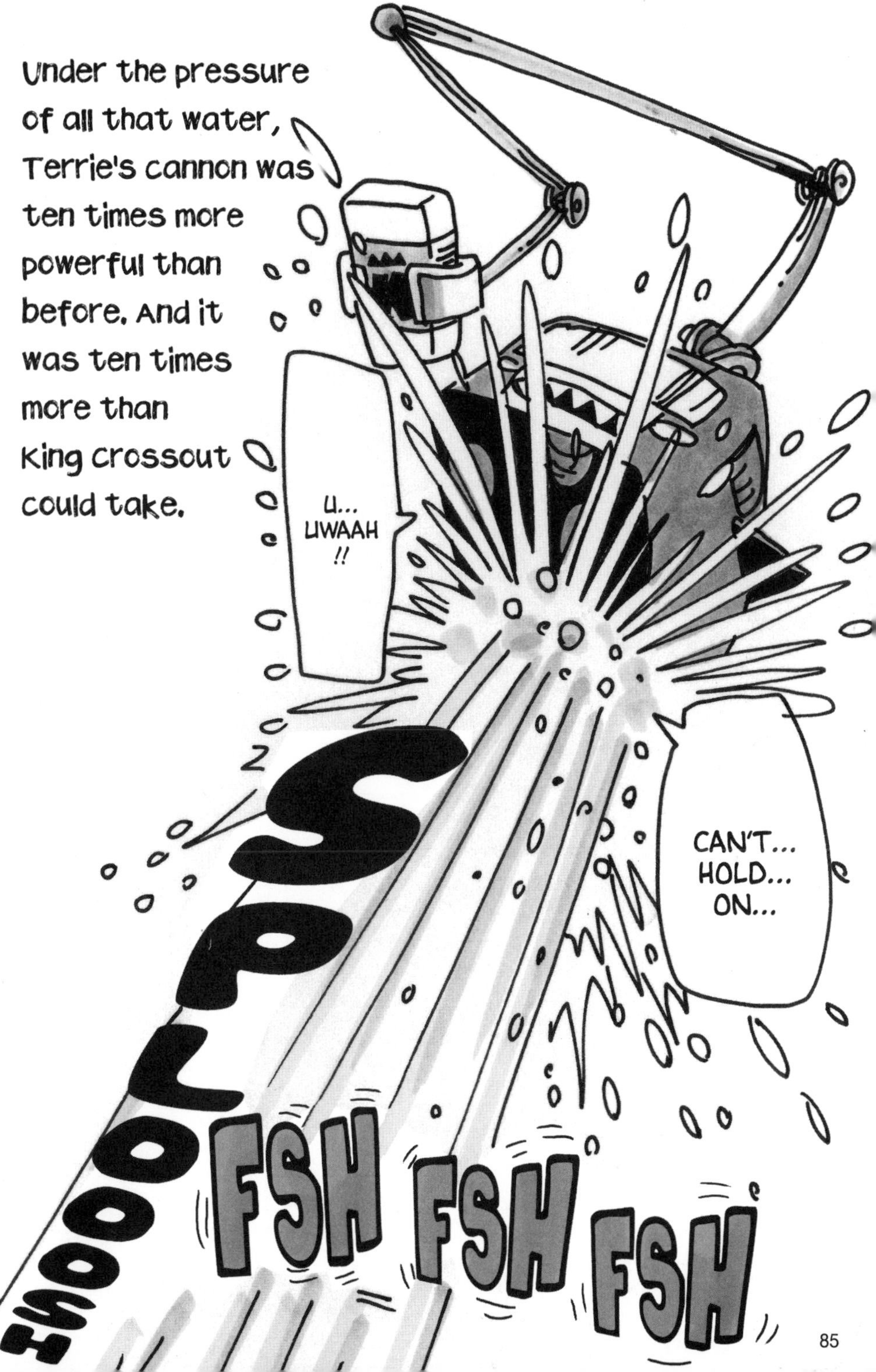
Under the pressure of all that water, Terrie's cannon was ten times more powerful than before. And it was ten times more than King Crossout could take.
U... UWAAH !!
CAN'T... HOLD... ON...
SPLOOOOSH
FSH FSH FSH

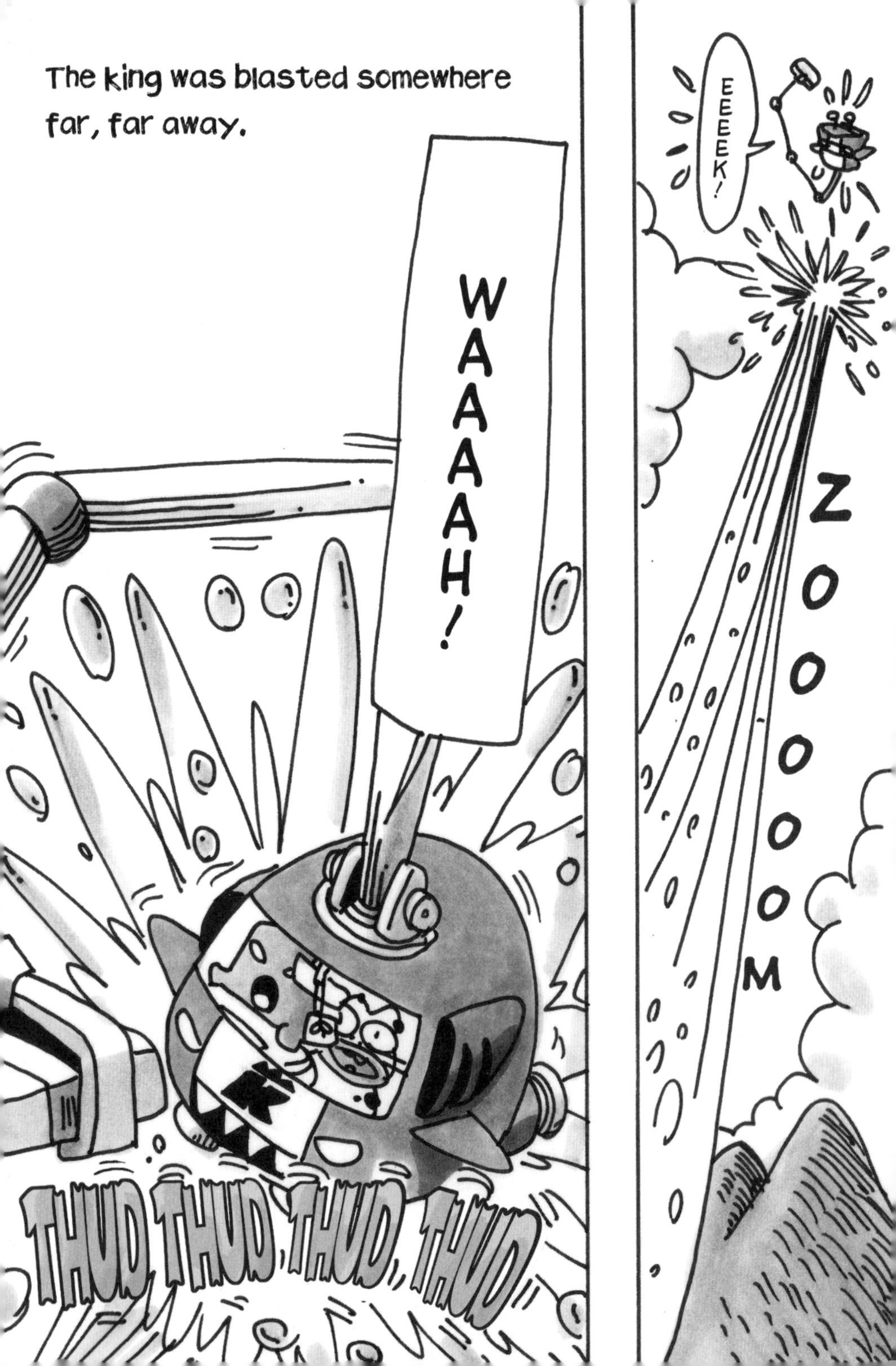
EEEEK!
ZOOOOOOOM
The king was blasted somewhere far, far away.
WAAAAH!
THUD, THUD, THUD, THUD

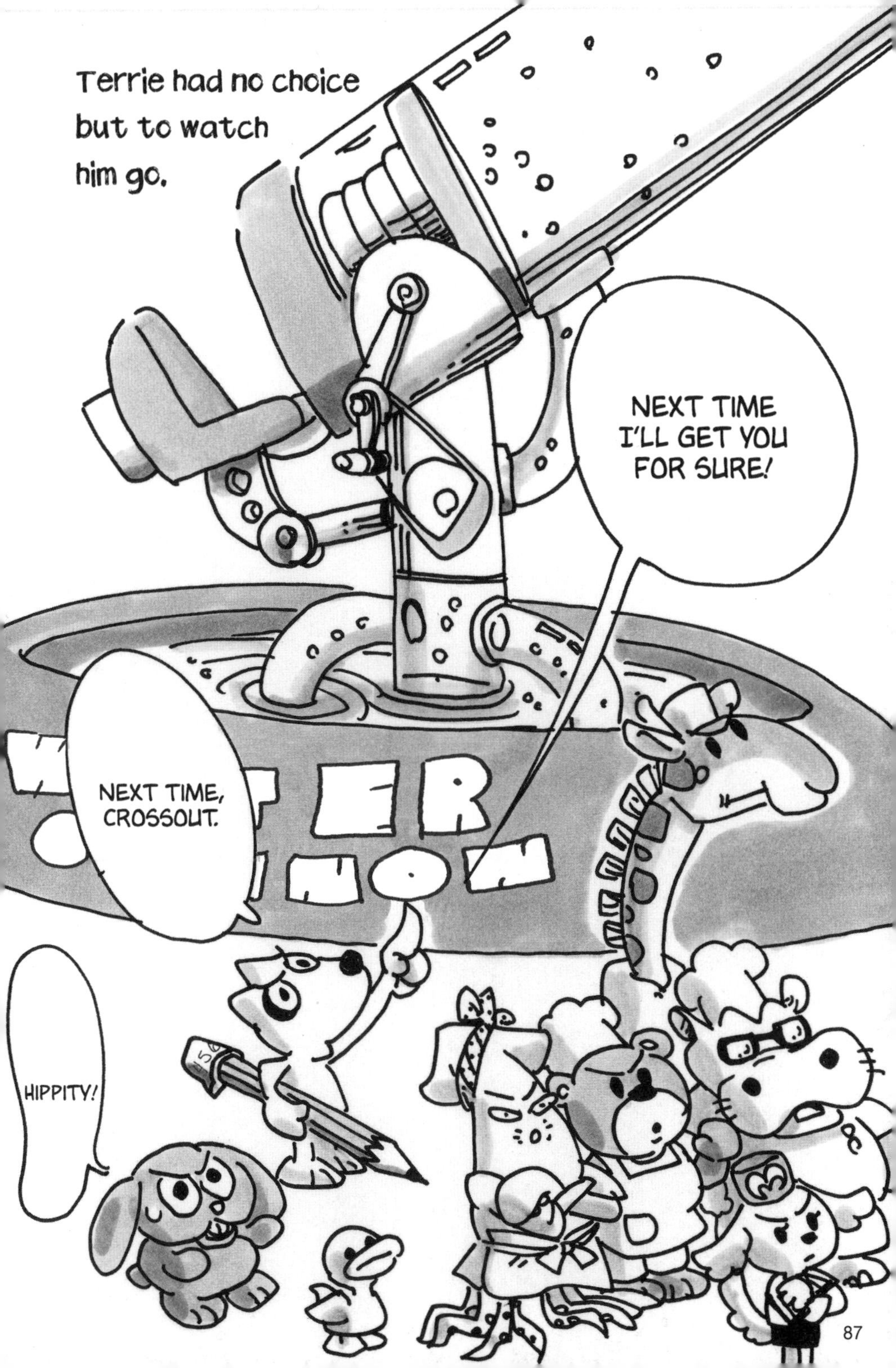
Terrie had no choice but to watch him go.
NEXT TIME I'LL GET YOU FOR SURE!
NEXT TIME, CROSSOUT.
HIPPITY!

To thank Terrie and Hippity for saving Eats Street, the chefs threw them a banquet.

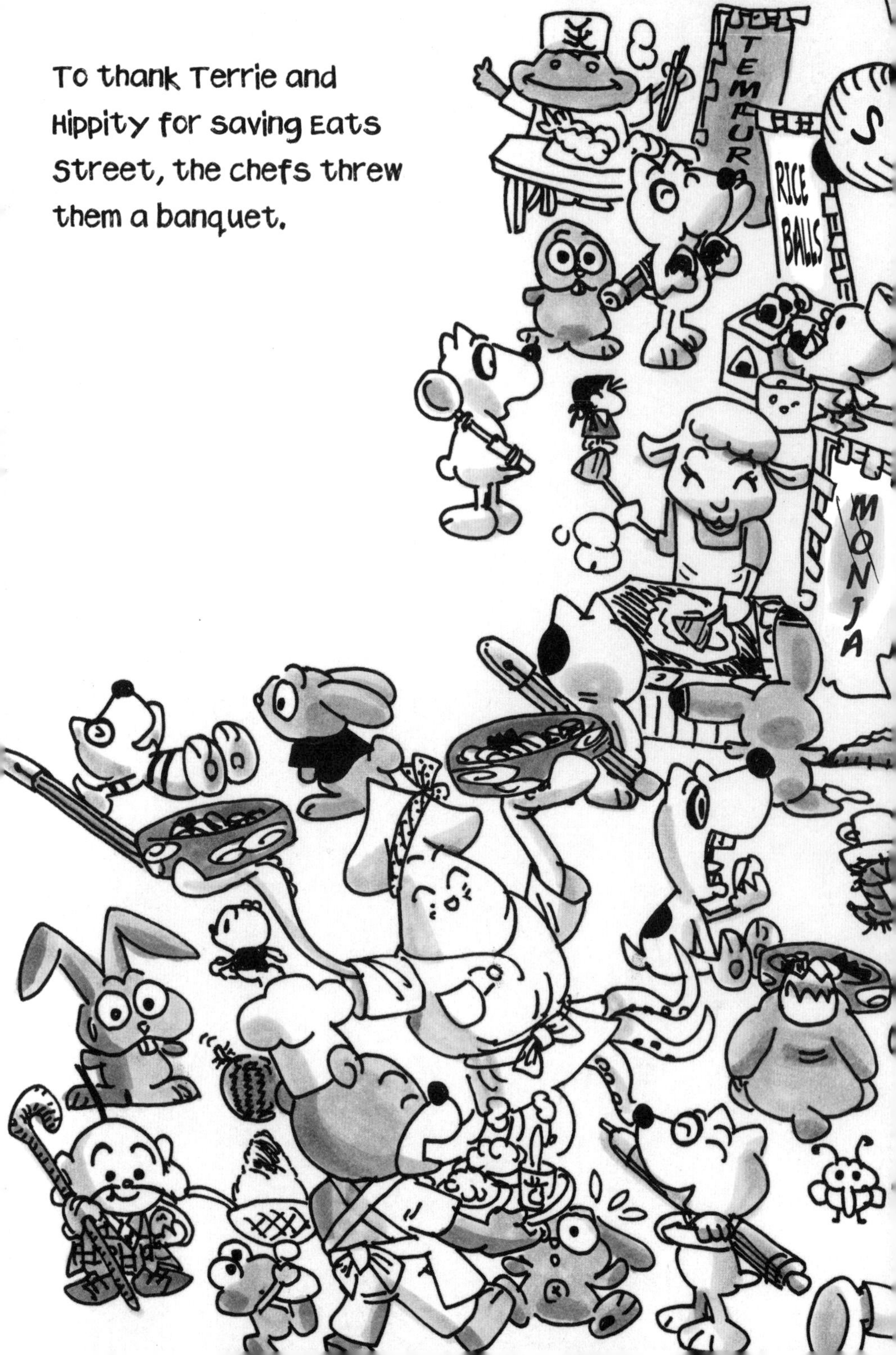
TEMPURA
RICE BALLS
MONJA

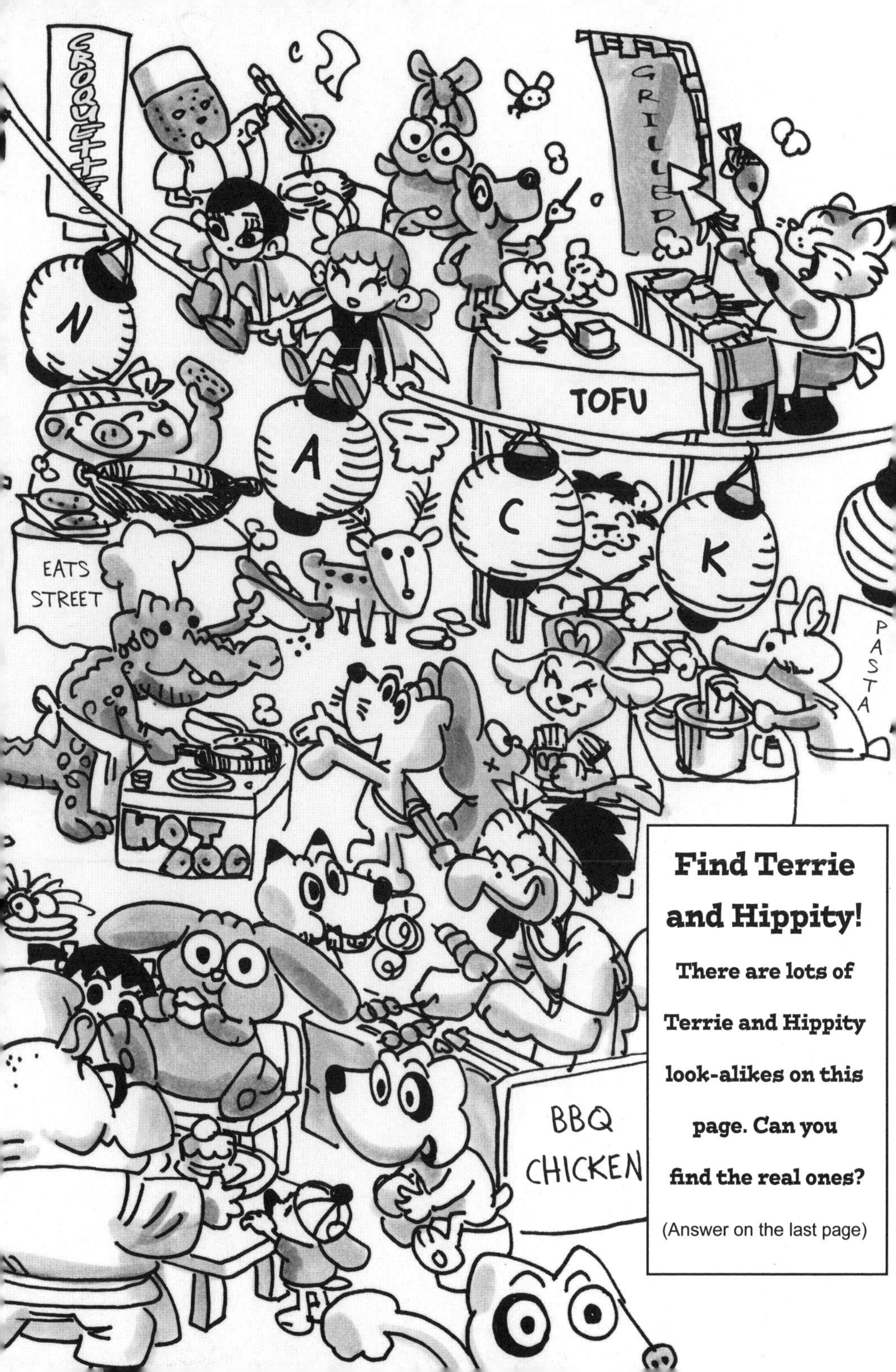
CROQUETTE
GRILLED
TOFU
N
A
C
K
EATS STREET
PASTA
HOT DOG
BBQ CHICKEN

Find Terrie and Hippity!

There are lots of Terrie and Hippity look-alikes on this page. Can you find the real ones?

(Answer on the last page)

Halfway through the feast, Terrie noticed that the tip of the Magic Pencil was low. When the tip of the Magic Pencil snaps or gets dull, Terrie has to return to the real world where he becomes Taro once again.

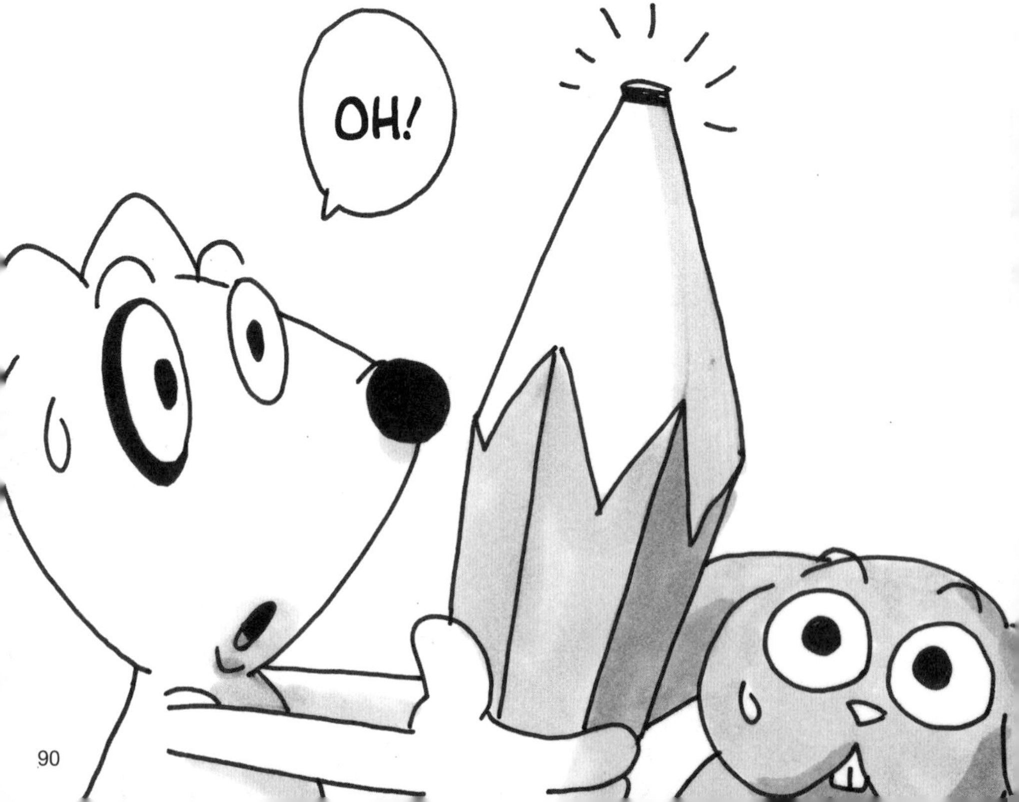
OH!

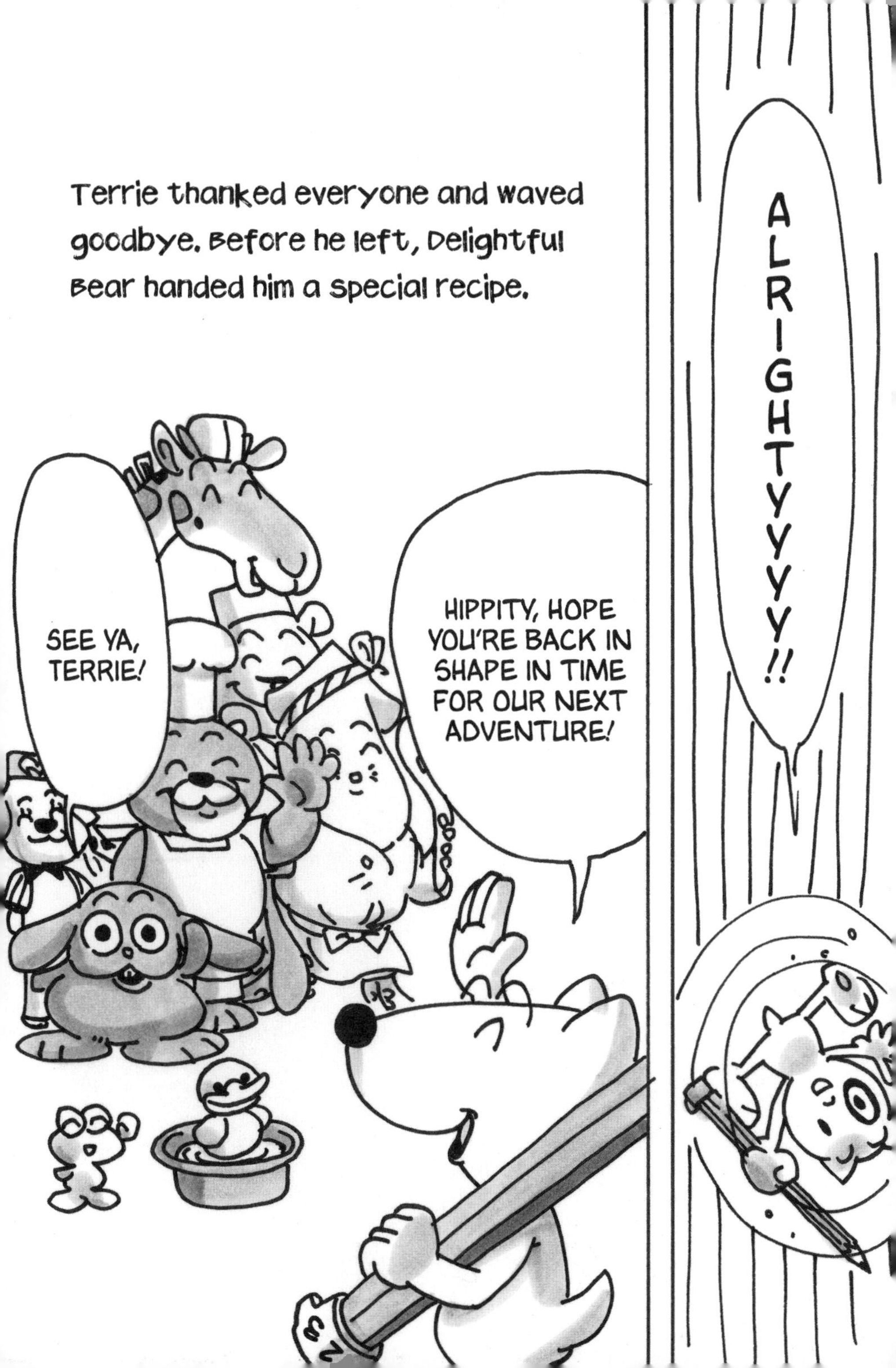
Terrie thanked everyone and waved goodbye. Before he left, Delightful Bear handed him a special recipe.
SEE YA, TERRIE!
HIPPITY, HOPE YOU'RE BACK IN SHAPE IN TIME FOR OUR NEXT ADVENTURE!
ALRIGHTYYYY!!

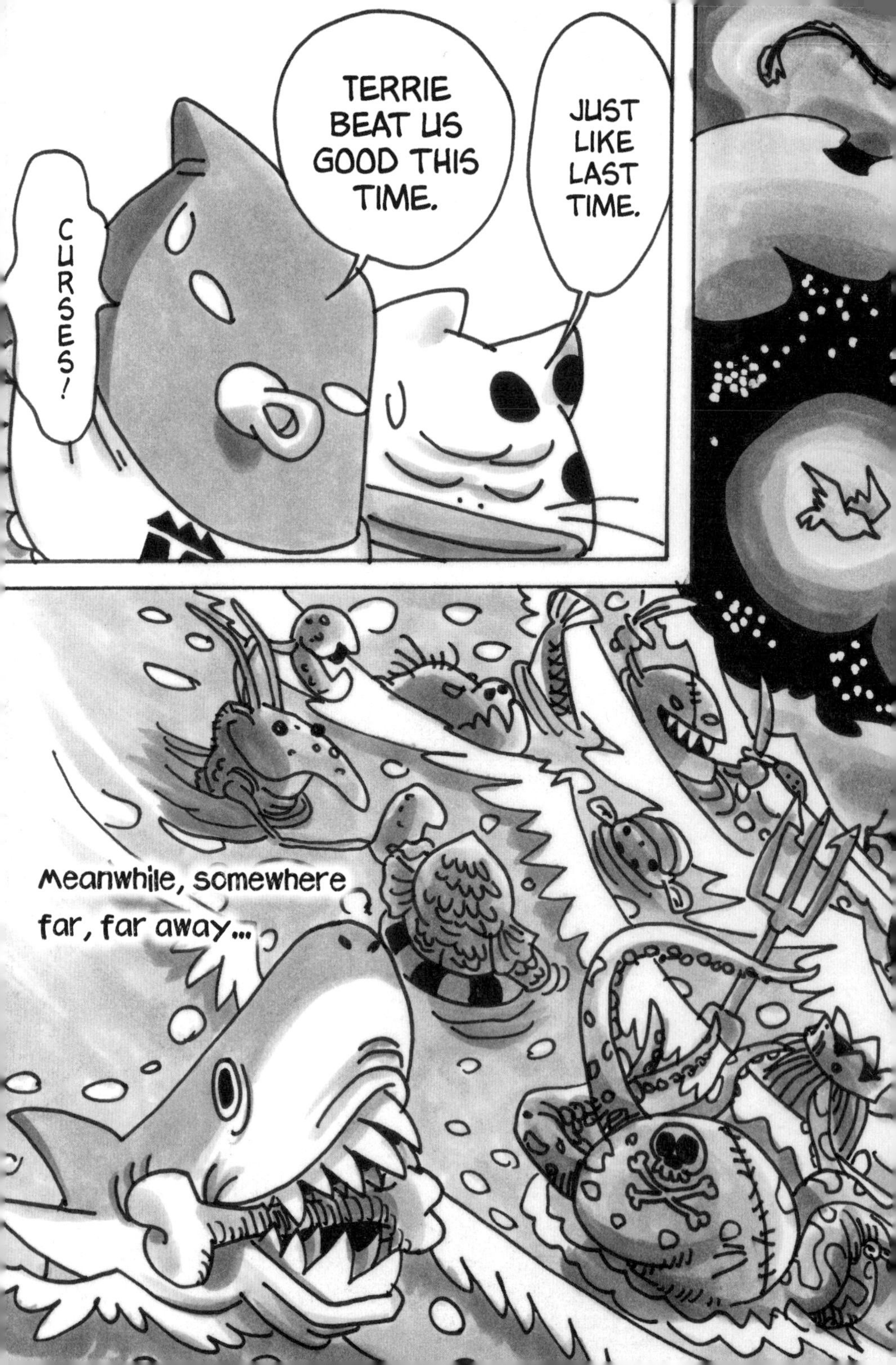
CURSES!
TERRIE BEAT US GOOD THIS TIME.
JUST LIKE LAST TIME.
Meanwhile, somewhere far, far away...

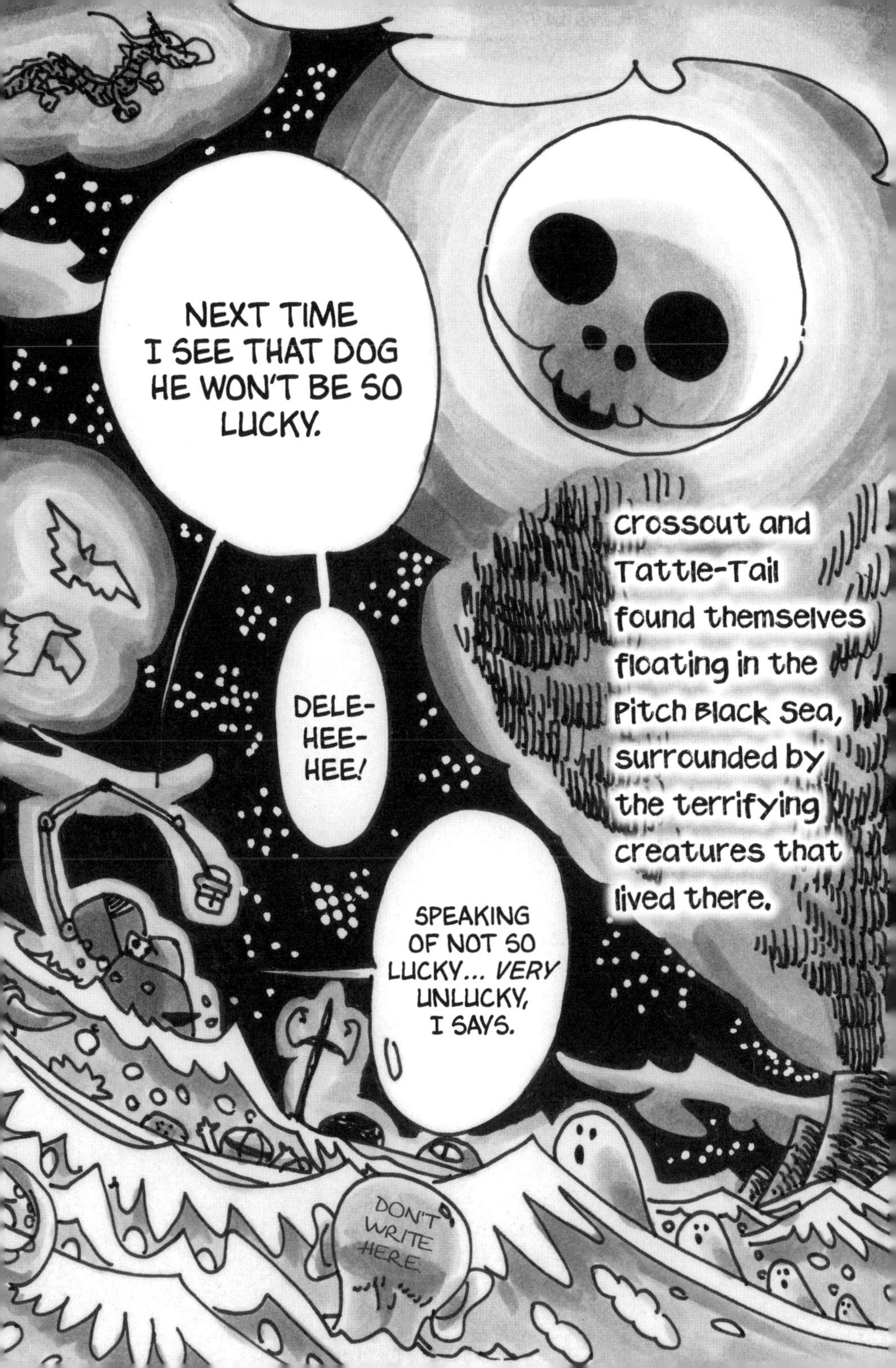
NEXT TIME I SEE THAT DOG HE WON'T BE SO LUCKY.
Crossout and Tattle-Tail found themselves floating in the Pitch Black Sea, surrounded by the terrifying creatures that lived there.
DELE-HEE-HEE!
SPEAKING OF NOT SO LUCKY... *VERY* UNLUCKY, I SAYS.
DON'T WRITE HERE.

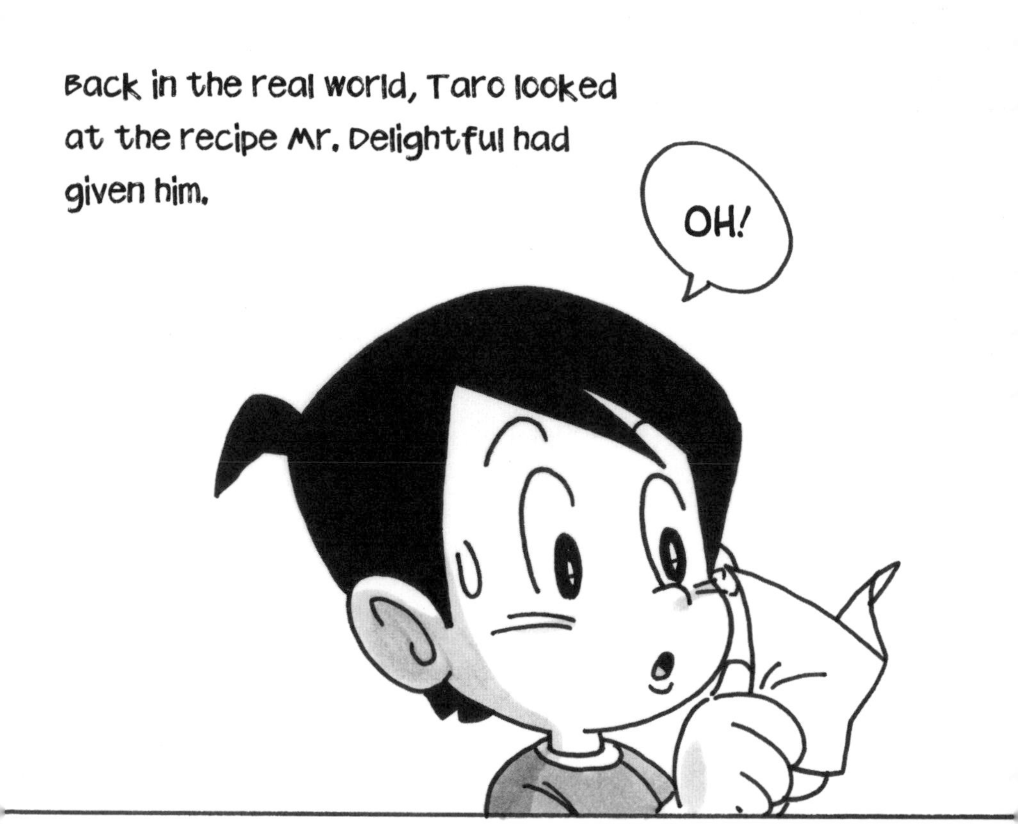
Back in the real world, Taro looked at the recipe Mr. Delightful had given him.
OH!

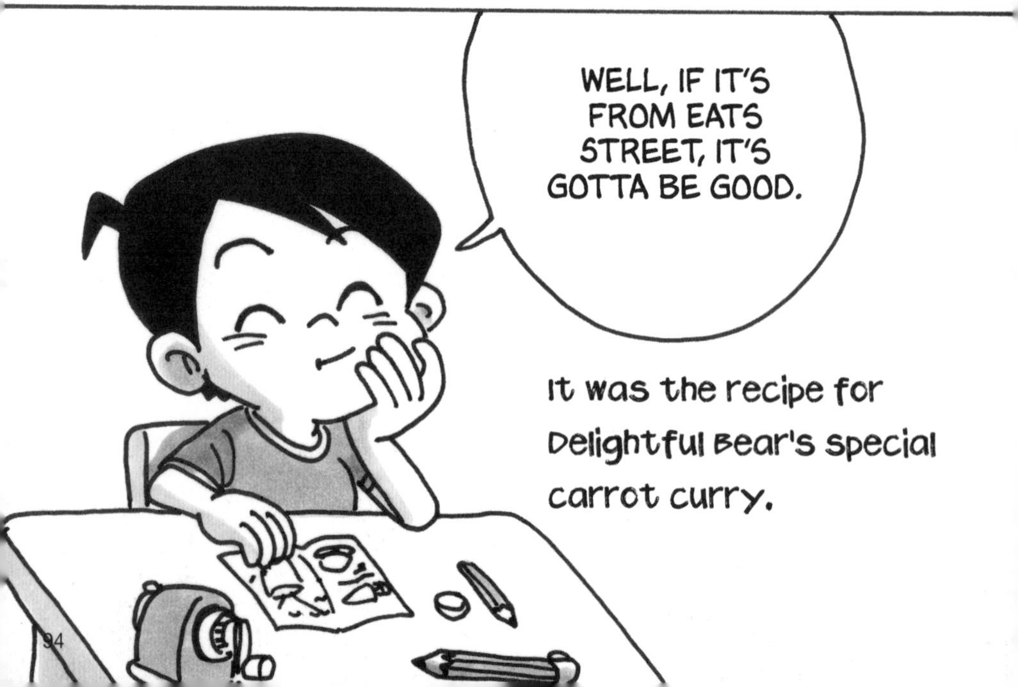
WELL, IF IT'S FROM EATS STREET, IT'S GOTTA BE GOOD.
It was the recipe for Delightful Bear's special carrot curry.

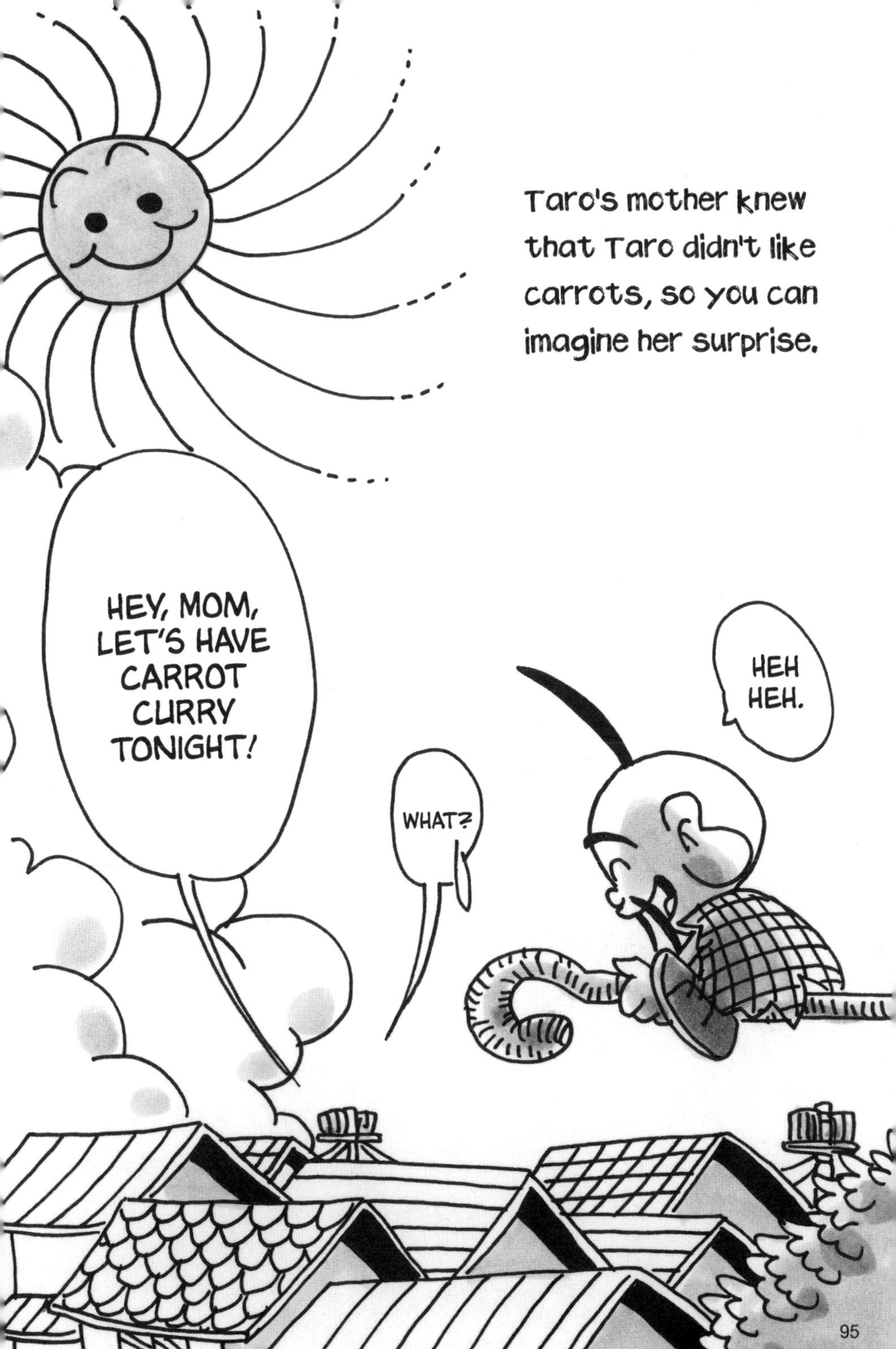
Taro's mother knew that Taro didn't like carrots, so you can imagine her surprise.
HEY, MOM, LET'S HAVE CARROT CURRY TONIGHT!
WHAT?
HEH HEH.

TARO AND THE TERROR OF EATS STREET

VIZ Kids Edition

Story & Art by **Sango Morimoto**

Translation/Katherine Schilling
Touch-up Art & Lettering/John Hunt
Graphics & Cover Design/Hidemi Sahara, Sam Elzway
Editor/Traci N. Todd

PIT BURU-TARO Kyoufu no okazu yoko-cho no maki
© 2008 by Sango Morimoto
All rights reserved.
First published in Japan in 2008 by SHUEISHA Inc., Tokyo.
English translation rights arranged by SHUEISHA Inc.

The stories, characters and incidents mentioned in this publication are entirely fictional.

Printed in China

Published by VIZ Media, LLC
P.O. Box 77010
San Francisco, CA 94107

10 9 8 7 6 5 4 3 2 1
First printing, March 2011

www.viz.com

www.vizkids.com

Answer to "Old Man Squid's Quiz of Doom" pgs 32-33

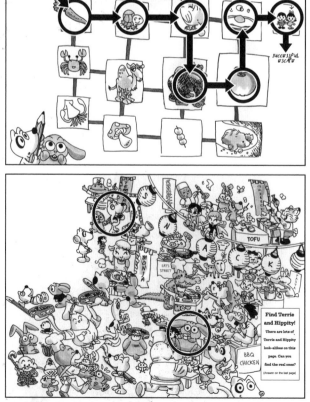

Answer to "Find Terrie and Hippity" pgs 88-89

About the Author & Artist

Sango Morimoto was born in 1955 in Tokyo. He is best known for *Friends of Harpo* and *Oshidori Chidori*, both published by Shueisha.